"I was far warmer when you were holding me,"

Rosaline said hesitantly.

The straw rustled as he moved nearer. He was kneeling beside her again. "Are you by any chance inviting me to share your sheepskin and my coat, fair lady?" he asked lightly.

"Pray, do not laugh at me," she begged him, already afraid that she had made a terrible mistake in suggesting such a thing.

"Laugh, ma'am! How could I laugh at such a wondrous offer, when I am almost turned to ice? You are an angel of mercy."

She was grateful for his levity, knowing that he recognized her fear. Whatever else he might be, this man was most decidedly a gentleman.

Moving to one side of the sheepskin, she made space for him beside her. When he lay down next to her, she draped the coat over both of them. Now she realized that he was shivering and she made a move toward him. "Come closer," she whispered.

"Are you sure?"

"Yes."

Instead of drawing nearer, he turned partially onto his back, at the same time enfolding her in his arms . . . drawing her head against his chest . . .

THE ELUSIVE COUNTESS

Also by Elizabeth Barron

Miss Drayton's Crusade
The Viscount's Wager
*An Amicable Arrangement**

Published by
WARNER BOOKS   *forthcoming

∾THE∾
ELUSIVE COUNTESS

Elizabeth Barron

WARNER BOOKS

A Warner Communications Company

WARNER BOOKS EDITION

Warner Books, Inc.
666 Fifth Avenue
New York, N.Y. 10103

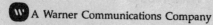 A Warner Communications Company

Printed in the United States of America

First Printing: October, 1987

10 9 8 7 6 5 4 3 2 1

Dedicated to my friends, past and present,
in the
RICHMOND SHAKESPEARE SOCIETY
Richmond-upon-Thames, England

and, especially, to the memory of
MARY WALLACE & EDDIE REDDING,
superb actors and beloved friends

⎯⎯⎯ Chapter ⎯⎯⎯
One

"I shall never marry you, Oliver, no matter how much you may beg or threaten me! Never, never, never!"

The words, spoken in a woman's resonant voice, rang through the wainscoted great hall of Beresford Castle, echoing among the oaken rafters high above the two protagonists who stood confronting each other beside the massive stone fireplace.

Mr. Oliver Prescott's thin lips widened into a sardonic smile. "My dear cousin, have I ever told you how very much greener your eyes become when you are angry? Or how the sight of your heaving bosom inspires me to even greater heights of passion?"

The Countess of Beresford's hands tightened into fists. "God, how I loathe you," she ground out through clenched teeth.

Her cousin laughed his hateful laugh. "It is my intention, my dear Horatia, to turn that loathing to love." His dark eyes narrowed. "If I do not succeed in winning your love, however, it is no matter for, willy-nilly, you shall be mine!"

"You sound exactly like one of those ridiculous villains in a Jacobean play!" declared the Countess with a derisive smile.

"Do I, my dear? Do I, indeed?" He took a step forward, bringing him within touching distance of her. "Then you would do well to recollect the fate of some of the heroines

1

in those plays. The Duchess of Malfi, for instance. One of your mother's favorite roles, I believe. The Duchess, you may remember, was murdered for marrying against her brothers' wishes.''

The Countess's hand flew involuntarily to her throat, and she passed her tongue over dry lips. ''Is it your intention, then, to have me murdered if I refuse to marry you, Oliver?'' she asked in an attempt at levity, raising her eyebrows at him. ''But of course it would be you yourself who would carry out the execution, knowing what intense pleasure you derive from hunting and shooting.''

Prescott hesitated for a moment, his dark eyes moving over her countenance, and then stepped even closer to her. They were almost of a height, for he was of only medium stature, and she was tall for a woman, the stiff black silk dress with its severe white ruff at the throat emphasizing that height. The Countess steeled herself not to move, not to run from him, as she had so often done in years past when he had chased her with a live frog or dead mouse or—oh, God, why must she think of this now?—the stiffened body of her favorite kitten, whose life he had so casually squeezed out with his steely strong fingers.

Now those fingers were clamped about her wrist. ''I do not believe that will be in any way necessary, Cousin,'' he drawled in a voice like velvet, pulling her closer. ''You heard your father's will read this afternoon. It was his wish that we be married as soon as possible—before the end of the usual period of mourning, in fact. He was deeply concerned by the thought of the fortune hunters you would attract when he died.''

He was now so near to her that she could feel his breath on her cheek and smell the brandy on it. Head swimming, she stepped back from him, but he did not release her, his fingers merely sliding down to clasp her hand in his.

She drew in a deep breath, striving to retain her composure, and slowly withdrew her hand from his. ''There was only one thought that ever concerned my precious father, as you well know, Oliver, and that was how to circumvent the strange quirk of Elizabeth the First, who granted the title of

Earl of Beresford, with all its many attendant estates, to one of her favorites, on condition that its inheritance *not* be confined to heirs of the male sex alone." Her green eyes glittered at him. "My father did not like women. To him they were for one use only. Although you are a rather distant cousin, you are like him in that, as well as in looks."

"Come, come, you are too harsh, my sweet Horatia. I—"

"I never wish to hear that name again. I detest it! From now on I am 'my lady' to you or, if you must, 'Cousin.' Nothing more!"

Oliver made a sharp, angry move. She held up her long-fingered hand, palm towards him, to ward him off.

"Hear me out. As you know, my father did everything in his power to try to change the order of succession so that you, his nearest male relative, could become his heir. The thought of a woman inheriting the title was an unbearable one to him, even if she was his daughter! When he discovered that nothing could be done, he brought you to live at Beresford Castle. And from the day that you strode into this hall at the age of twelve, with that superior air of yours, he considered you, not me, the rightful heir of Beresford and shut me out of his life. What a fool you were, Oliver! I was a lonely child of eight, with no friend but my mother. My love could have been yours for the asking, if you had not taught me, within a week, to view you with absolute loathing."

She swung around, the movement so sudden that he started back from her. With a sweeping gesture that encompassed the entire hall, she declared: "But now that is at an end. All this is mine." Her eyes shone as she turned to confront him. "Mine! It is I who am the heir, not you. You are merely Mr. Oliver Prescott, and I am the Countess of Beresford. *Nothing* can change that!"

For a moment she thought he would strike her—it would not be the first time—but then he began to applaud, the clapping echoing strangely in the vast hall.

"Bravo! Bravo! As I have said many times before, you have undoubtedly inherited your mother's extraordinary histrionic talents, *my lady.*" The heavy inflection of sarcasm was emphasized by the deep, mocking bow he made her.

"I shall leave you now," she said, suddenly very tired. "Give me another glass of wine to take up with me, if you please. I mean to sleep well tonight. It is unfortunate that Mr. Venables would not stay the night to keep you company. I thought he might as the weather is so foul. Ring for Barton if you wish anything."

"How exceedingly kind of you to show me such hospitality, considering this has been my home for the past sixteen years." He poured a glass of wine from the crystal decanter and handed it to her. "May I light you to bed?"

"No, I thank you. I have my servants to do that." She eyed him speculatively for a moment. "Although this has indeed been your home for many years, Oliver, now that I am mistress of Beresford, I must inform you that it is my wish that you remove from here as soon as possible. My father has left the Manor of Excombe to you. You may remain here until the manor house is put in order, but only upon one condition: that you never again raise the subject of our marriage. Is that understood?"

His thin eyebrows rose, but he inclined his head in a gesture of acquiescence. "Perfectly, my dear cousin."

His sloe-black eyes held an enigmatic expression that she was unable to fathom. But then, it had never been possible to guess what Oliver was thinking. His mind was more devious, more convoluted than that of any other person she had ever known. When he had first arrived at the castle, she had very soon realized that it would be to her distinct advantage to be able to gauge what was in her cousin's mind; but after enduring pinches, blows, and cruel practical jokes, and, in later years, his disgusting attempts to embrace her, she had learned that the only thing she could rely on was that Oliver Prescott never behaved in a predictable manner.

She took a sip of wine and stared into the fire, memories racing through her mind. Her mother had stood as a buffer between her and her cousin while she was alive, but when her mother died, Horatia at the age of fifteen had found herself without an ally. Her father refused to listen to any complaints about Oliver. "You are far too missish," he would say; and, when she had complained that Oliver had pushed her into a closet and fondled her, he had merely told her that she was "nothing but a confounded prude!"

From that day on, she had known that she must learn to defend herself, and she took to carrying a small silver dagger in her sleeve, which she did not hesitate to draw upon Oliver whenever the need arose—for the one thing she had been able to discover about her father's second cousin once removed was that he was terrified of knives.

"It would be most interesting to know what is going through your mind at the moment, my dear cousin," Oliver said.

She gave a nervous start, having forgotten that he was there. Now it was her turn to give him an enigmatic smile. The smile still hovering about her mouth, she raised her voice to summon the footman who stood in the shadows beyond the carved-oak screen. "My candle, if you please, William." She turned again to Oliver. "Good night and sleep well."

"Oh, I shall. I most definitely shall, my dear Horatia."

Before he could say any more, she turned on her heel and swept from the hall, her train brushing across the rugs that inadequately covered the vast extent of stone-flagged floor.

Horatia! She gritted her teeth as she mounted the stone stairs, worn at the center by four hundred years of footsteps. *Horatia.* How she loathed the name! And with what relish Oliver had used it, knowing how she loathed it. Well, she would be Horatia no more.

"From this day on I shall be known by the name my mother always called me in private," she informed her old nurse, who, although unmarried, was known to the staff as Mrs. Leaming and to her charge as Lemmy. "Rosaline. Rosaline, Countess of Beresford. It sounds well, does it not?"

Her nurse smiled into the mirror at her as she loosened the braids of rich auburn hair and brushed it until it gleamed in the candlelight. "Ah, my dearie, your dear, sweet mama would have liked that. Rosaline you were to her from the day 'ee were born. Rosaline were one of her favorite parts in Shakespeare, you know, my dearie.''

The Countess felt the strain of the long day slip from her. Lemmy's soft Devonshire accent always had a remarkably soothing effect upon her, and the rhythmical brushing was almost hypnotic. ''Will you sleep with me tonight, Lemmy?'' Her eyes met her nurse's gaze in the heavy wood-framed mirror.

''Course I will, my dearest lady. But don't 'ee be afraid of him no more. You're the mistress here now, and well he knows it.''

''Yes. But it is only three days since my father died. I fear that it will take a little longer than that for my cousin to realize that things have changed. Meanwhile, I intend to make sure—''

''Course 'ee do. I'll just tuck 'ee up in bed, then go down for a posset of hot milk and some of that saffron cake Cook made for the both of us. I'll be back sooner than a cat can wink.''

''Lock the door after you, then, and take the key with you. Be sure not to leave it in the lock!''

''What a little worrier it be, for all you're a grown woman of nigh on four and twenty and a grand countess now!''

Lemmy bundled her into the large four-poster bed, tucking her in and bestowing a warm embrace upon her before drawing the faded tapestry hangings around the bed. She pulled the heavy door to behind her when she had left the room, and turned the key in the lock. ''I've the key safe in my pocket,'' she called through the keyhole. The slap of her slippered feet retreated down the corridor.

The light of the candle danced before the Countess's weary gaze. Her eyelids seemed weighted with lead. She was determined to remain awake until Lemmy's return, but she was finding it impossible to keep her eyes open. She blew out the candle and, with a heavy sigh, burrowed into the down mattress. Clasping her hands beneath her cheek, she fought sleep no longer.

She was not sure what it was that had woken her. Possibly a log falling in the fireplace or the wind howling in the chimney or, all three. When she heard the creak of the door, she realized that it must be Lemmy returning with their bedtime supper.

"Do not forget to lock the door again," she called out.

Footsteps crossed the floor. Her very blood seemed to freeze in her veins. She sat up, heart pounding, eyes wide open in the enclosed darkness of the bed, for, although the footsteps had been almost silent, she knew that it was not her nurse who stood on the other side of the bed curtains.

God protect me was her one thought. Breathing fast, she began to slide backwards to the far side of the bed, but before she was halfway across, the bed curtains were swept open, and she was looking up into Oliver's gleaming eyes.

He had been drinking heavily—she knew that at once—for his usually fashionable appearance was disheveled. His black hair was tousled and he had removed his coat and neckcloth. His white shirt was unbuttoned, revealing the dark hair on his chest.

"How dare you! How *dare* you! Get out of my room this instant!" She reached through the curtains to pull the bell rope, but he was too quick for her, catching her wrist in a painful grip.

"It is no use, my love. The servants are either 'bought and sold' or sleeping an unusually heavy sleep."

The Countess gasped. "Never tell me you have poisoned them!"

Her cousin threw back his head and laughed, displaying his white teeth. "Why what a melodramatic female it is, to be sure! No, my delectable Horatia. Merely a little laudanum in the special punch prepared by me for the servants on the funeral day of the late, lamented Earl. Even your devoted Lemmy is snoring happily in the kitchen."

"And my wine? It, too, was drugged, was it not?"

"Indeed it was, Cousin, but with a very much smaller dose, for it was my desire that you be awake, not asleep, when I came to you. I should not find it half so pleasurable to make love to you while you slept, Horatia."

Her heart lurched in her breast. "Love!" she cried scornfully. "You mean *rape*, sir, not love!"

"Call it what you will, my dear; I intend to make you mine this very night." His eyes fixed on hers so that she felt incapable of looking away from him. "After I have finished with you this night, I believe we shall have no more talk of there being no marriage between us. And do not be thinking of running from the castle either, for I warn you, my dear cousin, wherever you may hide, I will hunt you down. Your father's generosity to me these past years has been put to good use. I have many in my pay. You will not even set foot outside these walls without someone being on your trail every step of the way."

"Oh, you are monstrously sure of yourself, aren't you?" said the Countess, trying hard not to betray her terror of him.

"Yes, indeed I am. But I give you one more warning. I am not always a patient man, as you well know. If you do run from me, the longer it takes to find you, the less likely it will be that I shall still be interested in marriage with you. For you see, my dear, if you were to completely disappear, I should become the heir to Beresford."

"Why not speak plainly? Either I submit to you tonight and then marry you, or you will arrange my death. Is that what you mean to tell me?"

"Precisely."

She must keep him in conversation long enough at least to allow her to get off the bed. Already, she had retreated several inches from him, but it was still a long way to the other side. "I always knew you to be evil, but I never realized you were actually insane, Oliver." She slid another inch or so from him.

He smiled. "My dear Horatia, it may suprise you to hear this, but I do not give one jot for what you think of me. Oh, I grant you your voluptuous body excites me, but I am excited far more by your hatred. To own the truth, my love, my greatest source of excitement is the thought of being earl—"

"Even if you marry me, you will not be Earl of Beresford. Have you forgotten that?"

"No, I have not, but my son will be, and I shall rule Beresford first through you and then him. Now, speaking of sons, let us waste no more time."

As he began to climb up onto the bed, she flung herself across to the far side. For a frantic moment she could not find the opening in the bed curtains. The she was outside them. Now he, too, was off the bed and coming towards her at the foot of it, his black eyes gleaming with the excitement of the chase. She tried to scream, but nothing came. It was as if her throat had been sealed over.

Her gaze raked the room. Where in the name of heaven had she put the knife? Then she caught sight of it on her dressing table, its silver haft glinting in the dying light of the candles. She ran to the dressing table and stood with her back to it, facing him, praying that he had not seen the dagger.

"Trapped, my sweet." His eyes roamed up and down her body, his gaze stripping her of her nightgown. Laughing low in his throat, he slowly approached her, like a wildcat stalking its prey. Pressing his lean body against the length of hers, he took her face in one hand, holding it fast between thumb and fingers. Then she felt his mouth on hers, hard and demanding, his tongue thrusting against her clenched teeth. "Open your mouth to mine, my love," he whispered.

She felt behind her for the knife, touching and instantly discarding combs and brushes. *Oh, God, please let me find it*, she prayed. Ah! She had it! Determined to do anything to distract him, she opened her mouth, willing herself to resist the waves of nausea and faintness his kissing evoked. Even as she slowly drew the dagger around and down into the folds of her nightgown, she vowed she would never, *never* again permit a man to touch her. All men were loathsome, despicable animals.

She jerked her head suddenly and at the same time pushed at his chest with the flat of her left hand, creating a space between them. In a flash, the silver dagger was pointing only a few inches from his heart.

A sickly pallor crept into his countenance, and he gave a nervous laugh. "Come, come, my dear cousin. You have been threatening me with that toy dagger of yours for years, yet you never had the courage to use it upon me. Why should I believe you would use it now?"

"Tonight is different. We both have a great deal more to lose. I warn you that this time I shall not hesitate to use it." Her eyes went to the door. "Is the key still in the lock?"

He stood, his thin lips flickering into a ghostly smile, but made no reply.

She made a threatening gesture with the knife. Beads of moisture broke out on his upper lip. "Answer me. Is it in the lock?"

He nodded slowly.

"Good. Then it is my intention to leave this room, lock you inside it, find a servant who is both awake and not in your pay, and bid him ride to Lord Ellington at Brampton House with a message from me. That message will inform him of your actions here tonight, so that even if you escape me, you shall be brought to justice."

Her eyes never leaving his, she walked backwards to the door, feeling behind her with her left hand but still keeping the dagger at the level of his chest. At first he did not follow her, but then he began to inch forward, anticipating her every move.

All at once, her feet encountered some impediment and she stumbled, realizing too late, that it was a rug that had become rumpled.

He was upon her instantly, his hand like a vise on her right wrist, bearing it down, seeking to shake the dagger from her grasp.

She kicked out at him, scratching at his face with the nails of her left hand. Cursing, he bore her backwards and she fell. But even as she felt herself fall, she grabbed his shirt and dragged him down with her. He gave a strangled gasp—and was still, the weight of his body heavy upon hers.

For a moment she lay, stunned by the fall. Then, dragging herself out from under him, she turned him on his back, to recoil at the sight of the dark stain spreading across his white shirt. A strangled sob caught in her throat. "Oh, my God," she whispered, "my God, I've killed him."

Sick and dizzy, she bent down to catch up his wrist. Pressing her fingers to it, she found a pulse. Thank God, he was still alive. But for how long? The pulse fluttered beneath her fingers, and then she could feel it no more.

Terror spurred her into action. Half crazed with fear, she ran across the room, tearing off her nightgown, which was now stained with Oliver's blood. Flinging open chests and wardrobes, she dragged on the most accessible clothing, all the while sobbing and muttering to herself like a madwoman.

"Must get away. Warm clothing. Money, money, *money*. Oh, dear God, I've no money here. Jewels? Yes, jewels. Pelisse? No, cloak. Old cloak. Raining. Gloves, gloves, *gloves*. Where are they?" She left doors swinging wide, drawers open, their contents tossed every which way.

Within minutes, she was dressed again in her black silk gown, which Lemmy, fortunately, had not put away, and a hooded cloak of black merino wool. Finding it impossible to drag on her riding boots without assistance, she had to make do with her half boots.

Not daring even to glance at Oliver again, she crept around his inert body, slowly opened the door, and sped down the corridor, fully expecting one of his servants to jump out at her from the gloom at every step. Now, instead of raising an alarm, she must do her best to escape without anyone hearing her. To fly from her home, which had now become a castle of death, was her only thought.

She tiptoed down the stairs, wincing at the scrape of her heels on the stone steps, and sped down the passageway to the new modern wing of the castle. Her easiest means of escape would be through the terraced room that had been her mother's favorite place. She crossed the pitch-dark expanse of the green saloon, bumping into chairs and tables as she went. Then she was in the neglected glassed-in terrace. The heavy scent of camellias carried poignant memories of her mother. *Dearest Mama, help me to decide what I must do*, Rosaline prayed as her shaking fingers unlatched the tall glass doors.

Flee this place, came the reply, *and seek out someone in whom you can place all your trust, someone who will help you to clear your name of the crime of murder and to secure your inheritance*.

The words were as clear as if they had been spoken.

She ran down the short flight of stone steps, casting a quick glance over her shoulder, fearful that she might see figures or—even more horrible to think on—one particular figure advancing upon her. Seeing nothing at all, however, for there was no moon that night, she raced across the soaking wet lawn, the rain like whips lashing against her.

Within minutes, she had left the castle walls behind her and was mounting the hill leading to the unprotected heights of Exmoor. "You will not set foot outside the castle without one of my men being on your trail," Oliver had said. A shudder ran down her spine. Even now someone might actually be close behind her. But she must not think of that now. She must concentrate all her energy on setting as much distance as possible between her and the castle.

Her brief term as Countess of Beresford was at an end. From now on, until she found sanctuary and assistance, she was no better than a hunted fugitive.

Chapter Two

The northern track across Exmoor ran close to the edge of the rugged cliffs that fringed the coastline of North Devon and Somerset. As Rosaline received the full brunt of the rain and wind high up on the bare moor, she could also hear the swell and hiss of the sea hundreds of feet below her.

The wind howled in her ears and whipped open her cloak. Soon not only the cloak but also her dress was soaked through. Striving to hold the edges of the cloak together, she bent her head and forced herself along the track.

She had known Exmoor all her life. Its heather-covered slopes had been her playground. She loved the austere beauty of the craggy hills, the grandeur of the harsh coastline, the immensity of the sea. Whenever her life at home had become unbearable she had only to take her favorite mare up on the moor and contemplate the ceaseless rush of the sea as the tide surged in, to find peace. But Rosaline was also aware that the moor had its savage side; in inclement weather it could be relentless. There were no trees to afford shelter, and on a dark, moonless night such as this it would be easy for a traveler to veer off a pathway and stumble over the cliff or down one of the precipitous inclines that scored its heights.

It was so dark that she was tempted to hold her hands out before her like a blind person, except that that would necessitate having to release her grip on her cloak, which she was desperately trying to keep from being blown open. As a compromise, she clutched the front of her cloak with one hand and held out her left hand, the one nearer the cliff's edge, before her.

She had been walking or, more accurately, battling the wind and rain for possibly the best part of an hour when she became conscious of a change in the sounds behind her. It was not exactly a new sound, for it would be almost impossible to hear anything above the roar of the wind; nor, had she turned around, could she have seen anything, for the night was inky black. No, it was more a feeling, a sensation at the base of her neck.

Someone was following her. Rosaline was certain of it.

In a strange way, it came as something of a relief. Ever since she had fled the castle, she had tried not to think of what she had left there, but now it forced itself upon her consciousness. It was inevitable. The person following her was either there to arrest her for the murder of her cousin or he was one of Oliver's spies, who quite possibly did not know yet about his master's death. She would soon find out, for now she could hear the scrunch of footsteps close behind her.

"Good God! I was right. There *is* another lunatic abroad on this godforsaken night!" declared a pleasant male voice. To her surprise, his accents were those of a gentleman.

As the man came up beside her, she was able to gauge, although she could not actually see him, that he was tall and broad-shouldered. Her heart sank. This would not be an easy man to escape from. "Good evening," she said, averting her face and drawing her hood more tightly about it. Whoever this man was, she was not about to make his task simpler by divulging her identity. If he should challenge her, she was prepared to deny that she was the Countess of Beresford.

"What the devil!" the man exclaimed. "You're a woman!" So he was going to pretend that he did not know whom she was, was he? That suited her well, for when it came to acting a part, she would be prepared to wager a fortune that she could outdo any other amateur.

"Yes," she shouted above the wind's fury. "I missed the stagecoach at Lynton and must make my way to Minehead in time to catch the early morning one from there."

Anyone who would swallow that tale was either a great gaby or was well aware of her true identity!

"How decidedly odd," came his reply. "That is exactly my intention, only I had to abandon the mount I had hired, the confounded animal having pulled a tendon. A breakdown in more than one sense!" His voice rang clearly and confidently through the noise of the storm. "Had I realized how appalling the weather was, I might well have risked staying the night at the inn on the edge of the moor. I decided, however, that I would prefer to brave the storm than to be smothered in my bed for my purse!"

How excessively convenient! He must think her an utter idiot if he expected her to believe such an incredible story.

Her mind feverishly working on her predicament, Rosaline made him no reply. It was obvious that he was not an officer of the parish. Therefore he must be, as she had first conjectured, someone in Oliver's pay. "If you run from the castle someone will be on your trail," Oliver had told her. "I have many men in my pay." There was no reason at all why this should not include some indigent, down-at-heel gentleman, was there? If that were the case, she must be at pains not to divulge anything, for it was possible that this man had been hidden *outside* the castle and had followed her once she had left it, on a prearranged order from Oliver. If so, it was likely that although he knew who she was, he would not know about Oliver's death. If, that is, Oliver was dead!

"Deuced dark, is it not?" the man said. "Perhaps I could assist—"

His words were lost in her scream, for she had felt his firm hand on her right elbow. The scream was torn from her as she imagined herself thrust over the cliff and falling, falling, falling, to crash onto the rocks beneath.

He sprang back as though stung.

"Do not dare to touch me again, sir!" Rosaline yelled. "I warn you that if you do, I have a knife and shall not hesitate to use it upon you." The image of her dagger buried in her cousin's chest sprang vividly into her mind.

"Good God, madam!" the man roared. "What the devil did you think I was about to do? Throw you over the cliff or some such thing? You must have been reading too many lurid novels recently!"

His anger sounded very realistic. Surprisingly good acting for an amateur, she thought.

"I can assure you, madam, that I had no such intention. Perhaps it would be best if we resume our former positions: I behind, you before."

"I should prefer it if you would walk ahead of me, sir, so that I may see you."

"See me! Ha! All I can say is that if you can see anything

at all in this confounded darkness and rain, you must have the eyes of a cat!"

Muttering to himself, he strode ahead of her and, after two or three paces, disappeared into the slanting downpour.

For a few minutes she experienced a sense of relief, but soon the violence of the rainstorm and the darkness and extreme discomfort began to prey upon her nerves. She began to shiver from the cold, the icy wetness seeming to permeate her very bones. Exhaustion from strain and lack of sleep made her stumble on the stony pathway.

Impatiently, she brushed away the tears that now mingled with the rain on her face, vexed at herself for indulging in such foolishness. But no amount of vexation could stop the flow of tears. The sobs Rosaline had been stifling for so long now welled up in her throat and she halted, unable to go one step further, enveloped in a blackness that was as much inward as outward.

This was utterly ridiculous! She must go on. But somehow her legs would not obey her, and she remained rooted to the spot, buffeted by the furious wind, the rain stinging her cheeks and eyes.

She sensed that the man had returned to stand before her. "I do not dare to touch you again, ma'am," he shouted at her through the wind's howl, "but I beg you to take my arm."

"I cannot go any further," she replied, striving to stifle her sobs but utterly incapable of controlling the violent shivering that assailed her. She was deeply ashamed of such a display of weakness before this man.

"Nonsense! Of course you can. Here, let me shift my bag to the other shoulder so that you may walk on my right, away from the edge of the cliff. Come now, no more of this foolishness. Take my arm and let us support each other."

She had no alternative but to take the arm he proffered. Her gloved fingers encountered the heavy folds of his riding cloak and then the firmness of his arm, which, once she had taken it, he clamped to his side, imprisoning her hand so that the warmth soon began to creep back into it. With this small speck of comfort, her desolation gradually diminished.

He shortened his stride to match hers. Now that she was so close to him she was able to confirm that he was, indeed, a large man, even taller than her father had been, and *he* had measured an inch over six feet. Yet, for some strange reason, she did not find this man's height as intimidating as her father's had been, despite her awareness that he might at any time swing her around and topple her over the cliff. By now, however, this fear had been superseded by an overwhelming desire for warmth and shelter.

"Do you know this part of the world?" he asked her when they had walked in silence for a while.

"Yes, very well," Rosaline shouted back at him and then wished she could take the words back. To admit she knew it well was tantamount to admitting she lived hereabouts and was therefore the woman he sought. *Ah well*, she told herself resignedly. *Too late now*.

"Then perhaps you may know if there is a farmhouse or even an inn nearby."

"No. There is nothing at all on this high part of Exmoor until we reach Porlock, which is a good few miles ahead. If we could strike out to the south of us, we would eventually reach Brendon, but it would be impossible to find the way on a night like this. We would run the risk of falling down one of the countless chasms about here. Our only hope in this darkness is to remain on the track."

God help me, she added to herself, for she was not sure that she could go much further without some rest. She had begun to realize that, in actuality, he was supporting her, for she was leaning all her weight upon his arm. It could not be easy for him while carrying a large bag on his shoulder, yet he did not falter. He also seemed remarkably surefooted, moving purposefully along the track as if *he* were the one with the eyes of a cat.

For a fleeting moment, she had a longing to see his face. Then she chided herself for even thinking such a thing at a time like this. Here she was, the fugitive Countess of Beresford, being assisted by a hired assassin or at the very least by the spy who was tracking her down, and she was wondering if he had a handsome face. All the strain of the past hours must be making her lightheaded!

"By God, I think I see something up ahead!"

His sudden shout startled her. He halted and drew his arm away to shield his eyes from the rain.

She peered into the rain-swept darkness. All she could see was this everlasting rain and the drops of water dripping from the edge of her hood.

"Can you see it now? A low building to the right of us, in the lee of that higher stretch of moorland." She sensed that he was looking towards her, but she could see nothing and merely shook her head, wondering what knavery he was up to now.

"Come, take my arm again. We must make our way down the slope here."

"I think it best if we stay on the track," Rosaline replied, her heart pounding. "Otherwise we may lose ourselves."

"Never tell me you are hen-hearted!" He sounded like a man coaxing a six-year-old child to jump her pony over a foot-high fence.

Wretched man! "No, sir, I am not hen-hearted. Merely very careful."

"Well, you may consider it careful to be standing out 'upon this blasted heath,' freezing to death, but I do not! Are you coming or not?"

Aha, so he knew a little Shakespeare, too. A well-read scoundrel! "No, I am not coming with you."

"Very well. Be stubborn. I shall go down to investigate. Remain here with my bag, if you please."

Before she could make any further protest, he strode off into the darkness. She had a good mind to walk on and leave him. He had an odious habit of giving orders as if he were accustomed to being obeyed without question. Yet he carried it off in such a reasonable manner, despite the fact that he had to shout to be heard, that she found it difficult to summon up the strength to berate him for it. Besides, she had not the faintest idea how one would berate a man who had been hired to spy upon—perhaps even to murder—one! All she did know was that he had been gone for a good few minutes. The thought of being abandoned on this desolate moor was now far more terrifying than was any conjecture as to his intentions.

Rosaline was about to shout into the void ahead of her when she heard the welcome sound of his voice hailing her.

"It's a small shepherd's hut built of stone," he said when he reached her. "Empty, but with signs of habitation. I daresay the worthy shepherd decided he'd best go home— which is where you and I should be also! Come, give me your arm. It is but a short scramble down a not overly steep incline."

She was still loathe to depart from the track and strike out into the hazardous unknown, but his hand on her elbow was insistent. He swung his bag over his left shoulder again. "I think it would be best if you were to hold onto my arm with both hands," he suggested. "Whatever happens, do not let go. There are patches of loose shale about, and you could slip."

Once again, as he guided her down the slope, she was amazed at his seeming confidence. He moved as if he were able to see way ahead of him. The strength of his arm renewed her self-confidence, and she stepped forward ahead of him—only to feel her feet slip from under her. For a horrid moment, she fancied herself sliding hundreds of feet down into one of Exmoor's ravines, but in a second both his arms were clamped about her and her slide was halted.

"All right?" he inquired as she stood, trembling, pressed close to his body. She could feel the rough folds of his cloak against her cheek and smell the odor of wet wool. "Good girl," he said. "You had the sense not to let go of my arm. It is but a few steps further now. Cling fast and walk very carefully, and we shall have no more mishaps."

It was a novelty not to be yelled at and called "a little fool" for having made an error in judgment!

He released her to swing his bag over his shoulder again, and Rosaline grasped his arm, keeping step with him.

The stone hut was indeed only a few steps further, its low, dark shape suddenly appearing beyond the rain. The thought of being sheltered from the gnawing cold and continuous onslaught of rain stirred her blood, and she ran forward to feel along the rough stone walls for the doorway. It was hard to find, for in this more sheltered part of the moor, the night was even blacker than it had been before, if that were possible.

He took her hand in his. She heard the screech of rusty hinges, and she was drawn into the hut after him, the door slamming shut behind them.

Once inside, the darkness became almost tangible. She could hear him breathing but could not see his face, even though she knew he was directly beside her. She wrinkled her nose at the damp, musty smell inside the hut and then began to strip off her sodden gloves.

Now she could hear him moving about, cursing softly as he bumped into some object. "Not much here," he told her, his voice booming upon her ears in the confined space. It was deep and warm, like the mellifluous tones of a cello. "Let me get out my tinderbox and see if there is a lamp somewhere about. If not, I have a stub of candle here in my bag."

Most resourceful! But then, from what Rosaline had deduced about Oliver's many nefarious activities, one of his spies would need to be resourceful.

She heard the sound of striking, but no light appeared. "Devil take it! Pardon me, ma'am, but this cursed rain has flooded it. I had not realized that the bag the innkeeper gave me in exchange for my saddlebag had a split in it. Ah well, perhaps the box will eventually dry out. For now, I regret to inform you, we must remain in darkness."

She wasn't at all sure that this was not actually for the best. Although she was extremely curious to see his face, she did not wish him to see hers. The continuation of the darkness preserved their anonimity, which in turn made her feel more secure. Surely, to acknowledge their true identities to each other would serve only to underscore the relationship of hunter and hunted.

"And now that we can at least hear, if not see, each other, allow me to present myself, ma'am. My name—"

"No," she cried. "I do not wish to know your name or

the reason for your having followed me. I beg you, sir, while we find ourselves in such—such unusual circumstances, let us remain unknown to each other. Let us pretend," she pleaded, "that we know nothing whatsoever about each other. I would rather go out in the storm again than acknowledge the true reason for our being thrown together like this."

"Very well, ma'am. Very well. Do not, I beg of you, become so overwrought. I own that I am all at sea when you speak of my having followed you, but I give you my word not to seek to know your identity, if that is indeed your wish." He moved forward to stand before her. "Give me your hand, if you please."

Hesitantly, she held out her hand and, finding it, he took it in his. He, too, had removed his gloves. As her cold fingers were surrounded by the warmth of his hand, a strange tingling sensation radiated from them to encompass her entire body.

"You are frozen." He reached up his hand to run it down her cloak. "Come, get out of this cloak immediately or you will catch a chill."

He was right. The cloak was heavy with water. The violence of her shivering had abated a little, but her teeth were still chattering together. Fumbling at the strings of her hood, she undid the top fastening and then the others, and dragged the cloak off.

"I fear it will not dry too well without a fire, but at least the water can drip from it if it is hung up." He took it from her, retreated to a corner of the hut, and then returned to stand close by her. "Now, my dear lady," he said softly. "What of your dress?"

To her horror, Rosaline felt his hands upon her, running down her back from her shoulder to her waist. She held her breath, suddenly realizing the terrifying possibilities of her situation. She cursed herself for not having grasped the opportunity to escape from him when he had gone off to look for the hut. Now it was too late. Here, in this confined space, she was utterly at his mercy.

Chapter Three

It was futile even to consider screaming or running from him. There was no one to hear her, nowhere to run to. *Stay calm*, Rosaline told herself. *If you speak reasonably to him, you may be able to forestall him.* But for how long? For the entire night? It was not likely! God, how she loathed men. They were all the same: animals beneath their fine exteriors. How naive of her to think that this one might be different!

Now his hands were on her hair, which hung loose down her back. She choked back tears at the thought of Lemmy brushing it in the warmth of her bedchamber. How strange to think that had happened only a few hours ago. It seemed to lie in the dim, distant past.

"Your hair is soaking wet also. I thought that all fashionable women chopped their hair off nowadays," he remarked in a surprisingly conversational tone. "My sisters have, I regret to say."

"You have sisters?" she asked brightly, clutching at the idea that a man who talked of his sisters might not be quite so disposed to do her harm.

"Indeed I have. Three of 'em, all younger than I. But let us not be talking of sisters while you are waterlogged and shivering with the cold. Have you a comb?"

"A comb?" she repeated, sounding like a half-wit.

"Yes, a comb. Oh, never mind. I have one here in my bag." He removed his hands from her and began to rummage in his bag.

Rosaline gave a nervous little laugh. "You appear to have everything in that bag of yours."

"Unfortunately not. I can neither light the candle nor get a fire going to dry your clothing. But I do have some provisions. As soon as I have you out of that wet dress, we shall eat."

His hands reached out to touch her again, this time brushing against her breasts, for she had turned to face him. Gasping, she sprang back from him.

"Forgive me, ma'am. I cannot see a thing in this confounded darkness. Turn your back to me, would you? I intend to dry your hair with this piece of toweling and I shall braid it so that it will not be soaking your back."

She began to think she was most assuredly locked up with a lunatic. "Braid my hair?" she repeated incredulously.

"Yes. Think I can't do it in this darkness? I'm not saying it will be a perfect job, but I braided my sisters' hair so often when they were younger that I am certain I could do it in my sleep, never mind in the dark. Now stand still, if you please, and I shall soon have it done."

She gave another little laugh, which came perilously close to hysteria. "You are indeed a resourceful man."

"Hm" was his only comment. He was evidently concentrating on the task in hand.

She felt the comb run down her scalp, dividing her hair into three sections. Then he smoothed the hair back from her face with the palms of his hands, sending shivers down her neck. His skin was smooth, and his hands smelled of sandalwood. Evidently he earned his living with his wits, not his hands.

Having a man braid her hair was a vastly different experience from having her nurse or one of her maids perform the task. As he twisted the three separate strands of her heavy hair into one thick braid, she found the deft movements of his hands on her hair, his fingers brushing against her neck and shoulders, strangely sensuous and relaxing. One small part of her, however, remained aloof and incredulous. *How can you bear having such a man even touch you?* demanded her alter ego. She could not answer the question. All she knew was that no man before this night had ever touched her thus—with gentleness, almost tenderness.

"There," he said. "That is done. I have tied it with a piece of twine. Not very elegant, my lady, but it will have to do."

She stiffened. Had he allowed the words "my lady" to slip out in error, or was it merely a funning term? She could not tell.

"Well, ma'am, do I get the position of lady's maid or not?"

"Why certainly, sir," she replied, employing the same bantering tone. "You have passed the ultimate test with flying colors."

"Now for your dress."

She jerked away from him. "My dress will do very well as it is, sir," she informed him in a haughty tone.

"Certainly it will, if you intend to be buried in it tomorrow morning! For heaven's sake, girl, the front of it is dripping wet. You cannot possibly keep it on."

"I cannot possibly remove it," she said in a less confident tone, fear catching at her throat.

For a moment there was silence. Then he moved closer to her and reached out to take her hand, to enfold it in his, a strangely comforting gesture. "You are not a child. I can tell that from your voice and manner and, if you will forgive me, from your body. It is also evident that you have a deep mistrust of the male sex in general and of me in particular. You will, therefore, lend me no credence when I assure you that I mean you no harm. So perhaps you will allow me to touch on your predicament in another way. You cannot go out again into the night or you will surely perish. You will also surely perish if you lie down and sleep in that gown, and sleep you must for I can tell that you are infinitely weary. If you were stark naked, I could not see you in this darkness, even if I wished to. As for ravishing you, I can assure you that if that were my intention, I could do so with your dress on just as easily as with it off." He gave her hand a reassuring squeeze. "I have neither the time nor inclination to carry your lifeless body down the hill to Porlock tomorrow, for I have heard it is a notoriously fearful incline. Nor do I have the time to make arrangements for your burial, for I am already late in my travel arrangements. So, I beg of you, humor me. I have a wonderfully warm flannel nightshirt in my bag—''

Rosaline could not help it. Whether from hysteria or not, the laughter burst from her, and she found she could not stop it.

"What on earth is so amusing?"

"That—that bag of yours," she spluttered. "That *infernal* bag is like Pandora's box!" She went off into another peal of laughter.

"By Jove, you're right! But, you see, my mother still thinks I am a young stripling of eighteen going out into the cruel world, instead of an aging man of two and thirty. She insists on my taking all these things 'just in case.' For once, however, I am glad of it. Now, what about that dress?"

"Oh, very well. I shall take off my dress, if you insist. But give me the nightshirt first, if you please, and then turn your back upon me."

"My dear lady," he said, his voice muffled. She surmised that he was once more delving into the depths of the seemingly bottomless bag. "How am I supposed to know my back is turned on you or not when I cannot even see you?"

He had a point there! The piece of toweling was thrust at her.

"Dry yourself with this as best as you can. It's a trifle damp from your hair, I'm afraid."

The towel was followed by the soft warmth of the flannelette nightshirt, which miraculously seemed to have escaped getting wet. Setting the towel and nightshirt down on a rickety stool, which her shins had encountered already, she began to strip off her wet dress, easing it distastefully from her clammy skin. Heavens, it was so good to remove it and be able to rub her skin to a glowing warmth with the rough towel!

Rosaline noticed that the towel bore the faint aroma of

sandalwood. She was drying herself with a towel he had used. The thought sent a rush of heat throughout her body, and for a moment she pressed her face against the towel. Then she dragged off her sodden hose, dried her boots, and pulled them on again, her bare toes curling against the feeling of hard, damp leather.

It was fortunate that her underslip had escaped a severe wetting, only the hem being damp. She decided that it would be best to keep it on, although the thought of the fleecy warmth of his nightshirt against her bare skin was an enticing one.

As she pulled it over her head, she caught an even stronger whiff of sandalwood and wondered if he had slept in it the previous night. Her face and neck were suffused with fire at the thought. The nightshirt was very large on her, the sleeves and hem far too long. She had been right. He *was* a large man.

"How is it?"

"Wonderfully warm, I thank you."

"Good. Give me your dress, and I shall hang it on the crossbar here, beside your cloak. Then for some food."

"One moment, sir," she said on impulse. "You have attended to my comfort, but what about yours? Are you not soaking wet also?"

"Do you wish to examine me to find out?" he asked, laughter in his voice.

She hesitated for a moment, then said in a low voice: "Yes, for it is not right that I should be dry and warm at your expense."

Her sensible other self looked on in astonishment. *You must have lost your mind,* it told her.

He came to stand before her, so that she could hear his rather hurried breathing. "Very well, ma'am," he said. "I present myself for your inspection."

Marveling at herself, she put out her hand and touched his coat sleeve. Damp, but not wet. She ran her fingers up to his lapel. Wet. The fabric was good, a fine broadcloth. Now his shoulders. She had to extend her arm to reach them. Very damp. Delicately, she ran her hands across his broad chest to feel his waistcoat and neckcloth. The waist-coat was slightly damp. The shirtfront was passable. The neckcloth was sodden.

He was shivering. But then so was she—and she was sure that it was not only the cold that was affecting her.

"Well?" he demanded. "Your verdict, ma'am?"

"You must remove your neckcloth at once, for it is extremely wet, and your coat is very damp. If only you had another—"

"I regret that I had to draw the line at carrying another coat in my bag. Capacious it may be, but it does have its limitations. I trust that does not disappoint you. My trunk with all my effects has been sent on ahead of me. At this rate, it is likely to arrive at its destination long before I do!"

For a moment, she believed him, so sincere did he sound. How gullible she was! Still, for now she must suspend all disbelief; otherwise the next few hours would be intolerable.

She could hear him tugging at his neckcloth. "There," he said after a short pause. "You were right. It is wet. That feels very much better. I thank you for your concern, ma'am. Now for that food I spoke of. I have bread and a wedge of cheddar and some ham, plus a small flask of wine. A veritable feast. Have you by any chance encountered some form of chair in this hovel?"

"There is a stool over here."

"Capital. I found a rough form of table by the door. I cannot guarantee that it will meet your possibly exacting standards of cleanliness, but beggars cannot be choosers. I know!" he suddenly exclaimed. "I have the very thing. A sheet of the *Western News* will make a fine tablecloth." He dragged the table across the room to her, and she heard the rustle of newspaper as he laid it on the table. "Good. Now . . . bread, cheese, ham, one leather flask of my father's best bordeaux—no glasses, alas—one knife. Before you, if you could but see it, ma'am, you have an exquisite feast. Have you your stool there? Draw it up and set to."

"What about you? What will you sit on?"

"First, I shall serve you your meal and then I shall sit on the floor. Have you a better suggestion?"

"No, I suppose not, if there is nothing else."

"Nothing. I have looked or, more accurately, felt. But there is one large sheepskin in the corner. I shall sit on that and, later, when you have eaten, it will serve as your bed."

The thought of bed effectively silenced her, but her misgivings were banished when she was handed her first meal since her father's funeral feast many hours ago. As she ate, she reflected that nothing had ever tasted half as good to her. Not even the delectable offerings at one of her father's infrequent extravagant banquets could approach the crusty bread cut in large slabs, with thick slices of ham and crumbly cheddar cheese between them.

"Mmm, the Earl of Sandwich is to be congratulated," her companion said. "A dish fit for a king—or queen! Some wine, my lady."

She wished he would not address her thus. It served only to underline his knowledge of her name and title. A shiver ran across her shoulders at the thought.

"Cold?" he asked quickly.

"Just a little."

"Put on my coat."

"No. I would not think of doing so! You would then have only your shirt and waistcoat, and they are damp. No, sir, I beg—" But her protestations were ignored. His coat, still warm from his body, was around her shoulders. "Thank you" was all she could say. In his good-natured, easy way he was an extremely *managing* person.

"Would you care for some wine?"

"If you please." Rosaline's fingers encountered his as he passed her the leather flask. She drank down a quite sizable draught. Within minutes, the wine was singing in her veins, making her pleasantly lightheaded.

"You say you have sisters. Have you brothers also?" she asked him.

"I seem to recollect being told that we were not to talk of ourselves to each other."

"Oh," she said, confused. "I do not wish to know your name, sir, merely your—your—"

"My origins? Very well. I am the son of a naval captain,

now retired. I have two elder brothers and one younger, in addition to my three sisters."

"A good-sized family."

"Yes, indeed."

"And do they all still reside at home?"

"Lord, no. My parents have a small estate near Ilfracombe, to which they removed from Plymouth when my father retired. Two of my brothers are serving their country as naval officers; the third is the master of a merchant vessel which plies its way between England and the West Indies. As to my sisters, only Andrea, the youngest, remains unmarried—though not for long, I imagine, with all the local gentry, both eligible and ineligible, wearing a path to her door."

"You did not follow your brothers into the navy, then?"

"No." His reply was as abrupt as a door being slammed in her face. "I am engaged in other employment."

Her heart sank. Why on earth had she asked him such a leading question?

"I am even now on my way to a new situation," he hurriedly added, probably realizing that he had given too much away, "the young man I was employed to tutor having taken his wild excesses up to Cambridge, where I doubt he will last half a term. It is because I am embarking on a new position that I did not wish to arrive later than the predetermined time."

"Quite so."

Now it was her turn to be abrupt. Rosaline wished that she had not started this conversation. She should have known that it could lead in only one direction: that of his involvement with Oliver. It was difficult to believe that for a short while she had completely forgotten who this man was and why he was here. She wished with all her heart that he had not found it necessary to lie to her. No doubt all his brothers and sisters, including the beautiful Andrea, were mere figments of his fertile imagination. The thought made her feel unaccountably depressed.

"More wine?" he asked.

"No, thank you." She felt overwhelmingly weary all of a sudden; weary and downhearted.

"Now it is my turn to ask about you," he said. "That you are from somewhere nearby I already know. What I do not know is your reason for having to run away on such a night as this."

She darted him a scorching look but then realized that that was useless, as he could not see it. "I have absolutely no intention of speaking to you about myself," she informed him haughtily.

"Not very fair, that. You glean all the information you can from me but then refuse to tell me anything about yourself. It won't fadge, you know. However top-lofty you may act with me, I know very well that you are in deep trouble, only I was sincerely hoping that you would feel able to tell me about it before I confronted you with it. You see," he added in a gentle voice, "I couldn't help but feel that bag in the pocket of your cloak."

Her blood ran cold. Her jewels. She had left them in her cloak pocket.

"Stole 'em from your employer, did you? I put you down as a runaway governess when I first caught up with you. I could tell from your speech that you were a lady, but it was not until I found the jewels that I understood why you were running away and also why you thought I was following you."

She heard the creak of the table as he leaned across it. "Whatever trouble you are in, it is not worth placing your very life in jeopardy, I assure you. Stealing valuable jewels is a hanging offence, you know. At the very least, you would be transported. Why not give the bag to me, and I shall undertake to return them for you? It is more than likely that your employer would be willing to forego the charges against you if the jewels were returned."

Rosaline almost laughed in his face. "Oh, you would like that, wouldn't you?" she said scornfully. "You must think me an utter fool if you think I would meekly turn them over to you! You will have to kill me first!"

"Very well," he said with a heavy sigh. "Let us not speak any further on the subject. But do not say I did not try to help you."

He sounded extremely dispirited. Ha! Why in the world should he be dispirited when he could quite easily take the jewels from her if he had a mind to?

"Do you wish to eat anything more?" he asked.

"No."

"Then I shall clear this all away. The mice can eat up the crumbs."

She shivered. The thought of mice running across her body as she slept was not at all conducive to slumber. She felt extremely cold and low-spirited. The warm rapport between them had been dissipated by her foolish questions.

She heard a rustling as he moved about nearby. "There," he said. "I have laid the sheepskin out on a bundle of straw."

"Your coat," she said, suddenly remembering that it was still around her shoulders. She took it off and held it out to him.

"No, no. Keep it. It is growing colder every minute in this place. Lie down and I shall cover you with it."

She was not about to argue with him. She lay down on the soft wool of the sheepskin and felt the weight of his coat and the touch of his hands as he tucked it around her.

"Good night, sir, and thank you for your kindness." Whatever his intentions, he *had* been kind.

"Good night, ma'am. Sleep well."

Despite her extreme fatigue, however, sleep refused to come. When she closed her eyes, she saw images of Oliver coming towards her—Oliver, with her dagger in his chest, his eyes glazed but still glaring venomously up at her. The wind gusted down the outlet in the roof that acted as a chimney, swirling around the earthen floor of the stone hut, and thoughts swirled in her tired brain until she was sure she was going out of her mind.

She began to shiver again, a sick shuddering that convulsed her entire body. She steeled herself, trying to control it, afraid that he would hear her, but the shuddering only intensified. The image of the gallows up at Brendon Cross, with her skeleton swinging from it, filled her mind. Oh, God, what was to become of her?

"What is the matter? Can you not sleep?"

She jumped, startled by his proximity, for she had not heard him approach. Now he knelt down by her, and she felt his hand firm upon her shoulder. So severe was the convulsive shivering that she could not reply. She felt his arms about her, lifting her up against him. "There now," he said in a soothing voice, as if quieting a child with a nightmare. "You are perfectly safe. Do not be afraid. Nothing here will harm you."

His cold hand stroked her face and hair, while he supported her with his other arm. Burying her face against his shirt-front, she at last allowed all her pent-up emotion to pour forth. As she sobbed against him, she could feel his hand all the time stroking her cheek and hair.

Eventually, she coughed, blew her nose in the handkerchief he offered her, and drew away from him. "Forgive me. I do not know what came over me."

"If only you would permit me to assist you in some more concrete fashion," he said, sighing as he stood up.

"I cannot," she mumbled.

"So you have said. Can you sleep now, do you think?"

"Yes. I—I believe I can." Then she remembered the coldness of his hand on her cheek. He had nothing, no coat, no warm sheepskin. "But I am still exceedingly cold," she ventured, amazed at her own daring.

"Oh, Lord, I regret I have nothing else to offer you. I admit that I myself am also frozen."

She swallowed. "I own I was far warmer when you were holding me," she said hesitantly. "Were not you?"

The straw rustled as he moved nearer. "Yes, I was." He was kneeling beside her again. "Are you by any chance inviting me to share your sheepskin and my coat, fair lady?" he asked lightly.

"Pray, do not laugh at me," she begged him, already afraid that she had made a terrible mistake in suggesting such a thing.

"Laugh, ma'am! How could I laugh at such a wondrous offer, when I am almost turned to ice? You are an angel of mercy."

She was grateful for his levity, knowing that he recognized her fear. Whatever else he might be, this man was most decidedly a gentleman.

Moving to one side of the sheepskin, Rosaline made space for him beside her. When he lay down next to her, she draped the coat over both of them. Now she realized that he was shivering, and she made a move towards him. "Come closer," she whispered.

"Are you sure?"

"Yes."

Instead of drawing nearer, he turned partially onto his back, at the same time enfolding her in his arms and drawing her head against his chest. She, in turn, put her right arm about his waist, feeling the metal buckle of his waistcoat against her fingers.

Since puberty, the term "sleeping with a man" had but one meaning for her: submission to a man's animal lust—terror and pain and disgust—and she had vowed to avoid it at all cost. Now here she was, actually inviting a man to lie beside her, being held in his arms, indeed relishing the sensations of intimacy and warmth his closeness evoked. Slowly, that warmth began to steal through her entire body, right down to her toes, loosening her muscles, unwinding the coil of tension in her neck—and she slept.

Chapter Four

Rosaline awoke with a start, her heart pounding as she opened her eyes to darkness and a strange environment.

For a moment, she lay on her back, yesterday's memories flooding into her mind. Then she tensed as she realized that his leg was thrown across the lower half of her body, and his left hand cupped her breast.

Her initial response should have been to strike out at him, but something held her back. For one thing, it was obvious from his deep, rhythmical breathing that he was sound asleep. She was also ashamed to admit, even to herself, that she found the weight and warmth of his leg and hand upon her body extremely pleasant. There was no sense of threat or demand in it, merely comfort.

She moved slightly to ease the slight numbness in her thigh. His response was to gently squeeze her breast, his thumb moving back and forth across her nipple. Her body quickened with the desire she had for so long believed herself incapable of experiencing.

No man had ever before inflamed her sensually as this stranger had. Indeed, she had long ago decided that she would never be able to respond to any man. It seemed unbelievably strange that Oliver's henchman would be the first man to arouse her at the considerable age of almost four and twenty. She would have laughed at the irony of fate had she not felt more like weeping.

For a long while she was content to lie beside him, listening to his calm breathing, enjoying, and yet frustrated by, all the new sensations his intimate proximity had summoned up.

Slowly, she came to realize that what had first woken her was the absence of noise. The deluge of rain had ceased, and the wind had died to a sighing moan. It was also growing light outside, for, although it was still pitch-dark in the hut, she could see a faint patch of sky in the chimney outlet in the roof.

Very reluctantly, she came to the conclusion that it was imperative that she escape from this man now, before he awoke. She lay for a moment longer, savoring what would be her last encounter with him. Then she slowly eased away from him, holding her breath when he groaned and turned over on his side—but he did not waken.

How cold and desolate she felt now that she was separated from him; it was as if she had left part of herself there beside his sleeping form.

This was no time for such sentimental foolishness. *Remember Oliver!* she told herself. By now, the murder would have been discovered and the search for her would have begun, and it would be this man who would betray her.

The thought was more than sufficient to goad her into action. Rosaline tiptoed across the hut, feeling her way with her hands, trying not to rustle the damp straw that was strewn on the floor. The hut was so small that it did not take her long to find her dress and cloak. Both were still extremely damp, but at least the rainwater had drained from them.

She dragged the dress on over the nightshirt. It was fortunate that she had lost some weight during the last few harrowing weeks of her father's illness, or the dress would never have fit over the bulky flannel shirt, which she was determined not to remove. By keeping it on she would not have the clamminess of the damp silk of her dress against her skin.

Now for her cloak. As soon as she pulled it on, she thrust her hand into the left pocket—to encounter the bag of brushed leather containing the jewels. She breathed a sigh of relief. If it had been his intention to take the jewels, he had evidently decided to leave it until morning. *Well, sir, now you are too late!*

Now for the door. It had been heavy and the hinges squeaked, she recollected. She must be extremely careful, or she would be sure to waken him. The thought of seeing this calm, warm-natured man in his true colors disturbed her deeply. She wished to remember him as he had been last night: good-humored and considerate. She was destined never to know what he looked like. Perhaps it was for the best. The prospect of visualizing her enemy was a chilling one. Far better to remember him as a nameless and faceless man who had befriended her in her need, whatever his motive.

Gritting her teeth, she drew back the bar, inch by inch,

and then slowly eased open the heavy door, lifting it to prevent it from scraping across the floor. Each time the hinges squeaked, Rosaline flinched and held her breath, praying that he would not waken—but no movement came from behind her.

Having opened the door a foot or so, she squeezed through the aperture and left the door ajar, not daring to close it again.

The rain had indeed ceased, leaving in its stead low clouds and the cold, wet mist that seemed to penetrate one's very bones. Having lived all her life on this northern coastline, Rosaline knew this type of weather well. Because of the poor visibility it was difficult to pinpoint the time exactly, but from the gray light and her ability to see a reasonable distance ahead of her, she guessed that it must be seven o'clock or thereabouts.

She glanced over her shoulder to see if the man was following her, but there was no sign of another human being. Scrambling up the slippery incline, having to cling to tufts of heather for support now that she did not have her escort's arm, she soon reached the track along the edge of the cliffs and began to stride eastward along it.

Knowing that she still had a good ten miles ahead of her and that she must pace herself accordingly, she fought down the temptation to run. It was extremely frustrating to know that the village of Porlock lay only two or so miles ahead of her. The thought of the warmth of the hospitable fire and the excellent breakfast she would no doubt have found at the Ship Inn there was tantalizing, but Porlock was far too close to Beresford for safety. Although she had seldom ventured from the castle and its immediate environs, there might well be an estate worker or servant in Porlock who would recognize her. Besides, he—she wished she knew the man's name so that she could think of him in some other way than merely as he—could catch up with her easily if she were to linger. No, she must pass as quickly as possible through Porlock and then press on to Minehead.

A few hours later—wet, weary, and ravenously hungry— Rosaline entered the small town of Minehead, to find that she had arrived there on market day. It was, consequently, her nose that guided her to the center of town. That, and the din of cackling hens and geese, bleating sheep, barking dogs, and the rumble and screech of cart wheels.

As she walked down the hill and entered the main street, it was like entering Bedlam, but at least she would probably be able to remain hidden in these crowds. From the time she had first entered the outskirts of the town, she had been on the lookout for a large man, in case Oliver's spy might somehow have caught up with her.

As she walked down the main street, she looked about her at the rows of attractive new houses. Although she had never been to Minehead before, she knew that the town had been rebuilt after a disastrous fire at the end of the previous century.

It was not houses, however, that interested her at present. Her pressing need was for food and shelter. Where was the main inn, she wondered. She must find it immediately. It would not do for a solitary female to enter one of the public houses frequented by the market folk, although the aroma of hot sausages that wafted from the doorway of a low-roofed inn of squalid appearance was extremely tempting.

Pushing her way through a flock of exceedingly muddy and scared sheep, she avoided the over-friendly attention of a large mongrel dog—not to mention the blatant stares and remarks she was receiving from the various farm laborers in the square, who had no idea what to make of her but made no bones about what they'd like to do *with* her—and continued to walk until she saw, across the street, a large stone establishment whose swinging sign on a tall post by its imposing front entrance proclaimed it The Crowing Cock. *Singularly suitable*, thought Rosaline as she dodged yet another yokel, who leered at her and tried to bar her way as she crossed the street.

Not wishing to enter through the main doorway in her present state of dishevelment, she went through the inn's arched coach entrance, darting to the side and pressing herself against the wall as a traveling curricle dashed through, heralded by a blast of a horn and an arrogant male voice shouting, "Out of the way, you stupid wench!"

The coach yard was even more noisy and bustling than the market square had been. Several carriages were being readied, with fresh teams of horses being harnessed or old teams being removed, all at a frantic pace. Such a hubbub did the raucous shouts and blasting horns and scrape of wheels over cobblestones create that her ears still rang with it when she stepped over the threshold into the relative quiet of the inn's interior.

Acutely aware of the decidedly odd appearance she must present, Rosaline drew herself up to her considerable height and moved down the corridor like a queen entering her throne room, pushing open the glass-paneled door to enter the carpeted reception area.

A man in flesh-colored pantaloons and an extremely tight coat with exaggerated puff shoulders, who was standing by the reception desk, raised his long-stemmed quizzing glass and surveyed her through it until she felt there was not one inch of her that he had not perused.

She cast him a withering look, but this apparently served only to increase his amusement. Realizing that it was best to ignore the popinjay, she approached the desk and the clerk who was leaning his hands upon it, looking down his long nose at her. "I wish to bespeak one of your best front rooms," she said in a firm voice.

"Oh, you do, do you?" the clerk replied with a supercilious smile, which caused the ogling man to laugh out loud. "I fear you're in the wrong establishment, miss. This is not a house for the likes of you!"

"I beg your pardon." Rosaline fixed the clerk with a haughty glare. She was about to bid him send for the landlord, when mine host himself bustled up.

"What have we 'ere, then?" he demanded.

Rosaline turned with relief, only to find that the expression on the landlord's plump face was one of extreme indignation.

The clerk rudely pointed his index finger at her. "This, er, lady—" He was interrupted by a derisive laugh from the ogler. "—wishes to bespeak one of our best front rooms, Mr. Crabtree."

"Does she? Does she, indeed?" The landlord surveyed her from the top of her hood to the toes of her muddy half boots and then back again. "And where might your luggage be, miss? And, begging your pardon, m'lady, your carriage? And your servants? Out back, are they? Just a-waiting to make sure as you gets your best front room afore they comes in?"

This exquisite wit was greeted with a mirthless smile by the angular-faced clerk and another odious, high-pitched laugh from the fop.

Rosaline lifted her chin and looked down at the landlord as if he were a beetle upon which she was about to set her foot. "My carriage has broken down about half a mile from town," she informed him. "I was forced to walk."

"And your ladyship's maid was sore injured with a broken leg so's she couldn't accompany you, I'll warrant! No, no, my girl, let us 'ave done with this farce right this minute. There's plenty places fit for such as you—the Fox and Duck down the road, for one. But not 'ere, m'dear, not 'ere. Now, be off with you. And no importuning my guests on the way out, neither."

He stepped forward and was about to take her arm, but thought better of it when he saw her furious expression.

"How dare you address me in that insolent manner!" As she confronted the landlord, her hood fell back to reveal an abundance of rich auburn hair, which had long since escaped its braid. "I have never before been spoken to with such a lack of common courtesy! Is it thus that you treat a lady who has had the misfortune to have an accident befall her? My friends shall know of this, sir." So incensed was she that she entirely forgot her intention to remain as inconspicuous as possible. "From henceforth," she cried, warming to the role of a lady severely wronged by an inferior, "this inn will be shunned by all those who consider themselves people of good taste. And as for you"—she spun around to face the ogling buck, who was treating it all as a tremendous joke—"you miserable little worm . . ."

She did not complete the sentence but tore the quizzing glass from his grasp. With one sharp tug, she wrenched it from his neck and then threw it on the floor to grind the glass beneath her heel. She bent to retrieve it and, with a sweeping gesture, returned it to him. "There, sir, is your glass," she said with a smile of infinite disdain.

His painted face reddened even more. "Here, I—I say," he stuttered, the smile most effectively wiped from his vapid countenance.

The clerk and landlord stood motionless, their mouths wide open with astonishment.

"I tell you now, my man," Rosaline informed the landlord, "I would not stay in your wretched inn if it were the last place on earth!"

And with these parting words, she swept regally from the reception hall—to be brought up short by a stout man of middle age who blocked her exit. "Bravo!" he cried ecstatically. "You were *magnificent*. Utterly magnificent! Worthy of a standing ovation, no less."

Rosaline was in no mood for any further facetious comments. "Out of my way, if you please," she snapped.

"No, no, madam. I assure you that I am in earnest," the man insisted. "In all my forty-six years in the profession, I have never seen anything like it. Such fire! Such hauteur! Not even Siddons at her best could equal it. Ah, what a Lady Macbeth you would make. What a Portia!"

"I beg your pardon, sir?" Her tone was more curious than angry, for she was sure that she was being accosted by a madman.

He drew her into the corridor. "It is, of course, most evident to me, who am a venerable member of the profession, that you are not what those imbeciles in there took you for—a woman of the streets. Ah, 'what fools these mortals be!'" he intoned in a hollow voice and then gave her a shrewd glance from his small pale-blue eyes. "Fallen on hard times, eh? It happens to us all, dear lady. And we must give succor to our own, must we not? Will you do me the honor of joining me in the public parlor?" Seeing her hesitation, he hastened to reassure her. "No, no, my dear young lady, I assure you that my intentions are entirely honorable. I am an honorable man. We are all honorable men. I have a proposition to put to you.''

Still she hesitated.

"You must be hungry. You *look* hungry. The body must be assuaged before the mind can be forced into action, you know. Have you partaken of luncheon?''

She had not partaken of breakfast, never mind luncheon.

"I have a monstrously large steak-and-kidney pie and a bowl of mashed turnips on my table this very instant, a-growing cold. Will you not join me, dear lady?''

The thought of food of any kind was too enticing to resist. "That is exceedingly kind of you, sir,'' Rosaline replied, employing a cool tone so as to dispel any doubts he might still harbor as to her character. "I must own that I am feeling a trifle hungry.''

"Capital! Come along, then.''

With a flamboyant bow, hand pressed to his magenta and silver-striped waistcoat, he ushered her into the public parlor and held a chair for her to be seated at the small round table. Although the oak-paneled parlor was full, it was not overly noisy. Upon their entrance, two men glanced up from their game of backgammon, and a young sprig in muddy top boots and a bright yellow waistcoat was about to saunter over, until he caught sight of the lady's stout companion behind her.

Having called for and received another plate, her benefactor served up a large plateful of the steaming pie, with a vast helping of mashed yellow turnips beside it.

"There you are, dear lady,'' he said, setting the plate before her. "Let us partake of our repast first and make conversation afterwards.''

This plan suited her admirably, for it would give her a little time to concoct a reasonably convincing explanation for her present predicament. As she ate the simple but delicious meal, her mind was racing, striving both to evaluate her present situation and to formulate plans for the immediate future.

Of paramount importance was the necessity to discover

whether or not she had killed Oliver. Even if his body had been discovered that morning, it was unlikely that the news could have reached Minehead yet. She would be safe for today, at least. During the long walk from Porlock, she had agonized over what was the best thing for her to do. Should she return to Beresford and throw herself on the mercy of Lord Ellington, whose estates marched with hers? He had avoided dealing with her father as much as possible in the past. And she knew that he was no friend of Oliver's. He was an aloof but just man. Yet surely, she thought with an inner qualm, would not that very love of justice preclude any show of mercy to a murderess? And if she did return to Beresford Castle, what if Oliver were alive? What then? She shuddered at the thought of Oliver bent upon revenge.

No, as her mother's voice had told her, she must seek out someone in a position of power, someone with influence, to help her. Whether Oliver was alive or dead, she must not divulge her identity to anyone until she could gain an influential ear—and that would take time. Meanwhile, she must hide. Even now, she found herself glancing at any tall man who entered the parlor, her heart beating faster at the thought that he—her night companion—had caught up with her. It was imperative that she find a hiding place as soon as possible!

Long after Rosaline had finished eating, the man opposite continued to ply himself with food. Marveling at his capacity, she surreptitiously surveyed him. His face was large and fleshy, as was his body, but he could not actually be called corpulent. *Portly*, perhaps, was the word. He was of a fair height, with a broad chest, which was at present draped with his linen napkin to protect his neckcloth from splashes. His coat was of a gaudy blue with scuffed gilt buttons, the worn cuffs having been carefully patched with black velvet. He was all affability, nodding and smiling at her as he ate, but the few glances he gave her when he thought she was not looking were shrewd and calculating. Whatever this proposition of his was, she was determined to be extremely wary of it.

"Aah." With a contented sigh, he leaned back in his

chair, having picked up with a moist index finger the last crumbs of a boiled currant pudding with raspberry jam sauce. "Now, to business."

Rosaline pressed her napkin to her lips, set it down on the table, and waited.

"First things first. My name is Pepperell, Percival Pepperell—at your service, ma'am." He inclined his head slowly in a grand manner.

"And mine is Rosaline Fitzgerald," she told him, having already decided upon this name. Fitzgerald had been her maternal grandmother's maiden name and only a few of her closest servants had know that her mother had called her Rosaline, for she would have incurred her husband's wrath had she done so in public.

"Aha! I knew it all along," cried Mr. Pepperell, his face beaming. "Fitzgerald! You are from Ireland. All the greatest actresses come from Ireland. Must be the famous Irish temperament that does it. Not yet found a position, eh?"

She met his penetrating gaze with equanimity. "That is correct, sir. I had hoped to be engaged by one of the circuit companies but have been unfortunate in my attempts so far."

"Hm, not surprised at it, not surprised at all. March is a singularly bad time of the year. Besides, there are dozens of actors with years of experience behind 'em begging for employment in the provincial and circuit companies—many of 'em willing to work for nothing but their food and lodgings. So, my dear lady, it is not likely you'd get far unless you have experience. Just come over from Ireland recently, have you?"

"Yes."

"I ask because you have very little of the Irish brogue to your speaking."

"My mother taught me to speak without it. She said it was not suitable for Shakespeare and the classical dramatists."

"Quite right. Quite right. Rosaline, eh? Very pretty, very pretty. A woman with hair as black as ebony and two pitch balls for eyes," he declaimed. "That's *Love's Labor's Lost*, you know," he informed her.

She knew, despite his rather muddled quotation.

"Doesn't quite fit your green eyes and red hair, does it?"

She smiled sweetly at him, biting back the hasty retort that had sprung to her lips. She loathed having the dark auburn color of her hair described as "red," but for the moment at least she must humor this man; therefore, she smiled sweetly.

"Well now, Miss Fitzgerald, here is my proposition. Ours is a modest little company, comprising less than a score of performers. We are what you might call a 'fill-in' company. We fill in where the circuit companies do not venture: little towns on market days and holidays, the outskirts of larger towns. Although, occasionally, we are fortunate enough to perform in a real theater, most of the time we put on our pieces wherever we can. Sometimes we pitch a tent in a field; sometimes we perform by request in a private house; sometimes, as here, we set up stage in the courtyard of a respectable inn. We are true ladies and gentlemen of the stage, the noblest profession on this earth, bringing entertainment and learning to the deserving public, wherever they may be found."

His voice had risen majestically as he spoke, and his arms opened wide symbolically to embrace his imaginary audience, so that heads turned to look at their table.

Draining down his tankard of ale, he leaned back in his chair, evidently waiting for her to speak.

"You spoke of a proposition, Mr. Pepperell," Rosaline prompted him.

"So I did. So I did. Unfortunately, my dear sister, the incomparable Mrs. Stiggins, is finding it impossible to continue as first female tragedian while attending to the day-to-day business of a thriving theatrical company—attending the box office, writing playbills, designing costumes, et cetera, et cetera—as well as looking after the nourishment, both physical and intellectual, of her five children. Ah, my dear Miss Fitzgerald, if you had but seen my sister in her heyday; what gestures, what eyes, such speaking eyes! But, alas, love and Alfred Stiggins—confound him, wherever he is—have been her undoing. We are in dire need of an actress, Miss Fitzgerald, one who would be willing to undertake the onerous duties of both leading female comedian and tragedian. Are you a quick learner?"

"Why, yes, I believe so," Rosaline replied.

"You would need to be a quick learner! For if we stay in a place more than one day, we are expected to provide our audience with a new play each night. A new piece together with a ballet and singing piece, and one or two solo soliloquies, of course." He bent his piercing gaze upon her. "I take it that you do sing and dance?"

"Oh, yes," Rosaline lied. She sang well enough, having had lessons, but the heiress to Beresford Castle had not had much occasion to perform solo dances in public. Still, she could learn—for at least as long as she was forced to remain with this man and his troupe.

"What do you say? Will you accept my offer?"

"That depends on the salary you are willing to provide, Mr. Pepperell. Unlike some of my colleagues, I am not willing to work for my board and lodging alone, you know. I do have my pride."

"Ah, yes. Yes, of course." He surveyed her unblinkingly, but if he expected her to be intimidated, he was to suffer disappointment, for she met his gaze with an equally candid, unwavering look, until his mouth widened into a smile. She had been assessed and not found wanting. "Shall we say ten shillings a week to start?"

"Ten shillings!" It was very little.

"If you prove to be as able as you say you are, then we shall raise it to twelve shillings after a while, depending on our takings, of course."

She still hesitated, not certain what she should do. To be sure, a traveling company would be an ideal place to hide herself, for it would be constantly on the move, but . . .

Seeing her hesitation, Mr. Pepperell hurriedly intervened. "Tell you what, my dear lady. If you are willing to share a bedchamber with my sister's children in whatever lodgings we find ourselves, we shall make it ten shillings with board and lodgings thrown in. What do you say?"

She was about to reply when the parlor door opened, and

a tall, shabbily dressed man entered. Her heartbeat quickened as he glanced across the room at her. He appeared to be looking for someone. Hurriedly, she ducked her head and picked up a fork to examine its bent tines closely. The man strode past her table but did not even look at her, hailing an acquaintance by the fire in a broad Somerset accent.

She breathed a sigh of relief. Then almost immediately she realized that Oliver's spy was no fool. He would be perfectly capable of imitating the accents of a Somerset farmer. This, more than anything, decided her.

"I will accept your offer, Mr. Pepperell."

He took her hand in a crushing grip, pumping it up and down. "You will not regret it, my dear Miss Fitzgerald, you will not regret it. We shall make you the star of the West. And when you tread the boards of the Royal at Drury Lane, you will turn to the best box, where I shall be seated, and declare to the audience: 'And there sits the man who is responsible for my success, the famous impresario, Mr. Percival Pepperell!' Oh, by the bye, can you write?" he demanded before she could make a reply to this highly imaginative scenario.

"Write? Why, of course I can write."

"Capital, capital. This gets better and better. Then you shall also be placed in charge of writing our bills."

"Bills?"

"Yes, yes, the notices for our shows. You will need to set to immediately to write up Saturday's playbill, with your own name in large script, of course."

"Saturday," she repeated, horrified at the thought of making her debut performance in only four days' time.

"Yes, Saturday. Now, my dear Miss Fitzgerald, I must inform you that our little arrangement is all subject to the approval of my sister. She is even now hastening to me, together with the rest of the company, I having come on ahead to make arrangements for the performance here. I do not consider, however, that once she meets you she will have any objections to your joining our select group."

He pushed his chair back and rose to his feet. "Meanwhile, I shall procure pen and paper, and you may set to work on the special notice." He stood, chin in hand, in an attitude of pensive thought. "It will read . . . now let us see, what shall it read? Aha! I have it! 'Mr. Percival Pepperell is proud to announce the auspicious debut with his traveling company of actors of Miss Rosaline Fitzgerald, fresh from her triumphs at the Abbey Theatre, Dublin—'"

"No, Mr. Pepperell," Rosaline said in a loud whisper, embarrassingly aware that once again Mr. Pepperell's stentorian voice had caught the attention of the entire room. "I cannot write that. I have never appeared at the Abbey Theatre."

"The audience will never know that." He caught her smoldering glance and hurriedly capitulated. "No? Ah well, never mind. Just put 'fresh from her triumphs in Dublin,' then."

Before she had time to make any further protests, he gave her a benevolent smile and, with a bow and a noble gesture of his arm, retired from the room like Julius Caesar from the senate, bestowing nods and smiles on all those he passed.

Chapter Five

Before the end of what appeared to Rosaline to be an interminably long day, she had become acquainted with several of the members of Mr. Pepperell's troupe of players, including Mrs. Stiggins, his ample—and decidedly hostile—sister. She had also been given a tattered copy of the script of *The Demon Usurper*, the melodrama in which she would be making her professional debut as an actress in the lead role of Lady Allardyce.

It was fortunate that her mother had set her to learning most of Shakespeare's plays and a great deal of poetry besides. Evidently that training was about to be put to good use.

As she lay on the edge of the lumpy bed which she was forced to share with the four young Stiggins girls, Rosaline willed herself not to fall asleep until she had organized her thoughts into some form of coherence, so that she could plan her strategy.

It would be best to remain in Minehead with Mr. Pepperell's company for the present. That way she would be able to discover whether or not Oliver was dead. Until then, it was impossible for her to make any definite plans.

Once she had news of Oliver, she would sell a piece of jewelry—those hideous, old-fashioned ruby eardrops would be the first to go; she would never be able to wear rubies. Then she would make her way to London.

Rosaline's mother had made many friends in London before her marriage to the Earl of Beresford. Several of them had been eager to take the beautiful, emerald-eyed actress as their mistress. One or two had even offered her marriage.

Rosaline squeezed her eyes shut to hold back tears. Perhaps if her mother had married another, less wealthy, man she would be alive still, not worn to an early death by her virtual imprisonment in Beresford Castle for almost sixteen years.

One of her mother's admirers had been a struggling barrister who was now, she recalled, an eminent king's counsel. Perhaps he would be able to help her. Yes, she must make for London.

"But first I must be sure to escape *him*," she whispered to herself, for through all her musings on past and future, she had been aware of the faceless image of Oliver's spy. If he found her, he would be sure to turn her over to Oliver, if Oliver was still alive, or the authorities if he was dead. Perhaps not. Perhaps it would be possible to buy his silence with her jewels.

For some reason she shrank from thoughts of such a

transaction. Although in one way she longed to meet with her nighttime companion again, common sense told her that such a meeting would be disastrous, even if he could be bought.

In the rustling darkness, she closed her eyes, permitting herself to dwell for a delicious moment on the memory of strong arms, tenderness, and the scent of sandalwood.

The next morning, one basin of water was employed for the ablutions of all the children, so that Rosaline had the choice of either using the leftover water or washing in fresh cold water. As the leftover water looked disconcertingly like the revolting stew she had been forced to eat the night before, she opted for the latter.

She was fast learning to appreciate, in retrospect, the comfort of her past life. Despite her confinement in Beresford Castle, she had always been warm and well fed and dressed in the finest fabrics.

The latter, her clothing, was one of her primary concerns. When Mrs. Stiggins saw the water-stained black silk with its sadly wilted white ruff, she too was concerned.

"Have you no other clothing at all, miss?" she demanded.

"I regret not, Mrs. Stiggins. My trunk was somehow lost on the boat coming over from Ireland."

"Hm! Had we known that you hadn't your own costumes, we might have thought twice about engaging you."

Mr. Pepperell coughed and loudly cleared his throat. Later, when his sister had left the room, he took the opportunity to address Rosaline on the subject.

"In mourning, eh, Miss Fitzgerald? My condolences. Would it upset your sense of the proprieties very much if you was to wear something brighter, do you think? Oh, I allow that black'll be perfect for the part of Lady Allardyce, but in general the public likes to see actors in colorful raiment. More attractive, you see. I trust you'll not take it amiss if I suggest that Miss Scudamore, our *costumier*, find some nice, bright gown for you to wear about town, would you? As a kind of advertisement, you know."

"Not at all, Mr. Pepperell," she replied, smiling wryly at the thought of herself as a walking advertisement. She stifled a spasm of guilt. Why should she care about discarding an outward show of mourning for a father who had cared so very little for her?

And so, two days later, on the morning of her first rehearsal of *The Demon Usurper*, Rosaline appeared downstairs in a chemise gown of green-and-white striped muslin which, having been hastily adapted from a costume Mrs. Stiggins had worn the previous year, was of a rather voluminous shape.

"Very suitable. Very nice," declared Mr. Pepperell, looking up from his dish of kippers to leer at the swell of her breasts above the rather low-cut bodice.

Rosaline immediately drew the paisley wool shawl Miss Scudamore had kindly lent her more tightly about her, crossing it over her bodice.

"Hm!" was Mrs. Stiggins's only comment. Then: "Know your part yet, miss?"

"Not quite, Mrs. Stiggins." Rosaline gave her a brilliant smile. "It is rather difficult to read without the benefit of a candle in one's room."

"I'm not about to have my girls burned to death merely because you wants to read in their bed, miss."

Rosaline bit back an acid retort. "Then Mr. Pepperell will have to be content with my carrying my lines on stage, will he not?" she said, her smile even brighter, as she poured herself a cup of the tarlike tea Mrs. Stiggins had brewed.

As it happened, however, Rosaline discovered that she had ample time to learn her lines, for there was so much other business to be rehearsed on the improvised stage in the courtyard of The Crowing Cock—the ballet, the singing and dancing for the burletta, and the sword fights and flame-throwing—that the rehearsal for the actual main piece had to be set aside for a while.

Having been greeted by the remaining players, most of whom appeared genuinely pleased to have her join them—most particularly the male members of the company—she moved away to a quieter part of the stable yard and began to pace back and forth by the stone wall that overlooked a sloping field, reading her lines.

She was working on the ridiculously overdramatic speech Lady Allardyce had to make when her son expired in her arms, and wondering how on earth she would be able to declaim "Angels, take him to your bosoms, and leave me here to mourn my darling's loss against the cold bosom of the earth" without breaking into helpless laughter, when she came into sudden collision with someone, so that the pages were jarred from her hand and fluttered to the ground.

"Oh, my goodness!" she exclaimed breathlessly, surprised by the impact.

The gentleman, for it was a gentleman with whom she had collided, immediately bent to gather up the scattered pages and handed them back to her. As he did so, she encountered one of the most handsome countenances she had ever seen.

He was an inch or so taller than she, of a slender but athletic build, and dressed in a multicaped greatcoat which hung open to reveal a coat of blue superfine and a pristine white neckcloth. His complexion was dark, with dark brown, almost black, hair. But his dark good looks were not the satanic looks of Oliver Prescott, for there was an expression of humor dancing in the gentleman's eyes and a twitch of amusement about his mouth. He appeared to be a man of about thirty.

When he spoke, his voice, too, was decidedly attractive, with the slight drawl of an aristocrat. "Pray accept my apologies for my clumsiness, ma'am."

"Not at all, sir," she replied. "It is I who must beg your pardon, for I was reading and was not looking where I was going."

His dark eyes widened with surprise at the sound of her refined accents, and he flashed her a charming smile. "Let us cry a truce, then, and admit we are both to blame." He bowed and extended his hand. "Lord Francis Kenmore, at your service, ma'am."

She shook his hand. "Miss Fitzgerald, my lord," she informed him, and then withdrew her hand from his tightening grasp.

"Not Miss Rosaline Fitzgerald, the actress, whose name

is upon the lips of everyone hereabouts? By the bye, you must sometime tell me how you came to be called Rosaline, or is it merely a stage name you have chosen?" He did not give her time to reply, which was, in the circumstances, a good thing. "But of course it must be *the* Miss Fitzgerald, for here are the worthy performers themselves engaged in their rehearsal."

He put up his quizzing glass and watched a sword fight being performed in slow motion before turning back to survey Rosaline.

She had stiffened at the note of sarcasm in his voice and lifted her chin to meet his slightly magnified eye through the eyeglass. Immediately, he let it fall, disarming her with his engaging smile.

"Are you appearing in tonight's performance, Miss Fitzgerald?"

"No, my lord, I am not. Saturday will be my first performance."

"Your first?"

"My first in England, my lord," she said hurriedly. "I have but recently arrived from Ireland."

"Ah, yes. From the Abbey Theatre, I believe." The dark eyes ran over her in an uncomfortably familiar fashion. "May I say how particularly fortunate we in England must consider ourselves to be graced by the presence of so famous an actress."

Again Rosaline stiffened. The inflection of sarcasm was there once more, and how dare he look at her thus! She was about to give him a severe setdown, when she suddenly recollected who she now was: not the Countess of Beresford, but an actress with a fourth-rate traveling company and therefore, it seemed, open to all kinds of insults and familiarity.

Observing her changes of expression, Lord Kenmore moved closer to her and again took her hand in his, his nearness playing havoc with her breathing. "Saturday. How can I bear to wait two entire days before beholding your beauteous face and figure again?"

His question being rhetorical, he did not expect a reply.

Besides, Rosaline was not about to give him the satisfaction of seeing her hang her head and declaring. "Oh, sir!" in response to his nonsense.

Her reaction appeared to interest him, for he raised his eyebrows and tilted his head in a semblance of surprise. "I shall return on Saturday, then, to attend your first performance, Miss Fitzgerald. Until then, I remain your most humble and devoted servant."

His eyes upon hers, Lord Kenmore raised her hand to his firm lips and kissed it lingeringly. Having released it, he bowed and then strolled across the courtyard, pausing for a moment to observe the sword fight, which had begun to speed up a fraction.

As she sorted the pages of the script into their correct order, Rosaline thought about the strange encounter. She was uncertain as to whether or not Lord Kenmore had seen her solely as an object of ridicule. The amusement in his eyes and about his mouth, together with his ridiculous speech about not being able to wait until he saw her beauteous face again, had surely denoted that he was laughing at her, had it not? Yet if it were ridicule, it was at least good-humored. Although she had learned to ignore the manner in which her father's and Oliver's friends had ogled her beauty, she had never become inured to their detestable innuendoes. To be the object of good-humored amusement was a new experience.

Rosaline was also bewildered by her own response to Lord Kenmore. She could still feel the imprint of his lips upon her hand and, although she had been indignant at the familiar manner in which he had looked at her, the frank admiration in his expression had pleased her.

He had said he would be there on Saturday. This knowledge made her even more determined to memorize her part and to bring to it all the poignancy she could muster to alleviate the cloying sweetness of the text.

By the time Saturday arrived, however, so intense was her concentration on the ordeal that lay before her that all thoughts of the enigmatic Lord Kenmore were banished from her mind.

The company dressed in the cramped little room at the rear of the inn, which served as both a storage room and a communal dressing room.

There was only one full-length mirror, before which had formed a line of players, anxious to view themselves, to preen and primp in its tarnished image, before they appeared before the audience. Feeling extremely self-conscious, Rosaline reluctantly joined the line.

When it was her turn to look in the mirror, the reflection surprised her. It was a younger version of her mother who stared back at her. She had not realized how like Mama she had become: not only the same deep auburn hair and jewel-green eyes, but also, alas, the same aloof, wary expression. Her own black silk dress, newly sponged and pressed by the kindhearted Miss Scudamore, with the white ruff, crisply laundered, at her neck, was a perfect contrast to the brightness of her hair and eyes and carefully painted face. Of course, part of the color would be bleached by the candlelight and the darkness surrounding the outdoor stage. The result, she hoped, would be the becoming pallor of a harried but still beautiful young widow.

Although Rosaline had had no time to feel apprehensive in the chaotic bustle of the dressing room, as she followed the actors out into the chilly night air a shiver of more than cold ran over her.

Until now, she had told herself that Mr. Pepperell's company was a minor troupe of traveling players, that whatever happened tonight mattered not one jot. But the image of her mother's face staring from the mirror had shocked her into realizing that, even if she were playing to an audience of one, she owed it to her mother's memory not to degrade the acting profession. She was part of a noble tradition and, by heaven, she would show these country yokels, and the grossly inadequate players themselves, what dramatic acting was all about, despite the appallingly ill-written text and the wretched songs.

Her heart hammering against her ribs, she mounted the wooden crates that served as steps, feeling like Mary, Queen of Scots, going to the scaffold. Remembering that tall, gracious queen, she took a deep breath and turned to face her audience.

The sight of Lord Kenmore in the front row, flanked by four or five fashionably dressed gentlemen, was almost her undoing. For one dreadful moment she panicked and turned her head, wildly searching for an exit from the stage. But it was too late. The music from the two fiddles scraped to a halt, and Mr. Pepperell's mellifluous voice started in on the doggerel that began the prologue.

Soon it was Rosaline's turn to declaim her brief opening verse:

"A hapless widow of great beauty, I,
Whose wicked brother full intends to die,
And turned from my glowing hearth and home,
Upon the snow-swept heath am forced to roam."

This poignant verse was greeted with stifled laughter from the front row. She cast a dark look at Lord Kenmore, at the same time determining to discover later which member of the company had penned this fulsome rubbish, so that she could strangle him with her bare hands.

As the play built to its climax, however, she began to realize from the applause that greeted every one of her speeches that she was a success. The exuberant audience even bestowed upon her the ultimate accolade: their silence when she spoke. This was infinitely preferable to the cat-calls and derisive whistles with which the other players were received. The exhilaration of her success propelled her to the end of the play and its ludicrous epilogue.

During the fourth tumultuous curtain call, Rosaline looked downward and saw, in the flickering lamplight, that Lord Kenmore and his companions were no longer there. She felt a spasm of disappointment. They had been an all too brief contact with her own world.

Now her brilliant success meant nothing. She would return to the dank house that smelled of stale kippers, climb into bed with the four rambunctious children, who would kick her and keep her awake with their pinches and chatter, and that would be the end of her debut as an actress. Tears filling her eyes, she sank into yet another curtsey and, with a last kiss of her hand to the audience, made her way to the side of the stage.

A hand was held out to assist her. She looked down—to see Lord Kenmore's handsome countenance gazing up at her, his dark eyes dancing.

"Hail, divine spirit!"

She took his hand, only to find it removed from hers. Placing both hands about her waist, he lifted her down from the stage but did not release her. She stood close to him, so close that she could see the slight creases at the corner of his mouth, the faint mockery in his eyes.

For a moment she thought he was going to kiss her, and even though that would be outstanding presumption on his part, she knew that she would respond to his kiss, for the sight of him had lifted her spirits immeasurably. To her slight chagrin, however, he did not kiss her but turned to retrieve something that lay on the top of the drum that had announced the prologue.

"For you, divine goddess of drama," he said, presenting her with a posy of crimson hothouse roses done up in silver paper.

"Oh, how lovely?" she cried. She had never before been given such a gift. "Thank you, sir," she said, unable to express her gratitude more fully. She looked up at him, feeling suddenly shy.

"My God, you're a beautiful, exciting woman," he said in a low voice.

She bent her head to smell the roses' delicious scent, not wishing to encounter the look in his eyes. His ardor excited her; yet at the same time it sent a shiver of fear through her.

She had seen too much of hot passion in her father, had witnessed the prologues to his savage attacks on her unwilling mother, made in the name of "love" or in his desire for a male heir.

"You are a thousand miles away, Miss Fitzgerald," Lord Kenmore said. "I am positively dashed to think that you find me so excruciatingly boring. My pride is in tatters at your feet."

Rosaline's mind leaped back to the present. "Pray forgive me, my lord. I fear I must be a trifle weary. The strain of the performance, I suppose."

"I do not doubt it for a moment. The strain of having to speak such abysmal drivel must be overwhelming! Dare I ask the name of the author, or has he already hanged himself in despair?"

She laughed out loud at this. "If he has not, I was prepared to murder him myself when I began that wretched prologue."

"Yes, indeed. Your sheer artistry raised an appallingly bad play to incredible heights. You realize, do you not, that you have prodigious dramatic talent, Miss Fitzgerald?"

She looked for the mockery that was never far from his eyes but this time found nothing but sincerity there. "Are you in earnest, my lord?"

"I have never been more so, ma'am."

"Were you not, perhaps, blinded just a little by my 'beauteous face and figure'?" She gave him a teasing smile.

"Not one whit, Miss Fitzgerald. When it comes to assessing dramatic talent, I am neither blind nor dumb."

She was about to demand what his qualifications were for the assessment of dramatic talent, to make him so supremely self-confident, when they were interrupted by Mr. Pepperell. The manager was all bows, all effusive compliments.

"My dear sir, I must humbly beg your pardon for not having made allusion to your illustrious presence in my introduction. Great heavens, to have the famous Lord Kenmore here, unacknowledged! Your fame as a connoisseur of the theater, of the drama in its entirety, has spread to the far ends of the kingdom, as has the fame of your own private theater at Luxton." With an arch smile, Mr. Pepperell paused to mop his brow with a red handkerchief. "Dare one ask what it was that drew you and your companions to our little performance?"

Lord Kenmore drew himself up to survey Mr. Pepperell haughtily through his quizzing glass, the light from the lantern that hung above them catching the glitter in his eyes. "Nothing or no person but Miss Fitzgerald would have persuaded me to sit through even five minutes of such arrant claptrap as you have just presented, sir." His cold disdain was palpable.

For once, the indomitable Mr. Pepperell was at a loss for words. Expressions of dismay and amazement chased across his face. He closed his mouth, which had fallen open, and smiled his close-lipped smile. "Well, yes, my lord. I—I must concur that it is not, perhaps, the best of our little plays, but . . ."

He looked from one to the other of them and then, with an obsequious bow, slid away, to leave them confronting each other in the now almost deserted yard.

"That was inexcusably rude of you," Rosaline declared.

Lord Kenmore looked decidedly taken aback at this onslaught. "I beg your pardon, ma'am," he said coldly. "I spoke but the truth."

"You were insulting," Rosaline said flatly. "Besides, I strongly suspect that he himself is the author of *The Demon Usurper*."

"Ah, now there I am fully in agreement with you."

She met his eyes and caught the spark of amusement in them. It was impossible not to respond to it. "Although I think you could have couched your criticism in kinder terms, I own that you are in the right of it. It is an exceedingly ill-written piece."

"Then we are once again in accord." He proffered his arm. "Come, you are shivering with the cold, and it has started to rain. I wish to ask if you would join me and my companions as the guest of honor at our supper. I can promise you a passable dinner, good wine, and five admirers ready to worship at your feet."

She hesitated, something telling her that she was playing with fire. In the past, she would never have ventured unchaperoned into an exclusively male supper party. But she was an actress now, and not only did she find Lord Kenmore attractive, but she also saw in him the ally she had been seeking to assist her in her fight for her inheritance—even more, for her very life.

She wondered what her mother would have done in similar circumstances. *Devil take my father!* she thought. If only he had permitted her to move in Society circles more frequently, she would know how to behave in any circumstance. One season in sedate Cheltenham had been her only taste of freedom—hardly the preparation necessary for dealing with the Lord Kenmores of this world!

He leaned forward to whisper in her ear, his breath warm against her cheek. "I have a proposition to put to you."

Her eyes narrowed. "What kind of proposition?" she demanded, suspicion edging her voice.

He smiled. "An entirely respectable one, I assure you. So you need not bridle at me like a cat with its fur up."

"Tell me now what it is."

"Aha! So I have caught your interest. No, no. You shall not hear it until you send word that you wish to join me for supper. Now, may I escort you inside, out of the cold?"

She nodded, and they stepped past the last few members of the company remaining outside, who were busy rolling up the canvas drop and packing away the props before the rain could damage them.

Emily Stiggins pushed past them, carrying an armful of the gauze that had served as rolling mist. She cast a vindictive glance at Rosaline as she went by, but Rosaline was too caught up with her own thoughts to care.

A proposition. What in heaven's name could it be? Even to consider seeing Lord Kenmore again was the height of folly, was it not? She hardly knew him. Yet there was something about him that excited her. Most of all, he was the first person she had encountered since she had fled from Beresford Castle who had the power and authority necessary to help her clear her name.

Whatever lay ahead of her, she was convinced of one thing: that, despite her misgivings, she would be unable to resist attending Lord Kenmore's supper party.

Chapter Six

As soon as Rosaline felt that she could slip away from the rowdy back parlor without being thought a trifle high in the instep by the rest of the company, she hurried to the little dressing room and changed into the green-and-white striped muslin. Then she braided her hair, forming the braids attractively around her head, intertwining them with a length of green silk she had found in the costume hamper.

The act of braiding her hair aroused memories of a man's gentle hands upon her face and neck; of the sensuous warmth of his fingers against her cold, wet skin; of the scent of sandalwood. Her nameless companion. And so he would be forever: nameless and faceless.

Although one part of her hoped that she would never again encounter him, the wave of longing that engulfed her whenever she thought of him demonstrated that it was not going to be easy to forget him.

When she had first met Lord Kenmore, the thought that the handsome aristocrat might be the nameless stranger immediately came into her mind, to be almost instantaneously rejected. Lord Kenmore was of a more slender build, and his accent and slight drawl denoted the aristocrat used to moving in London Society. Although it had been almost impossible to hear anything above the roar of the wind that night, the stranger's voice had been rich and deep, his speech more measured than Lord Kenmore's, and with a very slight West Country burr. There were other, more subtle differences which she could not readily identify.

No, what had occurred on Exmoor had, by now, all the semblance of a fading dream. What was decidedly not a dream was her daily search for news of Oliver. So far she had been able to learn absolutely nothing. On Monday the company was to move on to Dunster and from there to Bridgewater, even further away. The greater the distance between her and Beresford, the less likelihood there was of hearing any news about her cousin.

She must know. She *must!* Only then could she formulate her plan to go to London and seek help from her mother's friends.

The appearance of Lord Kenmore's servant at the door interrupted her musings. "Has your master not come himself to escort me upstairs?" she demanded of the servant, her anger rising.

"Oh, yes, miss. Only he said he'd wait for you in one of the front rooms."

As she followed the servant down the corridor that divided the back public rooms from the residential wing of the inn, an appalling thought struck her. Suppose one of Lord Kenmore's friends had also been one of Oliver's cronies? And if so, might he not then recognize her?

What a fool she was not to have thought of that before! But now it was too late, for she was being ushered into a small, well-furnished room which was empty but for Lord Kenmore. The sight of him in his exquisitely cut blue coat, buff riding breeches, and gleaming top boots swept away her misgivings.

Dismissing the servant, he advanced to greet her, bending his dark head to take both hands and kiss them.

"Pray forgive me for not having ventured into the nether regions to fetch you myself," he said, still retaining her hands. "I considered it best for all concerned if I avoided any further conversation with the redoubtable Mr. Pepperell. Pray be seated, Miss Fitzgerald."

He attempted to draw her to a small sofa beneath the window, but she, recognizing the inherent possibilities, demurred. "Where are your companions, my lord? I understood that I was to dine with the entire party."

"So you shall." His quirk of amusement vexed her. "Do not be alarmed for your virtue, ma'am. I had you brought here first so that I might hold private conversation with you before exposing you to my well-meaning but rather exuberant companions. Come, be seated. You have my word that my conduct shall be that of a gentleman, at least—"

"How exceedingly kind of you," Rosaline interjected in an acid tone.

"You did not permit me to finish what I was saying. I give you my word that my conduct shall be that of a gentleman—at least for the present. I offer you no guarantees for the future." His eyes grew even darker. She saw in them the look of smoldering passion she had seen before, and shrank from it.

He released her hands and gestured to the sofa. "Be seated. What I have to say should not take long."

His tone having lightened, she sat down at the end of the sofa, placing her reticule and painted ivory fan—both of which she had borrowed from the props basket—beside her, making it necessary for him to take the seat at the far end.

Crossing one leg over the other, he sat eyeing her with that slight tilt at the corner of his mouth which she found both vexing and intriguing, at the same time swinging his eyeglass back and forth on its ribbon. Then, without preamble, he spoke.

"What the devil are you doing in the company of these— these bumpkins, Miss Fitzgerald?" He did not wait for her reply, which, Rosaline thought, was fortunate, as his attack had been so sudden that no suitable response came to her mind. "You are evidently well bred. Your talent, although still very raw, is, as I said before, prodigious. And your beauty . . ."

He paused to examine her face and figure with a look of intimacy that made her feel as if she were being slowly divested of all her clothing.

"Your beauty is positively luminous. My dear Rosaline—I trust you will not deny me the pleasure of addressing you by that name. Rosaline! 'When tongues speak sweetly, then they name her name.' Most apt. Behold your love-struck, devoted slave."

"You promised to be brief, my lord," she reminded him in an unsteady voice, her pounding heart and the flood of warmth to her face and neck evidence of the effect of his words. No one in her entire life had ever displayed such ardent interest in her.

"So I did. Very well, then. I am, as you may have gathered from Mr. Pepperell's overeffusive address to me, something of an expert on all aspects of the drama and have my own private theater at Luxton."

"Luxton?"

"Luxton House, my family seat, which lies at the foot of the Mendip Hills, about ten miles south of Bath. But, of course, you will not know anything about the district, being newly arrived from Ireland."

She gazed at him, hurriedly assuming an expression of wide-eyed innocence. Naturally, she had heard of Luxton. It was reputed to be a veritable showplace and its present incumbent well-lined in the pocket. "Is that far from here, my lord?" she asked.

"A good forty miles. I am here for the spring stag hunting. Staying with Sir Basil Fortescue at his hunting lodge in the Quantocks. He's one of the fellows who is impatiently awaiting your appearance upstairs."

A spasm of terror gripped her. Exmoor and the Quantock Hills were perilously close to Beresford. She also recognized the name Sir Basil Fortescue but did not recollect that he had ever visited the castle. She knew, however, that in exposing herself to anyone who might conceivably know Oliver, she was treading on exceedingly dangerous ground. The question was, how on earth could she avoid this meeting with Sir Basil and his friends?

Realizing that it would be impossible to do so without some plausible explanation, which she felt far too fatigued to invent at present, she decided to abandon herself to God's will. If Sir Basil recognized her, so be it!

Lord Kenmore glanced up at the small gilt clock that stood on the mantel shelf. "You bade me be brief, my dear Rosaline. I shall therefore speak plainly. You cannot remain with this troupe of ruffians. Not only is it demeaning for

you, it is also dangerous. There are two or three in the
company, including even your worthy Mr. Pepperell, I'll
warrant, who, given the opportunity, would happily take
advantage of your unprotected position. Do I make myself
clear? In two years you'd be a blowsy wench dragging about
the countryside with an infant on your hip and no wedding
band on your finger.''

"You are insulting, sir!''

There was no trace of amusement in his eyes now. "Am
I? I assure you that I do not intend to be. Who would come
to your aid if one of these men were to attempt a quick
tumble with you one night after the play was over, when the
ale was singing in his veins? You are a singularly beautiful
and alluring woman. Who could blame him?''

"Not you, evidently.'' Her voice reflected the coldness
she felt at his words. "And exactly what is it that you are
offering me, my lord?''

A wry smile lifted one corner of his mouth. "I am an
honest man, my dear Rosaline, and so I shall admit to my
desire for you, but I also recognize that you intend to drive
a hard bargain. Therefore, for the present, my proposal is a
wholly professional one. I am about to mount a revival of
She Stoops to Conquer at Luxton, employing a cast of gifted
amateurs and one or two professional players. You know the
play?''

She nodded. Indeed she did; her mother had played the
role of Kate Hardcastle, and they had frequently read the
play together when their spirits needed lifting.

"Splendid! I thought you might, considering that Goldsmith was one of your countrymen. Here is my proposition,
then. I wish you to play the role of Kate Hardcastle. You
will reside at Luxton for the weeks of intensive rehearsal
and the performances thereafter. Do not be concerned; you
will be quite safe from my advances, I assure you—until,
that is, you are willing to accept them! You'll be safer at
Luxton than in your present company, I'll wager.''

She was not so certain of that. Safer from unwelcome
assaults, perhaps, but her feeling of attraction to Francis
Kenmore was, in itself, a danger.

Seeing her hesitation, he leaned forward to clasp her hand in his. "There is no need for you to make me an answer now. When does the company plan to leave Minehead?"

"The day after tomorrow." She sat without speaking, torn by doubts, and then turned to him. "How can I abandon them after only one performance?"

"Oh, as to that, you may remain with them for another week or so. I am not returning to Luxton myself for another three days and shall then have to make arrangements for the arrival of yourself and the other guests. As to fearing Pepperell's displeasure, you need have no qualms on that score. I'll wager you've not received any payment yet, this being your first performance. Am I correct? Thought as much. No, no. Leave the arrangements to me. I shall ensure that Pepperell receives ample compensation for the loss of his leading tragedian."

She flushed, humiliated by the thought of, in essence, being bought and sold. She met his eyes but saw therein only his habitual cynicism; there was no hint that he appreciated or understood her sensibilities. Momentarily she recoiled, but then, recollecting that she was the descendant of a noble line, she set her head proudly and rose to her feet.

"I must have time to consider your offer, Lord Kenmore. For now, I shall meet with your friends for a short while, and then I must take my leave of you. I do not wish to be walking alone through the town at this late hour."

He regarded her from his sitting position and then slowly uncrossed his legs and stood up, adjusting his white linen wristbands with fastidious fingers. "Have no fear, fair Rosaline. You shall be escorted home whatever the hour." He looked at her beneath raised eyebrows. "I see you are determined to bring our cozy tête-á-tête to a swift conclusion, alas. Let us, therefore, proceed to the upper room. I give you fair warning, however, that you may come to rue your decision not to remain here with me."

When she entered the large assembly room that ran the entire length of the inn, Rosaline was inclined to agree with Lord Kenmore. How in the name of heaven could five men make quite so much noise? They were standing in a group around the massive food-laden table, engaged in bawling a song whose tune she recognized but whose words she did not. When the song ground to a halt upon her entrance, her suspicion that it was of a ribald nature was confirmed.

The men converged upon her with cries of delight and extravagant compliments. Smelling the wine fumes on their breath and noting the dishevelment of their fashionable dress, she began to wish that she had indeed remained with Lord Kenmore in the downstairs room. Yet there, too, she had not been truly safe. Was there nowhere at all in this world where she could feel sheltered and secure?

A sudden image—no, more a series of sensations, for she had no true picture in her mind—conjured up the cold interior of a humble stone cottage and the warmth of strong arms about her. She turned, blindly, to accept a glass of brandy from a ruddy-cheeked, tongue-tied gentleman who was attempting to express his admiration.

"A-a-paragon, ma'am. Th-that's what you are." His face growing even ruddier, he turned to his companions. "I g-give you a toast. Will you j-join me in drinking to the exquisite, the b-beautiful Miss Fitzgerald?"

"Miss Fitzgerald!" they all cried in unison and downed the contents of their glasses.

"The divine Rosaline!" Lord Kenmore drawled, and they all laughed immoderately at this.

Without warning, two of them scooped her up and carried her in an extremely precarious fashion to the head of the table, where she was deposited in a large armchair.

Lord Kenmore observed this with his usual mocking expression. She wondered how far his friends would be permitted to go before he would intervene. The thought was not a pleasant one. It was high time she brought them all to heel before she found herself both presiding at and being the prime subject of a debauch.

"Gentlemen!" she called out, to no avail, for the gentlemen were busily engaged in drawing hairs as to who should have the seats to the left and right of Miss Fitzgerald.

Eyes flashing, she rose from her seat. "Gentlemen!" she

thundered. The silence that greeted this was absolute. "I wish to inform you that I mean to remain with you for one quarter of an hour only. If you care to dine with me, then pray be seated, for I intend to eat now. If you prefer to wait, then I beg you to have the goodness to permit me to dine in peace, for your noise is making my head ache."

From the sullen, disappointed looks being cast her way, Rosaline realized that they no longer considered her their darling; on the contrary, they thought her nothing but a kill-joy. All the better!

Lord Kenmore sauntered up, his eyes glittering. "Tamed, by God, and without any sign of a whip, too."

Rosaline sighed. "For heaven's sake, sit down, my lord, and give me some food. I am weary and long for my bed."

He leaned down to caress her hair and then let his fingers trail along her shoulder. "As do I, my dear, as do I—long for your bed, I mean."

As he pulled out a chair to seat himself beside her, she gave him a long, silent look which he countered with a wry smile and shrug. "I warned you that I was an honest man, fair thespian."

She found him an exceedingly difficult man to fathom, never knowing when he was in earnest or when merely funning. Too weary to concern herself at present with Lord Kenmore's enigmatic personality, she allowed him to serve her with a dish of roast pork accompanied by a delectable gooseberry sauce, and a small portion of squab pie with crisp apple slices. He sat watching her as she ate, swinging his eyeglass to and fro, until his gaze began to make her feel self-conscious and she pushed aside her plate.

"Some junket, perhaps?" he asked. "I can recommend it highly. From the aroma, I believe the cook has laced it lavishly with brandy."

It sounded too delicious to resist. A crystal dish of junket with an enormous helping of clotted yellow cream was set before her. As she took a spoonful it slid down her throat, cool and refreshing after the heavier meat and pie.

Before she had completed her meal, the port and brandy

decanters were passed and two of the men lit up cigarillos, puffing their smoke in her direction.

This was a new experience. Despite the preponderance of male guests at Beresford, no one would have dared to pass the decanters or smoked until the ladies had quit the room. This was the height of insolence, indeed!

The conversation came mainly from the center of the table, for Lord Kenmore appeared to be in a contemplative vein, being presently engaged in comparing the merits of two decanters of fine old cognac—doubtless smuggled—by holding them up to the dazzling light from the central chandelier. As most of the conversation revolved around hunting or shooting, Rosaline was about to make her excuses and take her leave when, out of nowhere seemingly, came the name she had for the past week both dreaded and yet longed to hear.

"Heard about that fellow Prescott?" asked the large man who had been introduced to her as Sir Basil Fortescue.

"Prescott?" a slurred voice drawled from behind a wreath of smoke. "Don't know the fellow. Know the name, though. Demmed rum touch, I believe."

"That's the man. Oliver Prescott. Some sort of cousin to the Earl of Beresford. You'll recollect the Earl died a week or so ago."

Rosaline held herself utterly rigid. Then, fearful of betraying herself, she bent down to pick up her reticule and held it on her lap, gripping the metal clasp with trembling fingers, willing the fiery blood to drain from her cheeks.

"Don't know him," another voice said. "Heard he's a bruising rider to hounds and also a devil if he's crossed. Anyone else know him?"

To Rosaline's relief, the response was in the negative.

"What about him, anyhow?" came the question.

"Stabbed. By his cousin, the new Countess, apparently."

"Good God! Why?"

"She's mad as a March hare, they say. Has been for years. She's been kept locked away for all this time. Seems her father's death made her worse. Prescott's keeping it quiet, naturally. Doesn't want a scandal."

"He's alive, then?"

"Oh, yes. Mending nicely. Touch and go, though. Just missed the heart. It was Wharton who told me. Friend of Prescott's."

"And the mad Countess? What of her?"

"Prescott's making arrangements for her to be certified insane and shut away somewhere privately. Once that's done, he'll be the new Earl."

"Lucky man. Wouldn't mind an earldom myself, particularly one with all the Beresford holdings!"

Rosaline's teeth were clenched so tightly together that a spasm of pain shot along her jaw.

Oliver was alive! This was the only thought that filled her whirling mind. Then came the rest. She was to be certified insane and then Oliver would be the new Earl. But there was no word of her having escaped from the castle. No, of course not. He would keep that quiet, so that he could hunt her down himself, and then . . .

She scraped back the heavy chair and stood up, forming her rigid mouth into a semblance of a smile. "Gentlemen, I have stayed with you far longer than had been my intention. I thank you for your hospitality."

"No! Not yet!" came the cries of protest. She moved towards the door, hoping that she would be able to reach the back room downstairs before the sick spinning in her head overcame her. Turning in the doorway, she raised her hand in a theatrical salute . . . to find the ever-attentive Lord Kenmore beside her.

"Permit me to escort you home, my dear," he begged once they had left the room and were descending the narrow staircase. "You do not look at all the thing,"

"No, I do not wish—that is, I prefer to walk home with Mr. Pepperell and his sister," she said distractedly. At the foot of the stairs, she turned to face him. "Were you in earnest when you issued your invitation to participate in your play, my lord?"

"Why certainly I was. How could you doubt it?"

She swallowed, seeking the words to explain her sudden decision. "Then I shall accept it, with gratitude. You must understand, however, that my acceptance is tempered with a certain reluctance. It is not what I—I should do in normal circumstances.'' She summoned up a proud little smile, but her eyes wavered from his direct gaze. ''Not only am I alone, however, and without a protector, I am also ambitious. To appear in one of Lord Kenmore's productions would be, I gather, a stepping stone to greater things.''

He laughed at this, throwing back his head in genuine amusement. ''You are exceedingly good for me, Miss Fitzgerald. When I become overbearingly conceited and self-centered, I shall look to you to set me in my place. I must inform you, however, with the greatest humility, that many would consider an appearance in a leading role in one of Lord Kenmore's productions to be the very pinnacle of success; but who am I to take issue with you on the subject?''

He walked her to the far end of the corridor and turned to smile down at her.

''You see before you a very happy man, my fair Rosaline. I shall speak with Pepperell tomorrow. Never fear, he will be amply rewarded for his loss.''

His words put her in mind of one of the Stiggins boys and his ''What's in it for me?'' when she had once asked him to run an errand for her. She, too, was for hire, except that her rewards were shelter . . . and time. Shelter to hide from Oliver. And time to seek someone who could lend her assistance.

For one brief moment, Rosaline was tempted to pour out the entire story to Francis Kenmore; but something held her back. Men were not to be trusted. To tell him would mean that she would be entirely at his mercy. No, she would need more time to get to know Lord Kenmore before she could be certain that she was right to place her trust in him.

Yet during that time Oliver would be hot on her trail, using the information his spy would have conveyed to him by now to track her down. She must seek refuge for a while. The last thing she should do at present was sell her jewels and make a dash for London. To do so would be folly indeed. She would be far safer hidden away at Luxton.

At the thought of confronting Oliver once again, terror

gripped her. *Oh, God*, she cried inwardly, *it would have been better if he had died!* Involuntarily, she clutched at Lord Kenmore's arm.

"What is it?" he asked her, placing his hand over hers.

The kindness in his voice reminded her of another, so that she was tempted again to tell him everything, but did not. "Nothing. Nothing at all. It is just that I am extremely weary." She put a trembling hand to her forehead.

"It does not surprise me." He took her hands and held them fast. "Will you not permit me to escort you home?"

She shook her head. "Thank you, no. I shall go with Mr. Pepperell and Mrs. Stiggins."

"Then I shall bid you good night, my dear Rosaline. Meanwhile, I shall be sustained by visions of you at Luxton, playing Kate to my Marlow. Now, before I leave you, I must make sure that your escorts are still here."

He pushed open the door, recoiling at the noise from the smoke-filled parlor. "Are you absolutely certain that you would not prefer me to escort you back to your lodgings? It is a madhouse in there!"

Rosaline shivered. In the circumstances, it was a singularly unfortunate analogy. She shook her head again, by now too exhausted to speak. He bowed and was gone before she could form the words of a response.

Chapter Seven

True to his word, Lord Kenmore presented himself at the lodging house around noon the following day and was closeted with Mr. Pepperell for little more than fifteen minutes.

While she was waiting to hear the result of their negotiations, Rosaline paced up and down the muddy lane outside the squat little house, barely noticing the greening of spring that was evident in the trees and bushes. Her mind was taken up, as it had been most of the night, with the realization that Oliver was alive and was planning to lock her away forever.

No, not forever! Doubtless he would arrange for her to be incarcerated at Beresford, but she would most likely meet with some "unfortunate accident" shortly thereafter. Living with Oliver all these years had taught her not to harbor any illusions about men in general and Oliver Prescott in particular.

When she heard the front door slam, she turned back and hurried to meet Lord Kenmore. *My new owner*, she thought wryly.

"All done," he announced with a satisfied smile when he reached the end of the cinder pathway.

She stood before him with lifted chin, shoulders thrown back, confronting him eye to eye. "I should like to know the extent of my present worth in the marketplace."

One eyebrow rose. "Forgive me, but that is none of your business."

"I must take issue with you on that, sir. It is very much my business. How much?"

He gave her his one-sided smile and turned to walk toward his horse, a black gelding which his groom was holding a little further down the lane.

"How dare you turn your back upon me when I am still talking to you!" she yelled at him.

He swung around so suddenly that she recoiled. With three strides he was before her, his hands gripping her upper arms so tightly that she winced.

"How dare you take that tone with me, madam! You appear to be forgetting that I have just rescued you from penury at a not inconsiderable cost. If you say one more word on the subject, I shall regret having done so."

She shook herself free of him and glared at him, gritting her teeth to hold back her fury. Her breathing came fast as she caught the dangerous glitter in his eyes, but slowly and deliberately she calmed herself by relaxing her tensed shoulders and breathing deeply. It would not do for her to lose her temper now, when she was most in need of him.

"Pray accept my apologies, my lord. I do not find it easy to accept charity from strangers."

The apology appeared to mollify him. "Strangers? Surely we have progressed far beyond being mere strangers to each other?" He spoke in a low, vibrant voice.

Aware of the proximity of his groom, she was relieved that he did not enlarge upon this theme, but the look he gave her was expressive enough to make her wonder, once again, if it were not exceedingly foolhardy to be contemplating a remove to this man's house. Would she not be entirely at his mercy there? On the other hand. would that not be preferable to being at Oliver's mercy?

Apparently unaware of her misgivings, he kissed her hand and strode away to mount his horse. Once in the saddle, he half turned his mount as if he were anxious to be gone. Rosaline had the uncomfortable impression that now he had "bought" her he no longer considered it necessary to preserve the niceties.

"Pepperell tells me you are making for Glastonbury in the next few days. Send word to me when you reach there. I shall send my carriage to the George and Pilgrim there in exactly ten days, to convey you to Luxton. Ten days, mind."

Uneasily aware that the groom could overhear everything they said, she clutched at Lord Kenmore's bridle. "You are forgetting that I have few clothes or possessions," she told him in a low voice. "Certainly nothing suitable for a sojourn at Luxton House."

Raising his eyebrows in an amused response, he reigned in his restless mount. "You may leave all that to me" was his terse reply.

"I will not have you buying clothes for me!"

"We shall deal with that when you arrive at Luxton." His

tone announced that he would brook no further protest. "Now stand back, if you please. Ten days, mind. *Au revoir, ma chère* Rosaline."

He raised his hand in farewell as he trotted his horse down the lane. She waited until he was out of sight before going back into the house.

Mr. Pepperell's reaction to her imminent departure was predictable and couched not in his habitual flowery language but in the baldest terms. "Well, I'll say this for you, miss: you're a demmed fast worker."

This comment appeared to sum up the general reaction of the members of the company. Once they knew she was leaving, they made no further effort to be friendly, all—apart from the kindly little costume maker—closing their ranks against her.

It was, therefore, with a decided sense of relief that, ten days later, Rosaline mounted the steps of the crimson traveling chaise with Lord Kenmore's arms prominently displayed on the side panel.

The interior was upholstered in the softest leather and the whole infinitely more comfortable than her father's old-fashioned, lumbering coach had been. Everything possible had been provided for her comfort: a rug of warm, soft wool; a hamper containing a variety of delectable foods, enough to feed six people; and a basket of books for her entertainment, one of which, "Monk" Lewis's *Ambrosio, or the Monk*, immediately caught her eye, for her father had expressly forbidden her to read it.

With a sigh, she sank back onto the soft cushions, relishing this return to the lifestyle to which she was accustomed.

For a few hours she was able to enjoy this luxurious hiatus in the midst of all her seemingly insurmountable problems. It was, therefore, with a feeling of reluctance that she leaned forward as the carriage bowled through the great wrought-iron gates which the gatekeeper had run out to fling open.

A shiver ran over her as the gates clanged to behind her.

She wondered, not for the first time, if this might not be a case of "out of the frying pan, into the fire."

To her surprise, Luxton House was a vast, low mansion built in the style of a Gothic castle. She had heard of such houses but had never before seen one. Set on a rise in a beautifully landscaped park, complete with a suitably romantical bridge over an artificial lake, the castellated mansion was a wondrous sight. Having lived all her life in a real castle, she was glad to see that the Gothic revival extended only to battlements and graceful arches. The large expanse of windows and generous, open aspect were a pleasant contrast to the massive, forbidding appearance of her own home.

The footman who had descended the steps to greet her cast a swift glance of surprise at her one small cloth bag. It contained her black silk dress and a few additional items of clothing, all of which had been given to her by Miss Scudamore as a farewell present, together with a warning that she was not, on any account, to tell Mrs. Stiggins. The bag held one other item of clothing, which might well cause more than a mere glance of surprise if it were to be discovered. She must remember to remove the nightshirt and hide it somewhere before some snooping housemaid found it. What a prime topic for gossip that would be belowstairs!

With a loud sniff, the footman picked up the bag and, with a muttered "Follow me, miss," carried it up the steps, holding it away from his body as if it were a fourteen-day-old haddock.

On the few occasions that Rosaline had been a guest in someone's home she had always been received warmly immediately upon her arrival; but when she followed the footman into the large hall, it was to find no one else there.

The hall was an agreeable mixture of marble pillars, a curving staircase with graceful cast-iron balusters, and a marble-tiled floor partially covered with a crimson Oriental carpet. Yet, despite this undoubted elegance, she shivered and felt a strong desire to run from the house to feel the April sun upon her face again.

An elderly man dressed in black suddenly materialized,

she was not quite sure from where. "Miss Fitzgerald?" he inquired in a thin, acerbic voice, his face devoid of expression.

She nodded in reply.

"I am Besley, Lord Kenmore's butler. His lordship will be with you directly."

His white-gloved hands at his sides, the butler inclined his gray head not more than one inch in her direction. The gesture eloquently conveyed his opinion of actresses who visited gentlemen's houses unchaperoned. Knowing what arbiters of good taste butlers usually were, Rosaline felt even more apprehensive. No doubt if she had swept into Luxton with an entourage of servants and dozens of boxes and trunks she would have been accepted, whatever her status; but to arrive without even one maid no doubt had damned her in the eyes of the servants.

To her great relief, she saw Lord Kenmore striding down the hall to greet her, looking remarkably handsome in a sapphire-blue coat and whipcord breeches.

"My dear Miss Fitzgerald." He took her hand and held it in his, his eyes perusing her face and figure with an ardor that assured her that he, at least, was genuinely pleased to see her. "Pray forgive me for not having been here to greet you. I have been shut away all morning with my auditor and had not been apprised of your arrival. Did you have a tolerably good journey?"

Why did his presence not warm her as she had hoped it would? Despite his ardent expression and welcoming words, there was an air of artifice about him, as if he were playing a role for her benefit.

Before she had time to say more than the "Yes, I thank you, my lord, a most comfortable journey" she gave him in reply, a door down the hall opened and from it issued a large man dressed well but unobtrusively in a dark brown coat and buff pantaloons with well-polished hessians. He moved towards them, walking, as many big-boned men do, with a light tread. There was no sense of urgency nor hint of servility in his step.

"Ah, Courtenay," Lord Kenmore said. "Have you completed the arrangements for the accommodation of my guests?''

"I have, my lord, and have also spoken to Mrs. Elliott regarding a personal maid for Miss Fitzgerald." Although he addressed Lord Kenmore, the man's eyes behind his gold-rimmed spectacles were fixed upon Rosaline.

Seeing this, Lord Kenmore waved a casual hand in his direction. "My secretary, Mr. Courtenay," he informed Rosaline. "This, as you will have already gathered, is Miss Fitzgerald," he told his secretary.

Mr. Courtenay bowed. "Richard Courtenay. Your servant, ma'am."

Recognizing from his voice and confident bearing that he was a gentleman, Rosaline held out her hand to Mr. Courtenay. "How do you do, sir. How very kind of you to arrange for a maid for me."

Her hand was taken and released in one swift movement. She was aware that she was being observed with singular intensity and had the sensation that she was being regarded with strong disapproval by the bespectacled secretary, although his countenance retained a fairly bland expression.

"Welcome to Luxton, Miss Fitzgerald," he said in his deep, pleasant voice. "If there is anything at all I can do to assist you, do not hesitate to apply to me."

Was it her imagination, or were the conventional words spoken with far greater emphasis than was necessary?

"I echo that," Lord Kenmore said. "And you may be sure, Miss Fitzgerald, that Courtenay means it, too. Though I'm not at all sure that I should say it to his face, for he'll be demanding that I increase his already exorbitant salary, but he's the most efficient secretary I've ever had."

He took her hand and placed it within the crook of his arm, looking down at her with such a warm expression in his eyes that she flushed, uncomfortably aware that Mr. Courtenay was observing them from his superior height.

Lord Kenmore's lips slid into a smile. "I had forgotten how very beautiful you are, my dear Rosaline."

She shook her head at him, casting a glance in Mr.

Courtenay's direction. "If you please, my lord," she protested with a frown.

"Oh, you need not worry about Courtenay. I have yet to see anything surprise him. He is utterly imperturbable. Is that not correct, Courtenay?"

"I regret I did not catch what you said, my lord." For a moment the secretary's eyes locked with Rosaline's, but she was unable to fathom their enigmatic expression.

"Never mind," Lord Kenmore said. "Wait for me in the library, would you? Meanwhile, you could work on that letter to the *costumiers*. Those costumes should have arrived by now." He turned again to Rosaline. "Come, my dear, let us go where there is a fire so that you may warm yourself and take some refreshment after your journey. Then you shall be shown to your room."

He turned to go and then looked back at his secretary. "I shall be with you shortly, Courtenay. Meanwhile, I shall be in the yellow saloon and am not to be disturbed on *any* account. Is that understood?"

The secretary inclined his head. "Perfectly, my lord."

As Lord Kenmore bore her away, Rosaline had the definite impression that those glass-shadowed eyes were following her all the way down the hall until she entered the aptly named yellow saloon.

Chapter Eight

When she went into the room, Rosaline's eyes were dazzled by every hue of yellow possible, from the palest primrose to the deepest gold. It was like walking out into a day of blindingly brilliant sunshine. The sheen of gold predominated—in the gilt furniture, the gilded drapery valance around the bay window, and the gold-painted mantelpiece. The one striking contrast was the scarlet lacquered Chinese cabinet, but even it had decorative scenes picked out in gold. Lord Kenmore's flair for the dramatic evidently extended beyond the merely theatrical. Yet, despite this striking use of color, the decor of the room remained just within the bounds of good taste. Besides, Rosaline found it a welcome change from the gloom of Beresford.

Lord Kenmore stood back, observing her with a quizzical look, waiting, she knew, for her to exhibit awe and admiration. Perversely, she determined to give him neither reaction. "What a pleasant room" was her only response.

His eyes narrowed at this. He was not pleased. "Ah, if only John Nash were present to hear one of his most famous rooms described as 'pleasant.' You disappoint me, Miss Fitzgerald. I thought you a female of natural good taste. If you think this room 'pleasant,' one wonders what will be your opinion of the theater?"

"Surely it does not matter what I think of it, so long as you are satisfied with it, my lord."

He moved closer to her. "There you are in the wrong, for I care very much for your opinion. My one desire is to meet with Miss Fitzgerald's approval at all times." His dark eyes met hers with burning intensity. "Rosaline, my darling," he groaned. She found herself crushed against him, his mouth insistent upon hers, his arms pinning her to his taut body. Instead of the sweet excitement she had expected from their first embrace, however, she was overcome with panic. His body was hard, unyielding, his mouth relentless, and she was suffering acute discomfort from the metal clasp of her reticule, which was pressing into her breast.

Rosaline endured his embrace, but when she found that he had no intention of releasing her and his hand began to roam alarmingly close to the side of her breast, she twisted her head away and said in a breathless voice: "Release me immediately, Lord Kenmore! You gave me your word that I should be safe from your advances at Luxton.''

He took her averted face in his hand and turned it towards him. "Shall we have done with all this playacting, my dear? It is no longer necessary here, you know.'' Still holding her face, he again crushed his lips on hers, his teeth grazing the soft inside of her mouth.

It was Oliver all over again! Oliver lying in wait for her in the dimly lit passageways of the castle. Oliver coming up behind her when she sat alone in the shuttered library. Her heart beating thick and fast in her ears, she struggled to release her arms so that she could push him away, but he merely laughed and pinned her even tighter. "God, you're an exciting wench!" he murmured against her mouth.

All of a sudden, his hold upon her relaxed. "What the devil!" He thrust her from him. "I thought I told you I was not to be disturbed!" he shouted at someone across the room.

Rosaline ran her tongue over her bruised lips, tasting blood. With shaking hands she smoothed her hair and then turned, to see Mr. Courtenay standing just inside the door, a portfolio bulging with papers beneath his arm. She was overcome with relief at the sight of him. His very size and attitude of calm assurance gave her a feeling of security.

"Pardon me my lord. I had understood you to say that you wished to see me about the letter to the *costumiers*.''

"The devil you did! You know damn well I ordered you to wait for me in the library. By God, I've a mind to turn you off immediately for this!"

The secretary appeared entirely unruffled by his employer's fury. Inclining his head a very little, he took a step backward, feeling for the door handle. "My lord, Miss Fitzgerald.''

"I should like to be shown to my room now, if you please," Rosaline said, determined to take advantage of this interruption to escape Lord Kenmore's advances. She also needed a great deal of time to herself to decide what she must do to fend him off for a while without incurring his wrath.

"Very well." Lord Kenmore flung away from her with a muttered oath, for all the world like a petulant schoolboy who had been denied a sweetmeat. "Take her to Mrs. Elliott, Courtenay," he snapped, "and then wait for me in the library, as you were told to do in the first place. I am going to the stables to inspect that new gray. That letter to the *costumiers* is to be ready upon my return. Understood?"

"Certainly, my lord. It shall be ready, never fear." The slight country burr in Courtenay's voice had an extraordinarily soothing effect. He sounded more like a father reassuring a distraught child than a servant who had just been severely reprimanded. He opened the door and stepped aside to allow Lord Kenmore to pass and then waited a moment to watch him go down the hall.

Sensing now that this was a man to be reckoned with, Rosaline examined the secretary more closely as he stood holding the open door. His large hands had long, well-shaped fingers, and he wore a plain gold signet on his right hand. His hair was a warm golden brown and fashionably cut, but its waves, she conjectured, were natural, not a product of the curling tongs. Somehow she could not imagine Mr. Courtenay primping before a mirror each morning before being prepared to face the world. It was his size, however, that fascinated her the most: his great height, broad shoulders, and muscled thighs strangely disturbed her. Great heavens, he was so large he could well have been . . .

"Oh!" The exclamation escaped from her before she could stifle it. She stood staring at him with wide-eyed amazement as her suspicions strengthened.

He turned, gave her a searching look, and then closed the door before walking towards her. He was taller than she by more than six inches. The stranger's nightshirt, which was still in the cloth bag in the hallway, had been several inches too long for her, never mind the immense breadth about the shoulders.

Her heart beating wildly, she took one step towards him—and breathed in the unmistakable aroma of sandalwood. "You!" she uttered.

He laid the portfolio down on the sofa table and regarded

her with an impenetrable expression. "So you have recognized me, have you? I wondered if you might." He was not smiling. "A trifle out of your depth this time, are you not?"

"What do you mean? And how in heaven's name did you know *me*? We couldn't see our hands in front of us in that—that hut."

Her hesitation was caused by a sudden flood of embarrassment as she recollected that she had lain in this man's arms for an entire night, that his large hand had cupped her breast most comfortingly. She thrust the thought away. What she must not forget was that this man was Oliver's spy and that in some mysterious way, he had engineered it so that he and she should meet again under the same roof.

"How did I recognize you, you ask."

She began to think that his slow, deliberate speech could prove intensely aggravating. Did he never say or do anything on impulse?

"Oh, there were several ways," he continued. "Your voice, your figure—I remember your body exceedingly well, you see." The appearance of his slow smile illuminated his face. "Then there is, if you will forgive me, the very scent of you, which I could never forget, having inhaled it for several hours, even though I was asleep much of the time. Last of all, there is your hair. That was what truly gave you away."

"My hair? But you could not see its color in the darkness."

"No, but you may recollect that I used my comb on it." He raised his hand a little, as if he would touch her coils of braided hair, but then let it fall again. "In the morning, after I had woken to find you gone, I discovered auburn-red hairs in my comb. It was not difficult to conclude, therefore, that the supposed actress Lord Kenmore had invited to Luxton and the governess-cum-jewel thief I had encountered on Exmoor on my way here were one and the same person."

His smile had disappeared; in its place was a stern schoolmaster expression that chilled her. He waited for her to respond, but she said nothing. "I must congratulate you upon your accomplishment. What will it be this time? The Kenmore ruby? The priceless collection of Hilliard miniatures? I take it that you have an accomplice stationed nearby to whom you will pass on your booty? I should not like to think of the dangers you might encounter were you to carry your ill-gotten gains from place to place. After all, you never know whom you might meet on some dark, stormy night!''

''You are insufferably insolent, sir,'' she informed him in a stifled voice. ''But once I have gained Lord Kenmore's confidence, no amount of bluffing shall avail you. He shall be told exactly who you are: a spy in my cousin's pay! Oh, a mighty clever one, I'll grant you. I should be extremely interested to learn how you managed to track me down to Minehead and then to inveigle Lord Kenmore to see me in the play. Once that was accomplished the rest was easy, I am sure, for you know well his reputation as a connoisseur of the drama and—''

''You're a little fool!''

So his passions *could* be aroused, after all.

''I have been in Lord Kenmore's employ only a short while, but I have heard more than enough from the servants to know that his reputation as a connoisseur of women is even greater than his knowledge of the theater.'' His voice grew harsh. ''I've a notion you're in over your head this time, madam. Luxton is notorious for its 'goings-on,' as the highly respectable Mrs. Elliott calls them with such morbid relish. I cannot keep bursting in to save you from Kenmore, you know, or I shall lose my position here.''

''Bursting in to save—'' she gasped. ''I'll have you know, Mr. Courtenay—and I don't suppose that is your actual name at all—I'll have you know that I do not need saving, so you may keep your Sir Galahad impersonation for some country wench who would better suit you.''

''Aye, I will, for I've no interest in a wench who's an inveterate thief, I can tell you. What came first, by the bye? Were you an out-of-work actress who turned thief, or vice versa? No, no, it must be the former. Only an actress could play all the roles your repertoire encompasses: governess, beleaguered gentlewoman chased by spies and a dastardly cousin, fine dramatic artist—or so I hear. A veritable galaxy of roles. I congratulate you, ma'am.''

His mock bow infuriated her. ''How can you have the gall to talk to me about playing roles! What, might I ask, is your position here as a secretary? It is but a role to ensure that I am constantly under your surveillance. And all this talk of—of Lord Kenmore's orgies is arrant nonsense, designed either to scare me away from Luxton or, at the very least, to deter me from confiding in him. If such things were happening, why would the housekeeper remain here? You said she was a respectable woman.''

''Mrs. Elliott remains here because, so she tells me, she is paid exceedingly well to be deaf and blind at certain times. 'I go to my room and bolt my door,' she told me.''

''It is truly remarkable how very quickly Lord Kenmore's servants have come to confide in you, is it not?'' Rosaline remarked in an acid tone.

Again, that slow, amused smile. ''Yes, it is. There must be something about me that inspires confidence, I suppose—in others, at least.''

He moved even closer, so that she was forced either to gaze at the top button of his waistcoat or to lift her face to his. He removed his gold-rimmed spectacles and drew out his pristine linen handkerchief from the pocket of his brown coat to polish them. The effect was so remarkable that she stared at him in astonishment. The owlish schoolmaster look disappeared, and she saw before her an exceedingly attractive man, with brown eyes flecked with gold. She suddenly realized how well he suited this room: *warm* and *golden* were words she might use to describe him. Yet at the same time how alien he was to it, for his golden warmth was that of the sun warming the brown earth, not of the artificiality of gilded furnishings.

Now he was looking down at her, those warm brown eyes fixed upon hers with a curious intensity, as if he sought to read her mind.

''Why do you wear those wretched spectacles?'' she asked impulsively. ''Is it to disguise yourself further?''

"I wear them because I cannot see without them," he replied with a wry smile.

"I do not believe you. I think it is a ploy to make you appear more trustworthy, more clerical."

He shrugged his immense shoulders. "Think what you please, Miss—ah, Fitzgerald, I believe the name was, was it not? Invented, of course. What was the name you used when you were governess to your last unfortunate employer?"

"You are changing the subject. We were talking of those ridiculous spectacles."

His reaction to this was to clamp the spectacles on his nose, pushing the side pieces over his ears, which ruffled the hair above them. Quite without thinking, Rosaline put up her hand to smooth it down, an intimate gesture born of the night they had shared together.

He looked down at her, his expression distorted by the glass that once again covered his eyes. Gently, he took her wrist in his hand and drew it down. She could feel an almost imperceptible tremor in his fingers.

The moment hung between them.

Eventually she spoke. "I think the reason I dislike them— the spectacles, I mean—is that I cannot read your expression clearly. It is hidden from me."

"And why should you wish to read it? You have dubbed me your enemy, a spy; your cousin's spy, I believe you said."

"And you have dubbed me a jewel thief."

"I have evidence."

"And so have I."

"Then we are at an impasse, ma'am."

She stole a look at his composed countenance. "Do you intend to give me away to Lord Kenmore?"

"I should do so. He is my employer. By the bye, what exactly is your relationship with him? Or is that too personal a question?"

She lifted her chin. "Yes, Mr. Courtenay, it is. But I shall answer it. I have been invited by Lord Kenmore to take part in his new production. That is all. We shall see what relationship, as you call it, will develop."

"Sweet on him, eh?"

"For a gentleman, sir, you employ remarkably vulgar terms. I find Lord Kenmore attractive, yes."

He released her wrist. "He's as attractive as a tiger! You may consider my plain speaking vulgar; nevertheless I shall continue to speak plainly. However considerable your talent as an actress, he's after one thing only, and that's your virtue."

She gave him an arch smile. "What makes you think the inveterate jewel thief has any virtue left, sir?" she asked, her tone honey sweet.

He drew even nearer, his size and proximity overwhelming. "Because," he replied in a low voice, "I have spent the night alone with you. I know that your fear of me was not because you suspected me of being a spy or murderer or whatever it was that you concocted at the time; yet your initial terror was no act. I believe that your fear of the male sex in general denotes that you are still innocent of the so-called commerce of love. I suspect, however, that something in your past has increased that fear to inordinate proportions.

"Very delicately put, sir," Rosaline said, her caustic tone hiding her surprise at his discernment. "But you have not answered my question about Lord Kenmore. What do you intend to tell him about me?"

He studied her intently. "I shall answer you thus: If I discover one item missing, even one small silver teaspoon from the canteen, I shall inform Lord Kenmore of your past activities. If, however, you abandon your design to rob him, then your secret shall be safe with me. But I repeat my warning about Francis Kenmore. It is a great pity that your mistrust of the male sex does not extend to my worthy employer. You may very well find that it is you, not he, who are the victim of a robbery!" He took her by the upper arms, his large hands encompassing them. "Give me your confidence, Miss Fitzgerald," he said earnestly. "Tell me who you truly are, give me your former employer's name and direction, and I shall undertake to settle everything for you. I beg you to believe me when I say that I wish to be your friend."

She felt the warmth of his hands through her thin muslin sleeves. His chest was solid before her gaze, and she knew a great desire to lay her head upon it as she had done that memorable night. One step, no, but half a step, and she could be within the security of his arms.

Remember Oliver! warned an inner voice. Her stomach clenched into a knot. Great heavens! She must be insane to be exchanging banter with this man, discussing inconsequentialities such as spectacles, even experiencing a strong pull of attraction towards him, when as soon as he had the opportunity he would be sending word of her whereabouts to Oliver. Why, by as early as tomorrow she could be once more in Oliver's power, deprived of her home, her title, and her freedom!

She stepped back and shook off his hands. "Trust you! Ha! You know, of course, that he is alive. You must know that."

"Who?"

"Oh, please." Her voice rose with her exasperation. "Spare me that look of innocent wonderment. If only you would be honest with me, I should at least know where I stood with you. But your refusal to acknowledge that you are in Oliver's pay, that he set you on to follow me as he told me he would if I tried to escape, so tries my nerves that—that—" To her utter consternation, she found she could no longer contain her tears, and she found herself gathered into his arms.

"My poor, dear girl," he murmured against her hair.

Furious with herself for her weakness and even more angry at her awareness that, unlike her response to Lord Kenmore's embrace, her foolish body desired nothing more than to press even closer against his, she thrust him from her.

"In the name of heaven, just this once, tell me the truth," she almost screamed at him. "Do you intend to betray me to Oliver?"

"For the umpteenth time, I tell you that I do not know

anyone by the name of Oliver. Nor do I know your true identity, or that of your cousin, for that matter.''

Angry tears again sprang to her eyes. "Oh, you—you devil!" She felt like ripping his face with her nails. She took a long, deep breath. "Very well, then," she said, her eyes narrowing. "How much will you ask not to betray me to Oliver? I have jewels, remember? Rubies, precious pearls. They are worth a fortune. How much?"

"But they are not yours to give away, you must recollect, my dear."

His quiet, reasonable tone infuriated her even more. She drew herself up to her full height and looked up at him with icy disdain. "Very well, then. If you are not willing to accept a bribe, I shall go immediately to Lord Kenmore and tell him the whole."

"I advise against it. To do so would mean you would be placing yourself in his power."

"It would also mean the end of you, sir!" Her eyes locked with his. He gazed back at her with that unruffled expression which goaded her far more than could any number of threatening words. The man was a dolt—an impenetrable dolt!

Rosaline felt utterly helpless. Nothing, neither threats nor pleas, appeared to move him. Her lower lip trembled. She was about to fling herself away from him to avoid displaying such a sign of feminine weakness again, when she decided that now was the time to make use of it. She looked up into his face, her eyes swimming with unshed tears. "I beg of you, Mr. Courtenay," she said in a low voice, clutching his arm. "I am terrified of what my cousin will do to me if he discovers where I am."

She felt the muscles in his arms tighten beneath her grip, and his eyes searched her face. "Very well," he said after a long pause. "I give you my word that I shall not betray you to Oliver." His words, although measured, were spoken with an expression of intensity.

The relief that swept over her was tempered with a sharp stab of disappointment. Her last thread of hope that perhaps this singular man was not in Oliver's service snapped. "You shall have my ruby eardrops as soon as I have unpacked my bag," she told him. "And," she added, her face burning, "I shall also return your nightshirt to you."

Amusement lit his eyes and quirked at his mouth. "The nightshirt, I accept. The eardrops can wait. In truth, I should prefer cash. It would not do for me to be selling the jewels openly, would it?"

"Why not? Now that we are both being frank with each other, you can acknowledge that they are mine, and not stolen."

"Ah, but then I could easily be accused of having stolen them, could I not? You could set the constable on me and have me locked up, thus neatly maneuvering me out of the way. No, no, my dear Miss Fitzgerald. I shall wait until you have the opportunity to sell them yourself. Meanwhile, you have my word that I shall not betray you to your cousin. Shall we shake hands on that?"

She released his arm and placed her hand in his, only to have it carried to his lips. He smiled at her. "Now we are friends, accomplices, in fact, and no longer foes."

"Yes" was her noncommital reply. She had bought his loyalty, just as Oliver had. She had no doubt at all that he could be bought back just as easily. All at once, she felt extremely weary.

"Heavens, is that the time?" she exclaimed, glancing at the gilded clock on the mantel shelf. "Lord Kenmore will return to find that letter to the *costumiers* still unwritten."

His eyes gleamed. "I thank you for your concern, Miss Fitzgerald." He turned away to pick up the leather portfolio. "You need not be anxious, however, as the letter is already written." He tapped the portfolio." I have it here."

"So you really did interrupt to rescue me from Lord Kenmore."

"I must confess that I did."

"Then I shall thank you, sir, not to do so again," she said, her voice strident with indignation. "I am perfectly able to take care of myself. Had you considered that I might welcome Lord Kenmore's embraces?"

"I had. That gave me even more cause to interrupt."

This response having left her speechless, he opened the door and sent the footman to fetch Mrs. Elliott. Then, bidding her a "Good afternoon, Miss Fitzgerald," he departed from the room before she had time to think up a suitably scathing reply.

Chapter Nine

To Rosaline's great relief, when the housekeeper came to escort her to her bedroom she appeared to be a perfectly respectable woman. From Mr. Courtenay's remarks Rosaline had half expected to be confronted with the sort of female who might preside over a bawdy house; someone akin to Shakespeare's Mistress Overdone, perhaps. But it was exceedingly difficult to imagine this of Mrs. Elliott, whose austere expression and sharp, ferrety features seemed better suited to censure than license.

"I understand from his lordship that you have not been in England very long, Miss Fitzgerald," Mrs. Elliott said over her shoulder as she led Rosaline up the graceful, curving staircase.

Rosaline was slow to answer, being too occupied in admiring the airy brightness of Luxton and contrasting it with the gloom of Beresford. As she looked about her, she felt as if she had been recently released from imprisonment—which, in a way, she had.

"Forgive me, Mrs. Elliott," she said when they reached the first-floor landing. "I was admiring those painted medallions on the ceiling. It is all so very beautiful, isn't it? In answer to your question, yes, I am only recently arrived from Ireland.''

"I see." The pale eyes swept over her, taking in the limp muslin dress and the reticule with the tarnished clasp. "And you were in the profession over there as well, were you?" A rather unpleasant smile touched Mrs. Elliott's thin lips.

Rosaline stiffened. "That is correct, Mrs. Elliott. I was an actress in—in Dublin."

"Well, well. You do surprise me. You have so little of the Irish brogue. Do you have any family there, might I be so bold as to inquire—any relatives?"

"I have an aunt and four cousins," Rosaline replied, quite truthfully. "Apart from that, I am an orphan. Now, I should be grateful if you would show me to my room, if you please, Mrs. Elliott, as I am anxious to wash off the dust of the journey."

"Certainly." The housekeeper led her down the corridor to a white door with gilt trim and, taking a key from the bunch that hung on a large ring at her waist, she opened it.

The bedchamber was a delightful room with a large bay window that appeared to open onto a balcony overlooking the gardens at the rear of the house. It was hung with oyster-colored silk draperies looped back with golden cords. The large tent bed was also draped in oyster silk, with an embossed needlework design on the coverlet. The carpet was of an oriental pattern worked in pale green, peach, and ivory. A leaf-green lacquered bedside cabinet, satinwood dressing table—equipped with every accessory imaginable for a lady's toilette—and a desk, large wardrobe, and opulently upholstered sofa and cane-seated chairs completed the furnishings of the room.

"What a lovely room!" Rosaline cried. "Are you certain that Lord Kenmore intended it for me?"

"Oh, yes. Quite certain," Mrs. Elliott assured her, a gleam in her pale blue eyes. "See, here are your dresses." She opened the mirrored door of the wardrobe with a positive flourish, like a conjuror's assistant at a village fair demonstrating her master's expertise.

Rosaline gasped at the row of dresses and costumes, a

sumptuous array of silks and muslins and jaconets of every color imaginable. She was aware that Mrs. Elliott was watching her reaction intently, as if she were deriving particular pleasure from it.

"Oh, yes, Miss Fitzgerald," the housekeeper said. "This is most decidedly your room. You see the door so cunningly concealed in the wall beside the bed? That leads to his lordship's dressing room." Now her eyes positively shone with excitement.

A coldness swept over Rosaline, as if the balcony window had been opened suddenly and an icy wind had blown through the room. She had not been wrong in her original expectations of Mrs. Elliott, after all. What were the words Richard Courtenay had used when he had been talking about her? Morbid relish. That was it. Strange words to employ in reference to a respectable housekeeper. Now she knew why he had used them. It was evident that this woman reveled in the amorous exploits of her employer. She was like an elderly spinster in Dublin her mother had told her about, who spent most of her time at the window, deriving all her pleasure in life from watching the comings and goings of the street from behind her shutters.

Rosaline grew even colder at the thought. Immediately upon meeting Mrs. Elliott, she had considered her an ally in this house of men. At Beresford, only the women could be trusted. She had learned that lesson at a very early age. All men were to be viewed with suspicion. Now here was a seeming anomaly: a woman who might very well prove her enemy.

"I should like the key to that other door," she said imperiously, holding out her hand.

"Oh, I couldn't possibly give it to you!" Mrs. Elliott cried, her eyes round with surprise.

"Very well, then. I cannot possibly remain in this room." Rosaline swept past her and started down the stairs again. "Which is the library?" she demanded when they were halfway down.

The housekeeper, who had been tutting nervously behind

her, halted. "The library? Why?" Her eyes grew even rounder. "Surely you cannot be intending to—"

"The library, Mrs. Elliott!" Rosaline repeated. "For heaven's sake, ma'am, do not be so utterly ridiculous. It is quite understandable for you to be in awe of Lord Kenmore, but I can assure you that I am not."

Mrs. Elliott's lips clamped together in a rigid line. When they reached the foot of the stairs, Rosaline could see that she was seething with resentment. Yes, she most certainly had made an enemy. Ah well, perhaps it was better to have the ill feeling out in the open.

She turned to a fresh-faced footman who hovered beside one of the marble pillars and asked him, with an accompanying smile, "Would you be so kind as to tell me which is the door to the library?"

The young footman reddened beneath his white wig and pointed back down the hall. "It be the second door on your right, miss. Shall I announce you?"

"No, most definitely not. Thank you." Bestowing another warm smile upon the bedazzled young man, she swept past the indignant housekeeper, marched down the hall, and, unannounced, flung open one of the large double doors into the library.

The two occupants of the room registered surprise, each in his own inimitable style: Lord Kenmore, who remained seated at a mahogany pedestal desk, with a dark frown and fiery expression; Mr. Courtenay, with a mere questioning arch of his golden-brown eyebrows.

"Lord Kenmore," Rosaline said heatedly as she advanced across the room. She halted, waiting for him to rise. When he showed no signs of doing so, she continued her march, to confront him across the desk. "I am not used to having people remain seated in my presence, sir."

Momentarily startled, Lord Kenmore set down the pen with which he had been signing documents and leaned back in his chair to survey her with a mocking smile. "By God, madam, that's rich! You storm into my library without even a 'by your leave' and then have the gall to tell me that you wish me to stand in your presence. Which role is it you're playing now? Cleopatra, Queen of the Nile, perhaps?''

Once again, in her anger, she had almost given herself away. She could not explain to him that she was unaccustomed to being treated with such insolence by a gentleman. If this was the manner in which actresses were received, Rosaline could understand why her mother had married her father. It was also apparent that Lord Kenmore was still smarting from her rejection of his amorous advances. Well, that was his misfortune. He would soon discover that she was not so easily seduced! He had sought to use her, but she had every intention of using *him* in her fight against Oliver. And if at the same time she could win the handsome Lord Kenmore's love—for she was convinced that he was indeed capable of such an emotion once the veneer of the inveterate Don Juan could be stripped away—all the better for both of them.

He was still leaning back, observing her now through his gold-rimmed quizzing glass; but by now she had become more intensely aware of Richard Courtenay's presence like a bulwark behind her, which gave her courage to speak her mind. She must remember, however, to employ tact if she was to achieve her object.

"I must first thank you for your exceeding generosity in providing me with such a magnificent wardrobe of clothes, my lord. I cannot think how you . . ." Confused, her voice died away and, to her vexation, she felt her face color up. Then, recollecting Mr. Courtenay's presence, she rallied. "But I came to tell you, sir, that although I find the bedroom you have assigned to me quite enchanting, the presence of a second, communicating door makes me feel uncommonly nervous." She gave a fluttering little laugh to illustrate this uncommon nervousness. "I should prefer to have another room, if that is possible."

She could see from his expression that her cajoling tone had not fooled his lordship for one moment. He knew full well that in rejecting the room she had once again rejected him. Yet, strangely enough, she cared more for Richard Courtenay's reaction. She sensed his sudden tension, as if he were standing with bated breath, poised for action, behind her.

Lord Kenmore said nothing, his glance sliding past her to Courtenay and then back again. Then he gave a light laugh which was at variance with the blaze of anger in his eyes. "Why, certainly, Miss Fitzgerald," he responded with a nonchalant wave of his white hand. "In truth, I am glad of it, as I am short a main chamber for Lady Hathaway, who is to play Constance Neville. And now that I come to think of it, such a chamber is far more suitable for a woman of her superior station. I had wished only to demonstrate, by assigning you such a room, that I did not underestimate your superior talents, Miss Fitzgerald. But on second thought, it appears that I *over*estimated them a trifle." His cynical expression left no doubt as to his meaning.

She drew herself to her full height and met his mockery unwaveringly. "In some ways, it appears that you did, my lord," she countered.

"Courtenay."

"My lord?"

Rosaline felt him beside her, silently supporting her.

"Instruct Mrs. Elliott to assign the second floor back bedroom in the east wing to Miss Fitzgerald," Lord Kenmore drawled, by now apparently extremely bored by the mundane subject of the assignation of bedchambers.

She looked sideways, to catch a glint behind Mr. Courtenay's spectacles. She could not be sure if it was of amusement or anger.

"If you would kindly come with me, Miss Fitzgerald," he said, adroitly escorting her from the library. It occurred to Rosaline that he played the part of secretary exceedingly well.

Once the door was closed and he had led her a little way down the hall, he halted and turned to her. She saw now that it was anger that flashed in his eyes.

"I warned you that you would not win this battle of wits against him, did I not?" He gripped her by the arm. "For God's sake, madam, have done with all this tomfoolery before you become so deeply embroiled that even I shall not have the power to extricate you."

This sudden display of passion, conjoined with his proximity and its accompanying waft of sandalwood, conjured up memories of that night on Exmoor, making her feel suddenly tremulous, like a young miss just out of the schoolroom confronted by her first beau.

Reminding herself that here at Luxton this man was no more than a servant, she gave a light laugh. "May I remind you for the last time, sir, that I am not in need of any rescuing, particularly not by you? I have not hired you to serve me. I have merely bought your silence. As for Lord Kenmore, he now realizes that I have no intention of occupying a room that is adjacent to his, that is all."

"I understand that it was your intention to win him to your side. No way better than through a communicating door, I should have thought." His eyebrows rose above the gold rims of his spectacles.

Rosaline's hands clenched into fists. "Oh, you are insufferable. I have no intention of becoming Lord Kenmore's paramour, as you well know, sir. That is not the manner in which I intend to achieve my objective. For now, I am content to fulfill my reason for being here: to appear in the leading female role in Mr. Goldsmith's comedy. If, in due course, I can solicit Lord Kenmore's assistance in my fight against my cousin, then I shall ask no more. Now, be so kind as to fetch Mrs. Elliott, so that—oh!"

The housekeeper herself glided from behind one of the pillars down the hall, her black bombazine dress rustling as she walked. "You wished to speak with me, Miss Fitzgerald?" Her mouth was pursed up like a prune.

It was fortunate that their conversation had been carried on in low tones, for Rosaline was certain that the housekeeper had been trying to eavesdrop. "I intend to remove to another room, Mrs. Elliott," she said coldly. "One on the second floor, was it not, Mr. Courtenay?"

"The second floor back room in the east wing," he told Mrs. Elliott curtly.

"Ah, yes. I see." The dry lips twitched a little, as if she

saw a great deal more than the changing of a room. "And the new clothing his lordship ordered for Miss Fitzgerald? Shall I have everything sent up there also?"

"Yes. Do so." His tone was even more curt.

"I doubt if the tiny clothes-press in there will take a quarter of them."

"Then store them somewhere else and advise Miss Fitzgerald where they can be found," he replied, not even trying to hide his impatience. It was evident that Mr. Courtenay was no admirer of Mrs. Elliott. "I trust you will soon be comfortably settled, Miss Fitzgerald." He inclined his head in the slightest of bows.

Impulsively, she reached out her hand, loath to see him still vexed with her. After a momentary pause, he took it in his. A tingling ran through her at the touch of his fingers and the warmth of his palm clasping hers. "I am most grateful for your assistance, Mr. Courtenay," she said in a low voice. Reluctantly, she withdrew her hand, but the tingling sensation remained.

"It is my pleasure to serve you, ma'am. I assure you that I am always at your service." She received the full force of one of his slow, vibrant smiles before he bowed and retired to the library.

Mrs. Elliott watched his retreating figure and then glanced up at Rosaline's flushed countenance. "Shall I take you to your room now?" she asked, her face devoid of expression.

Rosaline followed the stiff back and dry rustle of skirts up the first flight of stairs, along the carpeted corridor, past her previous room, and then up another, narrower flight of stairs to a small landing with a round window. From this landing they descended a flight of six stairs and walked the length of yet another narrow corridor.

Mrs. Elliott halted at the third door on the left, searched through her keys, selected one, and opened the door.

The room was more than adequate punishment for Rosaline's temerity in having repelled Lord Kenmore's advances. Small and dark, it was tucked beneath one of the slanting eaves, so that in places she would be unable to stand up straight. Moreover, it had no fireplace. She wrinkled her nose at the smell of dampness that pervaded the room. The bed was narrow—not much more than a servant's truckle bed, in truth—and when she tested it, she found that its hair mattress was as hard as a tombstone.

Yet, after having had to share one small, extremely grubby room with the Stiggins children, the little room was a haven. At least here she could be alone.

"Not quite up to the standard of the other room, is it, Miss Fitzgerald?" The housekeeper made no attempt to hide her pleasure at what she saw as a just reward for this upstart's refusal of her employer's desires.

"Thank you, Mrs. Elliott." Rosaline gave her a smile. "This will suit me admirably." She was tempted to laugh out loud at the housekeeper's surprised expression. "Now if you will kindly have some hot water sent up, I should be most grateful. Then I shall come down to sort out my clothing. Some, I shall wish conveyed here; I shall ask you to find storage for the remainder."

The housekeeper's mouth tightened. "I doubt if I'll be able to spare any of the servants, miss. We're busy preparing for his lordship's guests, who are to arrive this afternoon." The emphasis on the word *guests* was unmistakably intended as an insult.

"Oh, I doubt that Lady—Hathaway, was it not?—would wish to find the wardrobe in her bedroom filled with the garments of another lady, do you, Mrs. Elliott? I shall ring for you when I have finished," Rosaline added in a tone of dismissal.

Mrs. Elliott opened her mouth as if to speak and then closed it again, looking much like a codfish deprived of water. Having cast one look of loathing at this insolent female who behaved in a manner far above her station, she stalked out, slamming the door so that the decidedly inferior water color of Bath Abbey swiveled on its nail.

Rosaline looked about her and then sat down on the plain oak chair. If it was Lord Kenmore's plan to humble and dishearten her by giving her this dingy attic, he would not succeed. Indeed, it served only to strengthen her determination to win this battle of wits with him. She had no doubt at all that she would be able to bring him around eventually. Men were such fools! She had only to hold him at arm's length, at the same time employing tact and charm, to have him eating out of her hand before long.

But first she must assess the woman who appeared to be her rival for Lord Kenmore's affections: Lady Hathaway, who was to portray the secondary female lead in *She Stoops to Conquer*—and to occupy the bedchamber Rosaline had rejected.

Then she must tackle the part of Kate Hardcastle for she intended to entice Lord Kenmore not only with her charm and beauty but also with her dramatic talent, which entailed being word perfect from the very beginning.

Yet somehow all these considerations paled in comparison with the enigma of a man who was at one and the same time in the employ of her archenemy and, apparently, her only true friend in this house.

Dealing with Richard Courtenay, Lord Kenmore, Mrs. Elliott, and the various actors in the play would push Rosaline to the very limit of her resources. She would be like a juggler keeping several colored balls in the air at the same time.

For a moment her courage failed her. Then she squared her shoulders. Of course she could do it! After all, her inheritance and, indeed, her very life were at stake. She would turn Lord Kenmore's desire to love, and with him at her side Oliver Prescott would be vanquished.

First things first, however. A wash; she shivered at the thought of washing in this cold, fireless room. Then she would put on one of her modish new dresses—something extremely alluring. She had no doubt that Francis Kenmore's taste would tend toward the striking and sensuous.

For an idle moment she wondered what Richard Courtenay's favorite color might be. The thought was almost immediately squashed. What on earth was she about, to be musing thus about the man who had to be bribed not to betray her to her cousin? She must be out of her mind!

Chapter Ten

Having washed off the dust of travel with the most welcome hot water and a cake of sweet geranium-scented soap, Rosaline made her way down to the beautiful bedroom which was to be hers no longer. The door stood open, and as she approached she saw that Richard Courtenay stood inside the room, talking to a young chambermaid. The sunlight from the bay window behind him surrounded him with light, so that he looked like one of those knights in golden armor she had seen in paintings.

She smiled wryly at such a fanciful notion. An unlikely knight in armor Oliver's spy would be! She stepped forward. "Mr. Courtenay," she said briskly. "I am come to sort out my clothing so that it may be removed from here as soon as possible."

"Ah, Miss Fitzgerald." He gave her one of his slow, warm smiles that made the recipient feel that the world could not be such a hostile place after all. "This is Mary, who is to be your maid."

The girl cast her a quick, shy smile and bobbed a curtsey.

Rosaline smiled in return but turned resolutely to Mr. Courtenay. "I hardly think a personal maid will be necessary now, sir."

"Why, certainly you must have a maid, if only to convey to you any clothing you might need from this extensive collection." He grinned, his eyes twinkling behind his spectacles. Then his face became solemn and correct again.

"Mary will sleep in your room," he said, his tone indicating that there would be no further discussion of the matter.

"But that—" She had been about to tell him that one person in the tiny room was more than enough, but catching the slight shake of his head, she did not continue.

"Thank you, Mary," Mr. Courtenay said. "Take Miss Fitzgerald's bag to her room and unpack it for—"

Now it was his turn to halt, midsentence, in response to Rosaline's frantic signals, which she was trying to relay to him without the maid's seeing her.

Mary gazed from one to the other of them with wide-eyed astonishment.

Rosaline had to smother a giggle. It was evident that a bystander might find their conversation, with its mixture of secret signals and incomplete sentences, a trifle odd, to say the least. She glanced at Richard Courtenay, to find her amusement reflected in his eyes. Oh, Lord, why did she have to find the kindred spirit for which she had been searching all her life in this man, of all people!

"Ah, yes. Now I recollect your mention of having something that needed to be returned to its original owner," he said, his face expressionless bar the glint in his eyes. "Very well, Mary. Off you go and tidy Miss Fitzgerald's room for her. Return here in half an hour so that Miss Fitzgerald may give you her instructions regarding her belongings. *I* shall carry the bag upstairs. Oh, and do not forget to light the fire in Miss Fitzgerald's room to insure that it is not damp."

Rosaline lifted her chin. "There is no fireplace in my room."

He frowned. "No fireplace? Are you certain?"

She nodded.

"Then you must move to another room."

"But Lord Kenmore—"

"It is quite obvious that Lord Kenmore made an error when he assigned you that room. You are not sleeping in a room without a fireplace." He turned to the maid. "Go downstairs, Mary, and tell Mrs. Elliott that I wish to see her here in half an hour." He consulted his gold watch, which he had taken from his waistcoat pocket. "That is, at two o'clock precisely. No earlier, no later. Is that clear?"

"Yes, sir." The maid bobbed a curtsey in his direction and to Rosaline, and scurried away.

"Can you do that?" Rosaline asked.

"What?"

"Go against Lord Kenmore's orders. He particularly assigned me to that room, you know. You were there."

"Of course he did. You had rebuffed his advances, and it was his way of punishing you. But his spells of anger do not last long. However furious he might appear at present, he would be appalled at the thought of your sleeping in a cold, damp room tonight."

"Are you certain of that?"

"Yes, I am. Quite certain." He moved closer and looked down at her. "His aim, after all, is to seduce, not to antagonize, you."

She gave him a sweet smile. "Ah, but you have forgotten that it is my aim to seduce *him*, Mr. Courtenay."

"You are playing with fire, Miss Fitzgerald."

"Are you referring to my involvement with you or Lord Kenmore, sir?"

His eyes locked with hers. "With both, I imagine, ma'am." Then he smiled, the weather-tanned skin at the corners of his eyes crinkling in a most attractive fashion, and he shrugged his broad shoulders. "Enough! May I suggest that you give me back my nightshirt before Mary or Mrs. Elliott returns, for I collect that was the reason for your panic-stricken expression when I told Mary to unpack your bag."

A tide of warmth swept over Rosaline, and she turned away to hide the telltale flush in her cheeks. Her cloth bag stood by the wardrobe. She bent to rummage inside it; her fingers encountering soft flannel, she drew the nightshirt out.

Involuntarily, she clutched it to her breast, like a child with a favorite shawl, reluctant to part with what had been her one source of comfort ever since the time they had spent together in the hut on Exmoor. Not one night had passed that she had not slept with his nightshirt in her arms or with her head pillowed on its softness.

She held it out to him. As he took it from her, his fingers

brushed hers. A jolt of pleasure ran through her, and she was overwhelmed with a longing to be held in his arms once again.

For one fleeting moment he bent his bronze head to breathe in her perfume from his nightshirt, his action intensifying her longing, so that it became almost a pain radiating throughout her body. She ran her tongue over her lips to moisten their dryness.

He smiled, and she was utterly lost, dazzled by the sunshine and warmth that seemed to emanate from him, her golden knight . . . and once more she was in his arms. But this time it was different; this time there was a sense of urgency. His large hands ran the length of her back, pressing her soft body against his. Inflamed with desire, she reveled in his strength, his warm, hard masculinity.

She gazed up into his eyes, knowing that he was about to kiss her and wishing to see his expression before he did so. She also knew that she was eager for his kisses, that she had waited all her life for them. Her lips parted, ready to receive his and, not wishing to have any sort of barrier between them, she reached up to remove his spectacles.

To her dismay, he started, as if her action had jolted him back to reality. His hold upon her slackened. Taking his spectacles from her fingers, he turned away from her to put them on again. As he did so, she could see that his hands were trembling.

His jaw was rigid and his face pale when he turned back to her. "Pray accept my apologies, Miss Fitzgerald," he said, his voice remote. "It—I— There is no excuse I can give you for my conduct. Forgive me. I assure you that it shall not happen again."

Rosaline realized that she, too, was trembling: with both thwarted desire and anger at her own weakness in succumbing to him. This was, most probably, part of his plot to entrap her. Yet his remorse seemed genuine enough. So tangled were her emotions that her first instinct had been to lash out at him, but her better judgment told her that it would be preferable to have this man as a friend than an enemy. She must, however, insure that she never permit him to catch her off guard in such a manner again.

She drew in a deep breath. "I was as much to blame as you, sir." Giving him a faint smile, she held out her hand. "Shall we make a pact to remain friends, and only friends, while I am here? After all, it would not help my plan to gain Lord Kenmore as an ally if he were to find me in his secretary's arms, would it?"

Her brittle laugh sounded as full of artifice as did her words. Indeed, she felt more like weeping than laughing.

Outside the sun still shone, but the room now felt cold.

He took her hand, pressed it, and then released it as if her touch burnt him. "Thank you." His expression was inscrutable, covered by more than the mere glass of his spectacles. His face remained pale.

She could not bear to see him thus. So used was she to his usual aura of untroubled calm, his tension made her uneasy.

"Come help me choose a dress so that I may change, Mr. Courtenay," she said in a coaxing tone. "I am heartily tired of wearing the same two dresses for weeks on end."

She opened the wardrobe door to survey the row of dresses, but he made no move, standing in the center of the room like a stricken Samson. She went to stand before him. "Please, Mr. Courtenay. I need your assistance."

This appeal seemed to bring him to his senses again. He gave her a wry little smile. "What makes you think I would know anything about ladies' dresses, Miss Fitzgerald?"

"Why, because of your sisters, Mr. Courtenay." For her own sake as much as his she was determined to preserve the fantasy of the loving brother who doted on his sisters. "Besides, any man who could braid hair so dexterously is certain to be extremely knowledgeable about ladies' dresses."

This time his smile was almost its golden self again. "Ah, now I am to be put to the test! Very well. Let us see what we have here." As he surveyed the interior of the wardrobe, Rosaline began to take down each of the dresses for his inspection.

Despite her attempts at levity she felt decidedly embarrassed by the extravagant display of clothing Lord Kenmore had had made for her. But, in his inimitable fashion, Richard Courtenay soon put her at her ease, and before long they were arguing like brother and sister over the respective merits of a flounced muslin with an underdress of primrose yellow and a white French crepe with green beadwork and green silk ruching for her appearance at dinner that evening.

Only for a single moment did she recollect who this laughing man, holding two dresses up against himself for her perusal, actually was. She immediately pushed the thought back into the dark recesses of her mind, telling herself that Mr. Courtenay—or whatever his name might be—would be receiving ample compensation in the near future for his services to her.

So quickly and enjoyably did the time pass that both were surprised to see Mrs. Elliott surveying them from the doorway, an expression of shocked disapproval on her face.

"You asked me to come at exactly two o'clock," she reminded the secretary in a sharp voice.

"Why yes, Mrs. Elliott. So I did." He put down the two bonnets he had been holding up for Rosaline to see. "I understand that the room Miss Fitzgerald has been given has no fireplace."

"Oh?" The terse response was accompanied by what was unmistakably a smirk.

"Kindly see to it that she is given a room with a fireplace, Mrs. Elliott."

"There's none left. His lordship's guests are to arrive later this afternoon, and the rooms have already been assigned." Her eyes held a spark of triumph as she glanced at Rosaline.

"Have you the list with you?" Mr. Courtenay asked.

"The list?"

"Of rooms and their occupants."

He waited patiently as she reluctantly drew a piece of paper from the capacious pocket of her black bombazine.

"Lord Kenmore has gone over the list with me already," she said, confronting him with folded arms. "He would not wish anything to be changed."

"Nor would he wish Miss Fitzgerald to be put in a room without a fire."

"It was his choice."

He smiled. "You cannot be expecting Lord Kenmore to remember the state of every room at Luxton, you know, Mrs. Elliott. Give me the keys and the list, if you please."

"I must verify it with his lordship first."

"I shall do so, never fear." He held out his hand. "The list and the keys, Mrs. Elliott."

Not once had he raised his voice. He was utterly implacable, and the housekeeper knew she could not win. Rosaline, remembering his calm insistence that she remove her dress in the stone hut, had to hide a smile. She had never met anyone quite like him before. He achieved more with his quiet, determined reasonableness in a few minutes than did those who hectored and badgered in a day.

Within the hour, she was established in a comfortably furnished bedroom of medium size with a pleasant view overlooking the coppice. Although it was not a grand room by any means, it was such a vast improvement on the previous room, and the sight of a cheerful fire in the grate so boosted Rosaline's spirits, that when she came down to dinner that night, she felt in a positively sparkling mood.

Determined to make an instant impression on Lord Kenmore and his guests, she had chosen the white crepe with the green silk ruching and beading. She was tempted to wear her own set of emeralds, but knowing that that was impossible, she chose a simple gold chain from the jewel chest Lord Kenmore had thought to provide. With Mary's help she wound her hair into an intricate chignon, leaving a few feathery tendrils brushing her cheeks. The effect was extremely gratifying. She gazed at her image in the mirror. How good it felt to be dressed well once more! Lord Kenmore could hardly fail to be dazzled by the beautiful woman who smiled proudly back at her. Lady Hathaway had best be prepared, for battle was about to commence.

Rosaline had hoped to encounter Richard Courtenay before making her grand entrance, whether to gain his approval or his support she did not know, but as she descended the staircase she was greeted by one solitary footman. From the noise that issued from the yellow saloon it was evident that the majority of Lord Kenmore's guests were down already. All the better!

Drawing herself up to her not inconsiderable height, she nodded to the footman, who pushed open the doors, to announce: "Miss Fitzgerald."

She could not have asked for a better reaction to her entrance. All heads turned her way, the conversation died on everyone's lips, and Lord Kenmore hesitated for little more than a second before striding forward to greet her.

He bowed low over her outstretched hand, retaining it in his as he addressed her in a low, throbbing voice. "You are the most ravishingly beautiful woman I have ever met. Am I forgiven?"

She pressed his fingers and laughed, her laugh like the chiming of musical bells. "But of course, my lord. How could I not forgive you?" The tone of voice she employed was warm and intimate.

She was rewarded with a darkening of his eyes and a lingering kiss on the inside of her wrist and then on the cushion of her palm. Over his dark head she caught a glimpse of a slender, fair-haired woman in a blue dress, whose eyes were shooting darts of fury at her.

"Come, my dear Rosaline, permit me to present you to my friends and your future colleagues." Lord Kenmore led her forward. "Lady Hathaway, I should like to present Miss Fitzgerald, who, as you know, is to be our Kate Hardcastle."

Her rival's eyes were two ice-blue diamonds partially concealed beneath disdainful lids. Her painted mouth was voluptuously full, but her smile was a mere twist of the lips.

Rosaline bestowed one of her special brilliant smiles upon Lady Hathaway, most effectively turning the disdain to blazing anger.

Her victory was complete when, against all the rules of convention, it was to her and not Lady Hathaway that Lord Kenmore proffered his arm to take her into dinner.

Later that evening, when Lord Kenmore was taking his houseguests on a tour of his exquisite theater, Rosaline took advantage of the subdued lighting to approach Richard Courtenay.

"You look like a cat that's got the cream," he told her after brushing aside her offer of thanks for having procured such a comfortable bedroom for her.

She looked up at him with glowing eyes. "That's precisely how I feel!" In her state of excitement, she placed her hand on his arm. He was, after all, her dear conspirator, was he not? "I am convinced that I have Lord Kenmore exactly where I want him," she whispered. "And much of it is thanks to you, Mr. Courtenay."

"Is it, indeed? How so?"

"You are always so calm, so capable, that you make me feel that everything, *anything*, is possible."

His only response was a tightening of the muscles of his arm beneath her hand.

She looked up into his face, to find that his expression was hidden from her by the reflection of the flickering wall lights in his spectacles.

At last he spoke. "You have undoubtedly won the first engagement, Miss Fitzgerald. But let me warn you, once again, that yours may not be the final victory."

His words, and the tone of voice in which they were spoken, dismayed her. As she sought his face for further explanation, his grave expression softened a little. He took her hand from his arm and carried it to his lips, turning his back on the rest of the company, so that his gesture was hidden from them. "Whatever happens, never forget that you may call upon me for assistance at any time."

Far from giving her assurance, his offer of help served only to give her further cause for concern. But there was no time to continue their conversation, for she could see Lord Kenmore approaching from the center aisle.

"Thank you, Mr. Courtenay," she said in a cool, formal tone.

Richard Courtenay raised one eyebrow, bowed, and strode away to set about the task of insuring that Lord Kenmore's guests were suitably entertained, while Rosaline, all the secretary's warnings forgotten, enjoyed the privilege of being Francis Kenmore's preferred companion for the remainder of the evening.

Chapter
Eleven

" 'Pray, sir, keep your distance. One would think you wanted to know one's age as they do horses, by mark of mouth.' "

" 'I protest, child, you use me extremely ill. If you keep me at this distance, how is it possible you and I can ever be acquainted.' "

" 'And who can ever be acquainted with you? I want no such acquaintance, not I.' " Rosaline halted in the middle of the speech and moved from the circle of Lord Kenmore's arms, he, in his part as Marlow, having been attempting to kiss and fondle her. "Are you certain that my country accent is not too broad, my lord?"

"I have told you before, it is perfect. Naturally Kate would make her accent broader than the norm to ensure that Marlow would not penetrate her disguise." Taking her hands, he drew her closer. "Shall we start the scene again?" His eyes danced. "You cannot imagine what havoc you are causing in me by your struggles against my embrace, you provocative female." He spoke in a low voice so that only she could hear. "*And* before all these onlookers, which makes it even more exciting." He indicated the remaining members of the cast, who were seated in the front rows of the ornate theater, awaiting their turn on stage. "You do realize that I get to kiss you at the close of the play, do you not?"

"Is it written in the play? I certainly don't recollect seeing it."

"No, not exactly, but then I am chief actor and manager. Besides, an audience does so enjoy seeing the lovers embrace at the finish. We cannot disappoint them, can we? Now let us begin the scene again. From 'Did you call, sir?'"

"'Did you call, sir? Did your honour call?'" Rosaline said, reverting to her Devonshire accent, which was based upon that of her dear Lemmy.

"'As for Miss Hardcastle, she's—'"

"Pardon me, my lord," a voice called out from the center aisle.

Lord Kenmore sighed impatiently and shielded his eyes against the footlights' glare. "What is it, Besley? Did I not give strict instructions that we were not to be disturbed?"

"Yes, my lord," the butler said. "But you also instructed me to inform you when Mr. Kean arrived, and he is here now."

"Excellent!" Lord Kenmore clapped his hands together and advanced to the front of the stage to address the assembled cast. "Ladies and gentlemen, you will be glad to hear that our Tony Lumpkin is arrived at last from Weymouth. Take your ease for a moment while I go to greet him." His dark eyes gleamed. "You shall shortly witness a dramatic talent such as you have never encountered before. That is," he added *sotto voce* to Rosaline, "if he is sober enough to perform. I shall return shortly, my beauty."

Rosaline descended from the stage to take a seat at the far end of the front row. As the only "professional" there at present she was regarded with a variety of emotions by the aristocratic amateurs: by the gentlemen, with a mixture of curiosity and admiration; and by the ladies—particularly the blond and willowy Lady Hathaway—with suspicion and hauteur. It gave her the greatest of pleasure to imagine the expressions on their faces if she were to reveal her true identity to them.

As always, it was Richard Courtenay who came to sit beside her. "Your performance today is even more entrancing than yesterday's, if that is possible."

She glowed beneath his admiring regard. "Oh, do you truly think so, Richard, I—I mean Mr. Courtenay?" Her color flared at this giving of his Christian name, an error no doubt caused by her frequent use of that name in her thoughts when she lay in bed at night.

She rattled on, trying to cover her confusion, sincerely hoping that he had not noticed her slip. "I love this play, don't you? Kate is such a delightful character—so free, so independent. And your performance as Diggory this morning was a positive revelation. You will have the audience in stitches. You never cease to surprise me, Mr. Courtenay."

"I infinitely prefer 'Richard.'"

She met his eyes and could not look away again. He laid his hand lightly, unpossessively, over hers. "I collect that you have had no further difficulties with Lord Kenmore?" he said in a low voice.

"No, none. He has been the very soul of courtesy during this past week, praising me frequently for my acting and my knowledge of the part."

"Hm. It would be interesting to know what devious plot his lordship is hatching now to ensnare you."

"For heaven's sake!" She snatched her hand away. "Must you always be thinking ill of him? I am certain that beneath that mocking exterior there is a tender heart. He has been thoroughly spoiled, that is all."

"You have lived for too long in a world of subterfuge and unreality, Miss Fitzgerald. You appear to observe everything in a topsy-turvy manner, searching for good where there is none and suspicious of those who are so patently trustworthy."

"Meaning yourself, I suppose. Trustworthy enough when paid!"

"I hesitate to mention it, but may I remind you that I have not yet received any payment, Miss Fitzgerald?"

Her eyes flew to his in sudden fear. "You promised me—you said— You gave me your word that you would not betray me to my cousin." She drew in a ragged breath. "I have had no opportunity as yet to procure the money. I promise you that it shall be yours within the week."

Despite the subdued light in the theater, she could see the dark red that suffused his cheeks. "I have given you my word," he said with controlled vehemence. "I do not renege on a promise. But may I take this opportunity to urge you once more to put your entire trust in me and permit me to assist you in the matter of the jewels?''

"Have done, Mr. Courtenay. We have agreed not to speak of what lies in the past, remember? You shall have your money as soon as I am able to make arrangements. Meanwhile, we are being observed by the fair Lady Hathaway, I believe.''

He relaxed and took off his spectacles to look across the theater. ''No doubt you see her as a rival.''

"Ha! Some rival! It depends upon what we are talking about. Doubtless Lord Kenmore is already a regular visitor to her bed. I have other aspirations.''

He looked surprised. ''You surely cannot mean marriage?''

"Why not? I wouldn't be the first actress to marry a nobleman.'' She could think of several examples, including her own mother.

''That is true, but I cannot imagine that Lord Kenmore is interested in connubial bliss.''

"It is my intention to make him interested.''

"Is it, indeed? I can see that the next few weeks may prove to be even more fascinating than I had anticipated.'' His tone was decidedly acid. ''I wish you good fortune in your hunt. You will be in dire need of it, I assure you.''

She looked up into his face. ''Why do you mind so much?'' she asked him softly.

''Mind?'' He peered down at her, straining his gold-flecked eyes to focus upon her countenance. ''I was not aware that I *did* mind.''

"Can you see at all without your spectacles?'' she asked, suddenly changing the subject.

''Not actually. Your face is a blur with pools of darkness where your eyes and mouth and hair are. I am chronically long-sighted and, therefore, unable to see things that are close to me with any clarity.''

"What a dreadful pity.''

"Why?''

"Because, without your spectacles, you are an extremely handsome man.''

"And with them?''

She gave him a dazzling smile. "As you are given generally to modesty, Mr. Courtenay, I shall admit that even with your spectacles I consider you a handsome man."

"My dear Miss Fitzgerald, you have most decidedly brightened my day."

"Put them on again so that you can see me."

He did so, his eyes focusing on her face. "Now it is my turn. You know that you are an exceedingly beautiful woman," he said very slowly.

She had been told this many times before, by friends of her father or Oliver, but never in this way. His tone, his very manner of speech, suggested that he saw beyond the mere physical manifestation of outward beauty, which she had frequently cursed for its ability to inflame men with base desires.

She felt a burning at the back of her eyes and throat, and swallowed hard. A longing to lean forward and kiss his well-shaped mouth gripped her. She wondered what his reaction would be if she did so. What was it about this irritating man that made her heart—and body—ache, despite her determination to be indifferent to him?

He was still gazing at her with frank admiration in his eyes. "Although I abhor the idea of Kenmore buying clothes for you, I must allow that he does have good taste."

"Yes, you are right." She looked down at the classically simple blue-spotted muslin with knots of sapphire ribbon adorning the bodice.

"Pardon my curiosity, but how in the world was he able to gauge your measurements so accurately?"

"Oh, apparently he asked Miss Scudamore, the costume maker with Mr. Pepperell's company. Did you think that I had given them to him?"

His jaw tightened. So unusual was it to see him vexed that she gained great delight in teasing him further. "Or perhaps you thought I had invited him to take the measurements himself?"

She knew immediately that she had gone too far. His eyes flared with anger.

"I would to God *I* could afford to buy you all the

fripperies your heart desires, but I cannot now and never would be able to. You forget, madam, that I have seen all the bills for your dresses and bonnets and folderols. Only an excessively wealthy man could afford to keep you in such a manner." Bitterness edged his voice. "But if it were not evident that you care deeply about jewels and money and fine clothing, I would offer you—"

She was not to know what he would offer her.

"My dear Mr. Courtenay" came Lady Hathaway's silken voice from behind them. "I have been attempting these past five minutes to attract your attention. Reluctant though I am to tear you away from such an intimate tête-â-tète with Miss Fitzgerald, I must ask you about that book of French prints you promised to show me."

She bestowed a sultry smile upon the secretary, who, to Rosaline's great satisfaction, seemed oblivious to it. Indeed, like her, he appeared slightly dazed by what had just passed between them and permitted himself to be borne away by Lady Hathaway to the other side of the theater without even a backward glance at Rosaline.

Shaken, she gripped her hands together in her lap. It was patently obvious that Richard Courtenay was jealous of Lord Kenmore—jealous not only of her involvement with him but also of his rank and position. Still believing her to be a common thief, he thought her only concern was for money and the material comforts it could buy. Little did he know that she would willingly exchange all her wealth for contentment and peace of mind. Her wealth, but not her status. That was hers by right, by birth, and with it she would never part.

What had he been about to offer her? Some bargain, perhaps: all her jewels for his permanent silence? Or possibly he had been about to suggest some sort of liaison between them. But, no, he had said that he could not afford to keep her. It was possible that he suspected her of sleeping with Lord Kenmore already, despite her insistence that her goal was marriage.

"Oh, my goodness!" she said out loud. Could it be possible that Mr. Courtenay had been about to propose? For a fleeting moment, her mind's eyes was filled with the image of a little cottage somewhere in Devon, with a rose-trellised door and a large man with wind-tossed bronze hair striding up the pathway bearing a laughing child on his broad shoulders.

This idyllic picture was banished by Lord Kenmore's return to the theater. He walked down the scarlet-carpeted aisle, ushering before him the strangest-looking young man, dressed in a black coat that was decidedly the worse for wear.

"Ladies and gentlemen, here is Mr. Edmund Kean, whose manager, Mr. Hughes, has kindly permitted him to join us for two weeks and who will be playing Tony Lumpkin, the comic lead in our play."

Rosaline had time to observe Mr. Kean while he was being presented to the rest of the cast. His body was small but well proportioned, and he had a large head topped with black curly hair. His extremely thin body appeared coiled with tension, like a spring threatening to explode if released.

Now he was moving across the aisle, and she rose to greet him.

"May I present Mr. Kean?" Lord Kenmore said. "This, my dear Kean, is the only other professional player in our company: Miss FItzgerald, who is recently come from Dublin and is to play Kate Hardcastle."

Her hand was taken in a fierce grip and instantly released. "Your servant, Miss Fitzgerald," the actor said in a vibrant voice. She could smell the fumes of brandy on his breath. He did not give her even the faintest hint of a smile, and something in the way he looked at her, the penetrating dark eyes in the pale, thin face, caused her to step back involuntarily from him.

"Mr. Kean." She inclined her head and smiled, not quite sure whether she should engage him in conversation or not. He stood, balanced gracefully on his small feet, bearing himself with a mixture of bravado and uneasiness that made him appear decidedly unapproachable.

"Mr. Kean has recently completed a tour of the western circuit, where he played Macbeth, Richard the Third, and

Othello all in the same week," Lord Kenmore announced to the assembled group. "All this, in addition to farce and pantomime. His Harlequin is the *nonpareil* of the stage. You should see his handsprings!"

"I never feel so degraded as when I have to don a Harlequin costume," Mr. Kean declared in a cold voice, "and I abhor comic roles."

This certainly did not bode well for a production in which he was to play the leading comic role. Rosaline saw Lady Hathaway cast a speaking glance at the portly Sir Roger Vanier, who was to play Mr. Hardcastle.

Lord Kenmore laughed. "Do not look so concerned, my friends. Mr. Kean never does anything by halves." He clapped the smaller man on the shoulder. "I have sat through a dozen of his performances, comic and tragic, and never have I been more moved to laughter and tears and horror than I have been by the acting of Edmund Kean. Mark my words, he will be treading the boards of the Theatre Royal, Drury Lane, ere long, if I have anything to say about it."

This high-flown praise, which was taken as mere flattering hyperbole on Lord Kenmore's part, designed to put the taciturn young man at his ease, was proved to be far from exaggeration at the ensuing rehearsals. Offstage, Edmund Kean might have been ill at ease with those above his station, but once upon it he took complete command, so that eyes turned involuntarily to him even when he was merely standing by.

At first, Rosaline could not envisage this slight, nervous little man in the role of the boisterous Tony Lumpkin—or, for that matter, as Othello or Macbeth—but he insisted on donning his costume for all rehearsals, saying that the additional padding gave him the necessary bulk, and played the uncouth young squire with a frenzy and a hint of the sinister that gave one the feeling that Mr. Lumpkin was capable of far darker deeds than a few practical jokes. This was possibly not the author's intention, but it proved strikingly effective, making Tony Lumpkin more a villain than a stock comic character.

It soon became evident to the entire cast that they were in the company of extraordinary talent. Offstage, however, was another matter. Mr. Kean's boorish behavior and heavy bouts of drinking made him objectionable company. Unfortunately, because of his awkwardness with those whose status exceeded his, it was to Rosaline that he turned for companionship.

To begin with, she felt compassion for the frustrated and resentful actor.

"Ten long years I have been marooned in the provinces, striving to gain some entry to the London theaters," he confided in her. "My wife and children are sick, and I have not a penny left. I took a benefit last month and, would you believe it, lost money on it! Much as I detest comedy, I was forced to accept Lord Kenmore's offer. He is paying me well and, besides, he may provide me with an entrée to the Theatre Royal, for he's a close friend of Lord Byron."

Rosaline's compassion was sorely tried, however, when Mr. Kean drank to escape his frustration, which was a matter of frequency.

"Kenmore told me this would be a lively company," he complained to her one night after a late rehearsal. "Devil take it, it's more like a damned wake." He leaned towards her, engulfing her in the brandy fumes from his breath. "Don't you agree, Miss Fitzgerald? I've a feeling you'd like more excitement as well."

She stiffened as she felt his hand grasp her thigh. Not wishing to create a scene, she hastily stood up, leaving him lolling in his chair.

"Aha! So you've higher aspirations, my fine lady," he said with a sneering expression. "I wish you good fortune. Never you forget, pride comes before a fall, and I'll warrant you've fallen many times before." He staggered to his feet. "As for me, I intend to liven things up here, or Kenmore will have to stage all his rehearsals at the local tavern if he wants me to attend 'em!"

——— Chapter ———
Twelve

Before the end of the week, it was evident that the company would not need to repair to the nearest tavern for their rehearsals to satisfy Edmund Kean's whim. It was as if the actor's dissipation had set off a reaction in the other players, tainting them. Not that they appeared in any way reluctant to be tainted.

As the evenings grew rowdier and the drinking deeper, Rosaline became increasingly uneasy. She began to suspect that Richard Courtenay had not invented the stories of Lord Kenmore's parties, after all. Even so, she had hoped that Lord Kenmore would abstain from his excesses while she was there. But then, why should he? she thought bitterly. To him, she was an actress—and actresses were, by repute, notoriously easy women.

When she saw that Lady Hathaway and the Honorable Mrs. Goring were apparently eager to join in the drinking and whatever else might ensue, Rosaline determined to retire to her room, like Mrs. Elliott, and lock her door immediately after dinner each night. This hedonism could not last long, surely, for the rest of Lord Kenmore's houseguests were due to arrive from Bath and London that very weekend to witness the first performance of the play.

As if aware of this, after the dress rehearsal on Thursday night, before Rosaline had time to slip away after dinner, Lord Kenmore sprang up from his place at the head of the dinner table and stood, one hand on his hip, the other clutching a large crystal goblet of brandy. His handsome face was flushed with drink and a strange, feverish excitement.

"We shall have to be on our best behavior very soon, my friends, for my guests will be starting to arrive within twenty-four hours. Meanwhile, I consider we deserve a special celebration as we have all worked so hard." His dark eyes glittered in the candlelight.

Rosaline, who was seated on his left, stirred uneasily in her seat, aware that Richard Courtenay had ridden to Bath that day to make final arrangements for the dispatch of provisions and had not planned to return in time for dinner.

"I think I shall retire, if you will excuse me, my lord," she said.

His left hand shot out, gripping her wrist. "You will remain exactly where you are" was his menacing command. He smiled as he addressed the others. "To begin our evening of celebration, Kean and I have arranged for some exotic entertainment."

He clapped his hands and the doors were thrown open. Through them ran a band of barefoot gypsies, the women in voluminous skirts of myriad bright hues, the men in ragged breeches and with bare brown chests. Before Rosaline's amazed eyes, Kean and Lord Kenmore each took an end of the damask tablecloth, bundling up the dishes and glasses and food, and flung it into a corner with an utter disregard for the valuable Minton chinaware or the crystal glasses.

Earrings and necklaces clinking, the gypsies leaped onto the table and began to dance to the sensuous rhythm of castanets and tambourines. Despite her feelings of repulsion, Rosaline's blood was stirred by the primitive beat and the flagrantly sensual dancing.

When their dance was finished, two decanters of brandy were passed around, more glasses produced, and everyone, including the gypsies, drank liberally.

Everyone, that is, except Rosaline. Appalled, she watched the other ladies abandon all discretion under the influence of the strong spirits and the licentious atmosphere. The buxom Mrs. Goring had wound her arms around Sir Roger's neck, he being in no state to resist, had he so wished. And Lady

Hathaway was sprawled in her chair, her bodice dragged down so that her nipples were fully exposed.

Although she did not look at him, Rosaline was aware that Lord Kenmore had now moved to stand behind her chair. Her spine became a rod of ice.

He bent towards her. "Tonight I intend to break down that barrier you have set between us," he whispered.

She felt his mouth hot on the back of her neck and then his hands upon her hair. Jerking her head away, she attempted to rise, but his hands cupped her shoulders, forcing her to remain seated.

"You cannot escape me, so relax and enjoy, my sweet, adorable Rosaline." Again he kissed her neck, this time his kisses continuing along the slope of one shoulder.

Enraged, she tried to swing around to confront him, but still he held her fast. "Release me this instant, sir. You have gone quite far enough. Is this the way you keep your word that I should not be subject to your advances at Luxton?"

He merely laughed and began to kiss her again, his mouth trailing dangerously close to the curve of her breasts.

She flung away from him, flailing her arms and fists. Her blows struck his face, but made as they were from a seated position, they proved ineffectual. *God,* she thought, *how I wish I had my silver dagger!*

"What a little termagant it is, to be sure! Only not so little. A voluptuous tiger. My God, Rosaline, the more you resist me the more I want you!" His voice was so raw with passion that it was almost unrecognizable.

She could not believe that this was actually happening, here, in a brightly lit dining room, in full view of other occupants. A wave of fury mixed with terror engulfed her, but she must remain calm. She was convinced it was the only way to get herself out of this madhouse. Yet, even now she was finding it difficult to think coherently.

"Lady Hathaway," she called out in a shaky voice. "Is it not time for us to retire to the drawing room?"

Lady Hathaway was unable to reply, however, being locked in the arms of one of the male gypsies, her bodice now wrenched down to her waist, her hands convulsively clutching the man's curly black hair.

"As you can see, my beloved, Lady Hathaway is pleasuring herself. Why, then, should not you do the same?"

"This is utterly ridiculous. I cannot believe it is happening," she told him in a low voice. "I demand that you permit me to leave, Lord Kenmore. If you truly loved me, you would—"

"Loved you?" His laughter was more insulting than his actions had been. "Well, yes, I suppose I do love your voluptuous body and your beautiful face and that ravishing titian hair of yours. Come, let us see it as it should be. No, you vixen, it is no use struggling. I will have my way."

He put his left arm around her neck, holding her most effectively as his fingers unwound the coils and braids of her hair until it rippled down to her waist, falling about her like a mantle.

"My God," he breathed reverently. "How utterly beautiful you are!"

As the dancing and hypnotic beat of the tambourine became even more frantic, he hauled her up against him.

Her fingers curled into claws. "Release me instantly," she hissed. "I warn you, sir, I have almost killed a man for attempting to assault me. I shall not hesitate to do the same to you."

"I'll wager you would not, too. It is what makes you so devilish exciting beneath that ladylike manner of yours." His hands were at the bodice of her dress.

"I am not what you think me, my lord," she gasped. "I am of gentle birth. Surely you do not intend to ravish me?"

"Of course not. That will not be necessary. Have done, now. You have played the role of Virtue Assailed for long enough. I am not at all sure why you have maintained it for so long. Take a drink of brandy and admit you have been defeated."

She struck his hand away, so that the spirits splashed down his open waistcoat. "If you rape me, I shall report you to the nearest justice of the peace."

He grinned. "The nearest justice of the peace is myself, my treasure. Besides, you have lived here under my protection for two weeks. I have fed you, clothed you in fine style, given you shelter, all without once forcing myself upon you. On consideration, I believe I have been inordinately patient. You have been given ample opportunity to quit this house unmolested, if that had been your wish. You surely could not have been so naive as to imagine that I would not expect some sort of recompense. Good God, woman. You're an actress, not a duchess! I've seen too many greenroom Romeos not to know what goes on in the world of the theater, and, forgive me for saying so, the world in which I discovered you was, one might say, a substrata of the theatrical world I know. Come now, no more pretense at resistance, if you please. I wish to conserve my strength for our coming encounter."

She continued her frantic struggling as he crushed his mouth on hers. When he would not release her, she bit down hard on his tongue, which was most demonstrably effective.

"Devil take you!" he cursed, clapping his hand to his mouth and wincing with pain.

She turned to run from him, but he caught hold of the back of her dress, ripping the skirt, and swung her back to him. She could see now that his patience was at an end, for his face was pale with anger.

"Very well, madam. If that is the way you wish it to be, then so be it." He took her roughly by the back of the neck and dragged her against him.

Above the gypsies' music, the stamp of feet, and the clicking of castanets, she heard Edmund Kean's laugh ring out from the far end of the room and was convinced she was in hell. What was the use of further struggle? There was no one in this accursed place who would come to her aid.

The large double doors of the dining room suddenly burst open with such force that they crashed back against the wall.

Lord Kenmore jerked his head up, his eyes narrowing as he looked across the room. "Ah, it's you!" he shouted. "You have arrived just in time to join our party. Help yourself to brandy—and to the ever-willing Lady Hathaway if you wish. I believe she has been lusting after your gargantuan body ever since she arrived. She always did have an execrable taste in men! For God's sake, shut that door." He held Rosaline pressed against his side all the time he spoke. "Come in, man, come in. Tonight we are all equals. This is Liberty Hall, Courtenay, Liberty Hall!"

——— Chapter ———
Thirteen

"Rosaline!" Richard Courtenay's voice rang through the dining room. "Come here to me!"

"Rosaline, eh? So that's it." Lord Kenmore looked down at her flushed face, his eyes searching hers. "You're playing a devilish deep game, my girl. Deuced if I know what's going on."

She met his prolonged gaze steadily but found herself unable to resist sending a look of appeal to Richard Courtenay, who remained just inside the dining room doors.

"Release her, Kenmore." He barely raised his voice, but his words were heard by all, for the gypsies had ceased their frenzied dancing upon his entrance.

Lord Kenmore's grip on Rosaline tightened. "I think not. May I remind you, Courtenay, that you are in my employ?"

"Not any more. I hereby tender my resignation. I do not remain in the employ of men who offer insults to ladies."

"Ladies!" Lord Kenmore scoffed. "You know, this is all most unfortunate, Courtenay. You were an excellent secretary, with great potential for advancement. I fear in the circumstances that I shall be unable to offer you a recommendation."

"That will be unnecessary. I am not sure that a recommendation from you would be to my advantage. No more talk, Kenmore. Release her—now.'' He took a step forward, seeming, to Rosaline's eyes, almost supernaturally large in his many-caped greatcoat and spurred riding boots.

"Let me go, my lord," Rosaline said. "I refuse to demean myself any further by struggling with you. This is all so incredibly ridiculous. You are behaving like a head-strong child!"

The dancers stood on the table, observing the conduct of their betters with unconcealed grins. Rosaline was far more concerned about Richard's safety than her own. She was deeply afraid that everyone in the room would suddenly converge upon him and overpower him. "He will not release me," she called across to him.

From the pocket of his greatcoat he drew forth a small pistol. "Let her go, Kenmore," he said in a calm voice.

Lord Kenmore gave a great crack of laughter. "My dear fellow, you surely do not expect me to believe that you would attempt to shoot me. Confound it, man. I am at least thirty feet away from you, and you're as blind as a bat."

"For the last time, Kenmore: Release Miss Fitzgerald."

In reply, Francis Kenmore bent his head and kissed Rosaline's clamped mouth, and then smiled gaily in Courtenay's direction. Her back as stiff as a board, Rosaline glared at him. "You are utterly disgusting!" she informed him.

"And you, my dear, are utterly enchanting when you are angry."

With his left hand, Richard Courtenay carefully removed his spectacles, folded them, and slid them into his pocket. He raised the pistol, aimed, and pulled the trigger. Rosaline heard the whine of the ball as it passed just a few inches above their heads. Both she and Lord Kenmore glanced up to see that the candle in the wall sconce above them had been split in two.

"By God, Courtenay, that's incredible!" Lord Kenmore cried.

Taking advantage of his amazement, Rosaline broke from him and sped around the table and down the room to reach the safe haven beside Richard Courtenay.

His left arm drew her to his side, but his eyes maintained their vigilant watch on Lord Kenmore.

"Pack a bag," he told her softly. "A small one, mind— one that you can easily carry yourself. And be as quick as you possibly can." He gave her waist a reassuring squeeze. "Never fear, we shall soon be far from this place."

Lord Kenmore now was leaning nonchalantly against the wall, his arms crossed over his chest. "I grant you Courtenay's a good secretary, my fair Rosaline, but he's a wretched bargain for a woman like you, who's trying to climb the social ladder. Good God, woman. With your beauty you could have anyone you choose. Courtenay's not worth the proverbial brass farthing, you know. You deserve better than that. Stay here with me and I'll give you my word that I'll be exceedingly generous and treat you well. Though I am bound to tell you that I draw the line at the wedding band you were evidently hankering after."

They both ignored him. "Go quickly now," Richard said urgently. "When you are ready, go down the back stairs, call my name, and then go out the servants' entrance. I shall meet you there."

"Devil take it, let's have done with all this flimflammery," said Lord Kenmore in a weary tone. He moved to the table and dragged out the heavy chair at the head of it. Reaching first to pour himself a glass of brandy, he slumped into the chair, regarding them with a quizzical expression.

"My dear Miss Fitzgerald, there is positively no need for you to be slinking away like a felon from my house at this hour. Stay, and I give you my word that you shall be conveyed in my carriage to wherever you choose first thing in the morning."

"Thank you for your offer, my lord, but I believe we should prefer to leave immediately." She felt Richard's hand slide down to squeeze hers. She was almost inclined to giggle, so extraordinary was the change in the mood of the room.

"Very well, then. I offer you the use of my carriage tonight, but I regret I cannot extend the same invitation to Courtenay."

"I prefer to be accompanied by Mr. Courtenay and make my way on foot, sir."

"Do you, indeed? You consider the man so worthy of your trust that you will venture out into the night with him as your sole companion?"

She looked up at Richard Courtenay's profile, with its strong jaw and Roman nose. Lord Kenmore's question was a crucial one, but she had known the answer to it when Richard had first entered the room and her heart had leaped at the sight of him. "Yes, my lord, I trust him implicitly."

She was rewarded with a glowing look from Richard.

"You're besotted, the pair of you" was Lord Kenmore's disgusted response. He cast a jaded look about the disheveled dining room. "Have I your leave to dismiss this rabble?"

Richard Courtenay nodded.

Lord Kenmore waved a white hand at the dancers, who had descended from the table and were openly staring at the proceedings with shining black eyes. " 'Out of my sight; thou dost infect mine eyes.' "

The gypsies made no move, unaware that they had been addressed.

"Go!" Lord Kenmore cried. "My man will pay you. Leave by the other door."

Muttering amongst themselves, they stalked out, no doubt disappointed at this abrupt end to what had promised to be both a lucrative and pleasurable night. One of their party was missing, having been lured away earlier by Lady Hathaway.

"For God's sake put that pistol away, Courtenay. I want no more holes in my wallpaper. And as for you, you baggage," Lord Kenmore added, addressing Rosaline, "you have cost me a great deal more than mere money. You realize that you are leaving me high and dry without a Kate Hardcastle, and all my guests are arriving tomorrow? Devil take it, woman, I've a good mind to hold you to the verbal contract we had! Will you not remain another week at least," he pleaded, "so that we may do the play?"

Rosaline drew herself up to her full height, her pride and confidence now fully restored. "Not another hour, sir."

"I would have made you famous, you know. You are a marvelous Kate. How can you bear not to do it?"

It was a good question. The hardest part about leaving was having to relinquish her role in *She Stoops to Conquer*.

"I own that I am deeply sorry about that, for my own sake, my lord. But when you asked me to come to Luxton, you gave me your word that I would be safe from your advances unless I was willing to accept them."

Francis Kenmore signed. "You are in the right of it there. I did. Only, that damned fellow Kean would insist on having this party. Where is the wretch, anyway?"

Richard indicated the comatose figure lying curled up on a couch in a far corner of the room. In his drunken stupor, Edmund Kean no longer looked satanic, merely small and pathetic.

Lord Kenmore sighed again. "Confound the man! I shall have to keep him under lock and key if he is to be fit to play Lumpkin by Saturday."

"You intend to continue with the play, then?" Rosaline asked.

"Certainly I do. I am not that easily vanquished. I shall send off to Hughes this very night to see if he can find a replacement for you. Bound to be someone in the western circuit who can do Kate Hardcastle. Sure you won't change your mind?" he asked in a gruff voice.

"I regret not." She turned to Richard. "I shall go now and pack my things. I shall not take any of the clothes you provided," she informed Lord Kenmore haughtily.

"Confound it, woman. Take what you please. They are of no use to me. Have done with all this nonsensical pride, for the Lord's sake. Anyone would take you for a duchess, from your manner. Take what the devil you please." He turned from them to contemplate his glass of brandy, holding it up to the light and swirling the amber liquid.

With a quick, shy smile at Richard, Rosaline left the dining room and sped up to her room.

In less than a quarter of an hour, she returned. "Mr. Courtenay," she called from the back hall.

He came to meet her. "Kenmore is lending us the gig. We are to return it to him at our convenience." He grinned. "This has all turned into something of a farce, has it not? Here we are, escaping with the aid and reluctant blessing of the erstwhile villain!" His smile faded as his eyes searched hers. "Seriously, my—Miss Fitzgerald, did he hurt you in any way?"

She shook her head. "No. But I am not sure what would have happened had you not arrived when you did. He was growing extremely impatient with me. Oh, Richard, I have been such a fool." She turned her face away from him and fumbled in her sleeve for her handkerchief. "I thought—"

"I know what you thought. But however sincere his feelings for you, you were still but an actress from a traveling company to him, one whom he had elevated and placed under his protection. In the circumstances, one cannot consider his conduct entirely reprehensible, can one?"

"Oh, must you always be so full of common sense! Any man who would even think of forcing himself upon a woman . . . You would never do such a thing, would you?"

"No, I suppose not." He gave her a wry smile. "What a dull dog I must be, to be sure. But then, I am not a man of wealth and position like Kenmore. I could not afford to keep a *chère amie*, even if I wished to do so. For that matter," he added with a bitter note in his voice that she had not heard before, "I cannot even afford a wife." He bent to pick up her bag. "Heavier than when you first arrived, I believe," he said, his voice muffled.

"I must own that I did take some of the clothing Lord Kenmore had made for me. I had need of one or two things. I mean to repay him once I find a new position."

"Or sell your jewels?" he raised his eyebrows at her. "Remind me to bring up the subject of those jewels at some more convenient time," he continued when she made no response. "But let us waste no more time in setting off. I am uncertain as to what my grandfather will say to our arriving unheralded at his house in Bath in the middle of the night, but I have no intention of waiting here until morning.''

''Your grandfather? But—I do not think—''

''I assure you that it will all be perfectly correct. We shall have plenty of time to invent a plausible tale for him before we reach Bath.''

Upon seeing that she still showed signs of hesitation, he gently added: ''My grandfather, General Sir John Huntley, is my mother's father. He is the kindest old fellow imaginable, so have no fear of his turning you away from the door. Come now, let us be off before Kenmore changes his mind and sets the dogs on us.''

Chapter Fourteen

As they were bowling down the avenue in the little gig, Rosaline sat on the edge of the seat, her head swimming from all that had occurred that evening. Amidst the turmoil, one salient point emerged: tonight, all her suspicions and her mistrust of Richard Courtenay had been turned upside down. To cap it all, there had been the quiet, unheralded announcement that his grandfather was a knight and a general. There remained innumerable questions to be asked and answered on both sides, but for now she was so overwhelmingly happy that she preferred to remain silent.

Once they were through the lodge gates, which were opened, after a great deal of knocking, by the thoroughly disgruntled gatekeeper, she sank back against the cushioned seat, content to watch Richard as he held the reins easily in his large hands.

He glanced at her. "Comfortable?"

"Oh, yes."

They lapsed into a companionable silence, which was broken only by the rhythmical clop of the pony's hooves and the rustle of leaves and squeaks and hoots of night birds. It was a magical night. The scent of sweet clover filled the air. The sky was an inky blue with myriad stars, and the air was remarkably warm for early May.

"A singular contrast to the last time we spent a night together, is it not?" he said.

"Yes. It is." He might have been reading her thoughts, for her mind had been on that other night before he had spoken.

She closed her eyes and, as time passed, slowly conjured up the feelings she had experienced that night: the gradual awakening of desire, the yearning. Here they were, together again, this time without the restraint of suspicion—on her part, at least. This lack of restraint removed the control she had maintained that other night. The yearning became an intolerable ache that radiated throughout her body.

Her breathing quickened as she became intensely aware of the pressure of his firm thigh and hip bone against hers, his elbow against her shoulder. It was as if her flesh had become unbearably sensitive beneath the layers of clothing that covered it, like the princess feeling the dried pea through a score of mattresses. The longing to feel his arm about her, his hand upon her breast, his mouth upon hers, was almost unbearable.

A pony and gig was not the speediest method of transportation. By the time they had traveled a few miles, she was beginning to feel that she would scream with the longing, the aching, that was a mixture of intense pleasure and pain.

Whether or not he sensed her mood, for some reason he began to slow down the pony and drew the gig to a halt by the banks of a stream. She could hear the breeze lapping the water and the occasional splash when some night animal or bird submerged. From a nearby tree, a nightingale began its preparatory gurgling and then burst into a stream of melody so sweet that it brought tears to her eyes.

"I thought you might care to halt for a while, to stretch your legs," Richard said. His voice sounded strangely husky. "Perhaps you might like to eat something. I procured some bread and cold ham from the kitchen before we left Luxton."

"How very resourceful you are, Mr. Courtenay," she said with a shaky laugh.

He handed her down from the gig, releasing her hand immediately, as if it burned him, and then proceeded to spread the carriage rug on the sloping bank. She sat down, smoothing out her skirts and carefully folding her cloak across the front of her, as if she were striving to maintain some sort of barrier, some extra layer to cover that extraordinarily sensitive flesh of hers. But nothing could take away the mingled pain and exquisite pleasure that permeated her body.

"Here we are," he said, standing tall above her. "Bread and ham." He tossed down a package wrapped in greased brown paper. "That is all I could find in my haste."

"I am not sure that I am very hungry at the moment." He did not reply, nor did he move from his position, standing like a sentry above her. She could sense his extreme tension. "Will you not sit down, Mr. Courtenay?"

He hesitated for a moment, and then, like a man who had paused at the fork in the road and then chosen his path, he sat down beside her on the rug, knees bent, arms wrapped around them.

A little breeze wafted through the clearing, softly rustling the leaves. She shivered.

"Cold?"

"A little."

She held her breath, knowing and longing for what he was about to do and yet in a strange way fearing it as well. His arm closed about her, drawing her to his side. The familiar heady aroma of sandalwood emanated from him, its oriental fragrance fanning her desire.

She moved closer against him, turning her face to his

chest. "Oh, Richard," she whispered into the capes of his greatcoat. His body was as tense as a stretched cord.

They remained thus until she could no longer bear the intolerable ache of longing to be closer to him. Involuntarily, she stretched out her legs and turned on her side to face him, to find herself crushed against the full length of his body.

It was as if they had been made for each other. Their bodies pressed hungrily together as his mouth sought and found hers. She knew that the reason for her entire existence was in this very moment, this ecstacy of his lips upon hers, this molding of their bodies.

"Rosaline, oh, my darling, my darling," he groaned. He rained kisses on her eyes, her ears, the hollow of her throat, but always returning to her mouth again. His hand sought her full breasts, and even through the layers of clothing she could feel its warmth.

Now he ran both his hands down the length of her back, cupping her buttocks as he thrust his body against hers in a rhythm she was instinctively able to imitate.

"Please, please," she said, over and over again, not sure what it was she was asking for but knowing in her blind ecstacy she must have it. "Oh, please, Richard."

He muttered something to himself that she was unable to hear. All she knew was that, to her dismay, her voice had broken the spell. He gently drew away from her, kissing her forehead before he stood up, leaving her shivering with cold and disappointment and the ache of unfulfilled desire.

He sprang to his feet. She could hear the snap of twigs as he paced quickly along the track, away from her. While he was gone, she gathered up the discarded food and the rug, and returned to the gig.

The patient pony greeted her with a whicker and a toss of the head. "Yes, you are perfectly correct," she told it. "We should not have stopped here."

"Are you sorry that we did?" asked Richard's voice from behind her.

She spun around to gaze up into his face in the light from the gig's lantern. "No. Are you?"

He looked away down the track for a moment and then back at her again. "To own the truth, I am not sure. It was probably inevitable, but it has changed everything between us, hasn't it?"

"Yes. I believe so. Before we say any more on the subject, though, I must ask you if you still believe that I am a jewel thief?"

"No, I do not. And you? Do you still believe that I am in your cousin's pay?"

"No. But I still cannot fathom why you promised me that you would not divulge my whereabouts to him, when you didn't even know who he is."

"What a silly little gudgeon you are!" he said lovingly.

She reflected that only Richard would be able to consider her "little." It made her love him even more.

"It was the only way I could find to calm you down," he explained. "To my chagrin, it was far easier to convince you that I was being paid by your cousin than that I was not. Which does not say much for your opinion of me, does it?"

She grasped the lapels of his coat. "But, Richard, how was I to know you were telling the truth? Is it all true, by the bye: your sisters, and the three brothers at sea, and your home in Ilfracombe? Is that all true?"

"It is, indeed. And now it is you who owe me an explanation. Where did those jewels come from? And what in heaven's name were you doing on Exmoor on such a night?"

"Oh, my love. It is all so very easily explained." She was overwhelmed with relief at the thought of at last being able to share her dilemma with someone, most especially when that someone happened to be the man she loved. "It is a long story, so I shall relate it while we are driving, I think." She gazed up at his face, the moonlight glinting on the gold rims of his spectacles. "But before we start off again, would you be so kind as to kiss me just once more?" She reached up to remove his spectacles. "There. I give you my word that soon, very soon, I shall permit you to kiss me with them on, but for now I prefer them off when I kiss you.''

"I am not certain that I should kiss you again, Rosaline. You see what it almost led to?'' His voice was stern, but she could see the smile that lifted the corners of his mouth.

"Yes, Richard. Just one little kiss,'' she pleaded.

"Very well.'' He gripped her arms and bent his head to comply with her request, this time moving his mouth with an agonizingly sweet slowness over her lips, so that her mouth seemed to melt beneath his.

"Dearest love.'' He drew away with a shuddering breath and replaced his spectacles. "Despite my desperate pecuniary circumstances, I think we must marry. I regret this decidedly strange proposal of marriage, my love, but I have no idea as to whom I should apply for permission to pay my addresses to you. Our entire courtship has been, if you will forgive me for saying so, not only brief but also decidedly bizarre.''

His proposal did not surprise her, for although she felt she was in a dream world, all that had occurred since they had left Luxton seemed an inevitable consequence of the night they had spent together on Exmoor—inevitable and preordained. This was the right man for her. She now had no doubts whatsoever on that score.

"There is no one else. I am the only person you need ask.''

"Not even your cousin, Oliver?''

She shivered. "Particularly not Oliver.''

"That is reassuring, for if you had had any family, anyone at all who was in some way responsible for you, I should find it difficult to convince them that I was a good catch. Indeed, had there been someone, *anyone*, to care for you, I should not have proposed to you.''

Again, she heard the bitterness that had chilled her once before, in the hallway at Luxton.

"I have nothing at all to offer a woman, bar my birth and breeding; regrettably, birth and breeding do not furnish houses and feed mouths. I have a small allowance but no prospects whatsoever and, now, no position. That is why I am forced, very much against my will, to take you to Bath to my grandfather."

"Will he not assist you in finding a career?"

He appeared to tower over her. "Certainly he would, if I would permit him to do so, but I will not."

She had not realized how proud, how fiercely independent, he was. She had much to learn about the man she loved. "But, surely, as a younger son, you must take advantage of any assistance you are offered?"

"Not so. I prefer to make my own way in life, thank you. This position with Lord Kenmore might have proved a stepping stone. He has several influential friends in the political arena."

"And that is what you aspire too? The world of politics?"

He hacked at a tree stump with a large stick he had picked up from the ground "It *was*."

"And so I have been the cause of your hopes in that direction being dashed."

He flung the stick away and turned to her, grasping her hands tightly in his. "Nonsense! Kenmore's friends may not have proved to be helpful in any way to me. Besides, I had been with him too short a time to receive any recommendation from him."

"I should hate to think that I had been responsible for—"

"Shall we change the subject?" He looked down into her face. "I wonder what my mother will think of you. I have a feeling that, despite her initial disappointment, she will love you from the first moment she sees you."

Rosaline doubted this very much, but she was content not to mar his illusions. "Why do you think that she will be disappointed? Because I am an actress?"

"No, no, not that so much. Only because it has always been the fervent hope of my entire family that I would marry a woman of fortune and status, thus making it possible for me to pursue a political career. Although I am the largest of my father's sons, I fear I am somewhat of a disappointment to him. Indeed, both he and my brothers feel sorry for me because I could not become a naval officer."

"Because of your eyesight?"

"Not only because of my sight but also, I must confess with some chagrin, because I suffer greatly from seasickness, even if I am taken only in a rowboat around Ilfracombe harbor! I trust you will not divulge my shabby secret to another living soul."

"No, my love, I shall not." She also hugged to herself another secret: that she had ample cause to believe that, if it was a woman of wealth and high position that his mother wanted for him, she would not be disappointed. But that secret could wait until she began her story.

"You must not be thinking that it is only you who would be the cause of my mother's disappointment," he told her. "Before I left my home for this, my third position as a secretary, I made a solemn vow, and informed my family of it, that I would never marry a woman whose station or fortune was above mine. I could not bear to be subservient or in any way beholden to my wife. That, above all things, would be intolerable to me. I must be my own man, even if that entails starving in the process."

Icy coldness swept over Rosaline as the exact meaning of his words permeated her brain. She knew from his earnest tone that he meant what he said.

Dear God! She had fallen hopelessly in love with a man who had sworn never to marry above himself. How could she tell him now that she was the fabulously wealthy Countess of Beresford?

"At least, my dearest love," he continued, unaware of her sudden despair, "that is one thing that need not concern me when I marry you, it being so patently obvious that you are in far less fortunate circumstances than I."

She could not have responded had she wished to. Her tongue clove to the roof of her mouth.

He took her limp hand and drew her to the step of the gig. "Come, my dear unofficially betrothed, let us set off again. The faster we reach Bath, the faster we can begin to make the arrangements for our life together."

He helped her into the gig, his happiness so great that he failed to sense the change in her mood.

"Now, my dear Miss Fitzgerald," he said as the gig moved away from the grass verge and onto the track leading to the road to Bath, "I am eager to hear all about those jewels and Oliver and, most especially, to learn your true identity."

Chapter Fifteen

The urge to tell him the truth was so strong that Rosaline had to bite her lower lip to hold it back. No, she could not tell him until they were married or, at the very earliest, until after their engagement had been announced to his family, for then, she hoped, he would find it impossible to withdraw. She covered her eyes with her hands, striving to arrange her confused thoughts into some semblance of order.

"Tired, my love?"

She nodded and yawned widely, eager to grasp any opportunity to postpone the explanation for which he had been waiting so patiently. Again she yawned, finding it not at all difficult to convey the illusion of extreme weariness to him, for all her excitement had ebbed away, leaving her dispirited and fatigued.

"I am *so* weary, Richard. Would you mind very much if I tell you everything tomorrow? It is such a complicated story and, for now, I desire nothing more than sleep."

"Very well. I shall await your explanation with impatience but fortitude. Rest your head on my shoulder, my darling. Here, I'll tuck the rug around you." He shifted the reins to his right hand and pulled the rug over her.

His shoulder being higher than her head, he slumped a little in the seat to accommodate her. For a while, she thought that she might indeed sleep, so rhythmically even were the sound of the pony's hooves and the squeak of the wheels, but, alas, her thoughts were whirling through her head with no sense of rhythm whatsoever, and her peace of mind was at an end.

"Asleep?" he whispered.

"Not yet."

"May I ask you just one question, then?"

She nodded, dreading what it might be.

"Is your name truly Rosaline?"

Tears rushed to her eyes, and she turned her face to his shoulder. "Yes, my name is truly Rosaline" was her muffled reply.

"Thank God for that. I should find it extremely difficult to think of you as anything but Rosaline."

She made no reply, her mind already feverishly occupied with the creation of a new story, a convincing one that would cover the jewels, Oliver, and herself, together with her presence on Exmoor at night in one of the worst rainstorms of the year.

By the time they reached the outskirts of Bath, she had managed to invent a reasonably plausible story which she hoped would satisfy his rather too perceptive mind.

It was strange to be driving through the almost deserted streets of the famous town at this hour. In the dim lamplight, she caught tantalizing glimpses of elegant stone buildings and bow-windowed shopfronts. A shiver of anticipation ran over her at the prospect of exploring all the sights of the town with Richard.

She sat up and began to braid her hair. "I cannot arrive at your grandfather's house with my hair all over the place."

He glanced across at her before returning his gaze to the narrow street down which he was driving. "I deeply regret that I am unable to do it for you. By the bye, I must remember to add one proviso to our marriage contract."

"What is that?"

"That you give me your word that you will never cut

your hair. I eagerly anticipate the sight of you on our wedding night with—"

"Enough, Mr. Courtenay! You will be putting me to the blush if you continue."

He did not turn to look at her, but she could see by the lamplight of a passing curricle that he was smiling broadly.

He negotiated the gig up a narrow street, and all at once she found herself surrounded by a large circle of elegant terraced town houses; in the center was another circle of what appeared to be lawn and trees, although she could not see much at all in the lamplit darkness.

"The Circus," Richard announced, drawing the gig up outside one of the houses. "It must be after two o'clock. I fear everyone will be asleep."

He handed her the reins and sprang down from the gig. "Would you hold them a moment until I can get my grandfather's groom to take the pony and gig to the stables?"

Not waiting for her reply, he strode up to the door and knocked twice. The sound seemed to echo around the enclosed area, so that Rosaline fully expected to see several doors open.

In fact, not one door opened, not even the one at which Richard had knocked. She could hear him cursing softly, and then he knocked again. The yowling of tomcats fighting in the gutter appeared to be the only response, until the door slowly creaked open and a querulous voice called out, "What is it you want?"

"Good morning, Jennings."

In the stream of light from the interior of the house, Rosaline could see a small old man clad in an ancient dressing gown of faded green velvet. He peered at Richard.

"Bless my soul, it's Mr. Richard." His wrinkled face lit up with a smile, making him appear like some jolly old gnome.

At Richard's request, he went to wake up the groom, and shortly thereafter Rosaline found herself standing in the narrow hallway.

"Good morning, ma'am," Jennings said, giving her a sharp, inquiring look, as if trying to discover what sort of female this was that Mr. Richard was bringing to his grandfather's house in the early hours of the morning. "I regret we were not expecting Mr. Richard, or the door would have been answered sooner."

"And I regret having to wake you at such an early hour, Jennings," Richard said as the butler helped divest them of their outer clothing. "Thank you. I trust we didn't wake my grandfather. I do not wish him to be disturbed. This is Miss Fitzgerald, Jennings. If it were possible to find a room for her, I can sleep on a couch somewhere until morning."

Richard cast a warning look at her, no doubt realizing, as she had, that it might have been wiser if she had at least told him her real name before they entered his grandfather's house. It was not going to be easy to explain the reason for a sudden change of name the next day.

Rosaline was too weary to be concerned about anything so trivial as a name, however, when her entire future happiness was at stake.

"If you will go into Sir John's study, where there's still a bit of a fire," the butler said, "I shall waken Mrs. Jennings to attend upon Miss Fitzgerald."

Rosaline had to smother a giggle at the frowning looks with which the old butler was attempting to convey his disapproval of Richard's conduct and Richard's maintenance of a bland, smiling expression in response to them.

"No, no, I beg you, Jennings, do not disturb your wife," she said. "It is far too late to be waking anyone. If you will give me the candle and tell me where I am to go, I can light my own way up."

"Is there a room prepared, Jennings?" Richard asked.

"Yes. Sir John always keeps the blue room ready in case you or one of your brothers should arrive unexpectedly," Jennings replied.

"I thought as much. Be so kind as to put a warming pan in the bed for a few minutes, and then *I* shall light Miss Fitzgerald up to her room."

Now the butler openly conveyed his disapproval by twitching his eyebrows at Richard. This time Richard made no pretense of not seeing, but smiled and gave the old servant the explanation he was evidently expecting. "Miss Fitzgerald and I are unofficially engaged to be married, Jennings. Indeed, you are the first to be told, and it is to be kept secret for now, because of——"

"My father's recent demise," Rosaline interjected, having decided that her father's death would have to be part of what she would be telling Richard.

He shot her a questioning glance and then turned back to Jennings. "Quite so. And also because I have not as yet apprised any member of the family of the news of our engagement. You understand, Jennings?"

"Of course, Mr. Richard. Not one word of it shall pass my lips. Except——" He paused, his forehead even more wrinkled in a frown.

"Except for Mrs. Jennings, of course," Richard finished for him. "Naturally, she must be told."

Jennings's face brightened. "I am glad of that, Mr. Richard. It wouldn't have been easy to keep such a secret from her, especially with Miss Fitzgerald being here and all."

"I'll wager it wouldn't," Richard murmured to Rosaline as the old man toiled up the stairs to fetch a warming pan. "Mrs. Jennings, who is my grandfather's housekeeper, as you doubtless will have guessed, would worm it out of him in ten seconds flat."

"He's a dear," said Rosaline, her heart warmed by the easy familiarity of the old butler, which reminded her of Lemmy's easy manner. She was also warmed by the old-fashioned but tasteful comfort of the house.

"He's getting a little beyond the rigors of the position, but he's been with my grandfather for more than forty years, so it's unlikely that he will ever be sent into retirement. Come into the study. Jennings shall make you a warm drink when he comes down."

"No, let him get back to his bed, poor man. I need nothing but sleep now."

He led her into his grandfather's study. It was a small, cozy room furnished with heavy, old-fashioned furniture, with one wall lined with books. She smiled at the rather incongruous sight of a large vase filled with purple lilacs sitting on the otherwise decidedly masculine oak desk. The heady scent of the delicate blossoms filled the air, masking the underlying aroma of smoke.

Richard lit a branch of candles while she stood, suddenly shy, in the doorway.

"Come in and sit down, you goose. What are you thinking about, my pale-faced love?" He went to her and drew her to a comfortable winged chair by the fire that still glowed in the grate.

"I was thinking how strange it is to see you in a habitat in which you appear so much at home, one that suits you."

He laughed and stirred a log with the toe of his boot, so that sparks flew up from it. "I doubt that my grandfather would agree with you there. He is forever telling me that I am too large for this house and, most particularly, this room. 'You're built for a castle, not a house' is his favorite complaint when I visit him here."

Rosaline's heart jumped. She said nothing, but her mind was filled with the image of Richard striding through the great hall of Beresford Castle like a bronzed Norman knight in his baronial hall. The picture pleased her immensely. She had the distinct feeling that Richard's presence in the castle would help lay to rest all the nightmarish memories of her past life there.

"Richard," she began. "I should tell you now—"

The door opened and Jennings reappeared, bearing a copper warming pan. His slippered feet shuffled across the floor.

"Give it to me," Richard said. He took the pan from Jennings and filled it with hot coals from the fire. "There," he said, handing it back to him. "Put it in Miss Fitzgerald's bed and then off to bed with you."

"Are you sure, Mr. Richard? Would Miss Fitzgerald not like some tea or hot chocolate before she retires?"

"Nothing, thank you, Jennings." Rosaline smiled warmly at him. "I am most grateful to you for warming the bed. That is all I need."

"There is brandy and sherry in the decanters on the side

table, Mr. Richard. I am so sorry that the servants are not here to attend to you, Miss Fitzgerald. You see, I did not know Mr. Richard was coming. Had you sent word ahead, Mr. Richard, I would have—''

''I know very well you would have done everything in your power to make us feel comfortable, Jennings, as you have done already. Now please go back to bed.'' Richard kindly but very firmly escorted him to the door. ''Now are you certain that you can manage the warming pan by yourself?''

''I am perfectly able to carry a warming pan upstairs,'' Jennings replied with great dignity. ''You must not be treating me like a useless old fool, Mr. Richard. Sir John would not like that at all.'' He bowed stiffly, indignation emanating from him. ''Good night, Miss Fitzgerald.''

''Good night, Jennings, and thank you.''

Richard closed the door on him. ''Now I have ruffled the old boy's feathers. But it is impossible to stop him talking once he starts; and I do have visions of him tripping up the stairs and setting the place alight with that pan of hot coals.''

''Poor Jennings.''

He returned to the fireplace and stood leaning his back against the mantel, arms folded over his chest. ''You were about to say something to me when Jennings came in,'' he prompted.

She hesitated, wondering if it would not be better to give him her partly invented history when she was less weary. But something warned her that if she postponed it, she might find it even more difficult to lie to him in daylight than now, when the leaping shadows would hide her expression from him.

She folded her hands in her lap to steady their trembling. ''Sit down. I wish to tell you everything: about Oliver, the jewels—''

''And your father?'' He flipped aside his coattails to sit in the chair opposite her.

She met those slightly magnified, questioning eyes of his

without flinching and then had a sudden idea. "Take off your spectacles, if you please, Richard."

"But then I shall not be able to see your face properly," he protested.

"You do not need to see my face, only to hear my voice, and, as I have told you before, I feel there is a barrier between us when you wear them."

She knew instantly that he was annoyed.

"I regret to inform you that you will have to become inured to my spectacles, Rosaline, for I refuse to be taking them off every time I wish to talk to you or kiss you." He tapped the lens with his index finger. "These are my eyes, my love. They are part of me. I do not feel whole without them. Please try to understand that."

"Yes, Richard," she said in a small voice. "Pray forgive me. I was being foolish." She could not explain to him that she had not wished him to see her expression while she was lying to him.

He leaned forward across the hearth and took her hand, his expression as solemn as an owl's. "Do you mind so very much?" He blinked. "About the spectacles, I mean?"

"Oh, Richard!" She jumped up to fling her arms around his neck, tears stinging her eyes. "Oh, my darling, what a wretch I am to upset you. Of course I don't mind them." She knelt before him and took his face between her hands, gazing into his eyes. "I love you and everything about you, you foolish man, including your golden spectacles and your golden eyes. Did you know you have golden sparkles in your eyes, especially when you laugh? I love you, Richard Courtenay, and always shall."

He took each hand down from his face, pressing his lips to her palms, and then gathered her onto his lap, holding her fast. "And I adore you, my junoesque beloved, and always shall."

"You truly mean that, even if at times I am a trifle overbearing?"

"I truly mean it. With all my heart and soul and mind, I mean it." He laughed. "And body."

She lifted her face to his and closed her eyes to receive

his kiss, which was slow and warm and sweet. Its quality changed, however, when she opened her mouth beneath his. Slowly, tantalizingly, he ran his tongue along her lips and then darted it against hers, the pressure of his mouth on hers increasing. She arched her neck, daringly inviting his mouth to move downward. As his lips blazed a trail of fire down the creamy column of her throat, his hand slid from her back to her breast. Her dress being of a thin muslin with only a fine lawn chemise beneath, the thrill of his touch so close to her skin sent spasms of longing down her body.

Now she felt his fervent kisses on the bare curve of breast above the bodice of her dress. Moaning softly, she gripped his head between her hands, twining her fingers in his thick, springy hair as his mouth moved even further downward to press hot kisses on the fabric that covered her breasts.

This time it was she who broke away first. Placing her hands on his chest, she pushed away from him and stood up on trembling legs, face flushed and hair escaping from her braids. "I do not think it is at all safe for us to be left alone together."

He looked up at her, still dazed from their encounter. Then he smiled and straightened his spectacles, which had been knocked askew. "Decidedly not. We must draw an imaginary line across the hearth rug." He took up an iron poker and ran it across the rug. "I, this side; you, that."

She sat down, her fingers busy with pushing strands of her auburn hair back into place.

"Lord," he breathed, "how beautiful you are! I cannot believe my good fortune. Are you certain that you love me, that it is not a dream my feverish mind has conjured up?"

"Absolutely certain. *Dear God,* she prayed. *How can I bear even the thought of losing him?* "And you, my dear Richard, are a beautiful man. Did you not know that?"

He grinned self-consciously. "As beautiful as a solicitor's clerk, with my glass eyes."

"You are my golden knight. I remember thinking that when I saw you in Lord Kenmore's yellow saloon. But yours is the gold of sunshine, warm and glowing, not of cold metal."

"Aye, but there are times when sunshine's not enough and cold metal comes in very handy!"

She reached across to touch his hand, and the bitter grimace disappeared. He sat back in his seat, grinning. "No, no. We made a vow that we would not cross the line, remember? Enough, my dear one. It is time now to tell me your story, or I shall be begging you to keep it until morning if we wait any longer. This has been a long night."

She gave him a faint smile and sat on the edge of her chair, hands gripped together to still their nervous fluttering. Her heart was beating so wildly she was surprised that he could not hear it.

"First of all, my name," she began. "It is Rosaline, as I told you. Rosaline Fleming." That at least was the truth. As she would have to sign her own name in the marriage register, she had decided that it would be necessary to take the risk of giving him her true family name. Fortunately the name of Fleming was not uncommon.

She paused, but when he made no reply, she continued slowly, feeling her way. "A few weeks ago, my father died, leaving me utterly alone, for my mother died several years ago."

"What was your father's name?"

"My father's name? It—it was George," she faltered, giving him the second of her father's six names.

"And he was . . . ?"

"A minor landowner. He had a small estate, a farm, really, near Parracombe."

"Ah, I see. George Fleming," he mused. "No, I have not heard of him. But then I wouldn't have, not being from North Devon myself. My father retired only six months ago to his place near Ilfracombe. Before that, as I think I told you on the night we met, the family resided at Plymouth."

Rosaline breathed an inward sigh of relief. Thank the Lord for that!

"So you were left alone?" he prompted.

"Well, not entirely alone. Unfortunately, my cousin, Oliver, had resided with us ever since his parents had died. He was raised with me and, I fear, grew to think of our home as his. When my father died, Oliver refused to leave the house. In truth, he tried to—to force himself upon me.''

''Good God!''

Rosaline rushed on, not wishing to dwell on that dreadful night. ''I had no alternative but to run away.''

''Taking your jewels with you.''

''Yes. Oliver had taken all the money that was in the house.''

''Was there no one to whom you could apply for help? No family lawyer or, perhaps, someone in authority who lived nearby?''

''It all happened so suddenly that I did not have time to apply to anyone.''

It was impossible to explain that even her lawyer had taken Oliver's side against her, that it had been her father's wish that she marry the man she feared most in this world. In retrospect, the entire story sounded utterly incredible.

''He—I—Oliver terrified me so greatly that I felt compelled to flee from him. Knowing this, perhaps you now can comprehend why I thought he had sent you to follow me. It seemed too much of a coincidence that another solitary traveler would be out on Exmoor on such a night.''

''And after you had escaped my clutches—if you will pardon the expression—what then?''

''I walked on to Minehead and was discovered there by Mr. Pepperell and invited to join his theatrical company. My plan was to hide from both you and my cousin until I could find someone who would be able to assist me in my dispute with Oliver. You can imagine what a horrid surprise it was to find you at Luxton House!''

''I can, indeed. You poor darling. What an ordeal. Yet how resourceful you have been throughout. I salute you. You have even managed to get by without having to sell your jewels.'' His eyes shone with amusement. ''By the bye, speaking of the jewels, there is one thing that still puzzles me.''

She held her breath, wondering what was to come.

''If I am not much mistaken, those jewels—I take it that they are genuine, or you would not have shown such concern when I found them in the shepherd's hut—those jewels appeared, from touch at least, to consist of large stones. And you spoke of ruby earrings and priceless pearls, if I recollect aright. How do you come to have such valuable jewels in your possession?''

It was the question she had been dreading. ''My—my mother came from a very wealthy Irish family,'' she blurted out.

Too late, she realized her error. He visibly stiffened. ''Does that mean you have inherited some of this great wealth?'' he demanded.

''Oh no, no. Not at all. My mother's family cast her off when she married my father,'' she hurriedly invented. ''They said he was not good enough for her. She came to him with only her jewels as dowry. Believe me, Richard; they are all I have of hers.'' She was almost pleading with him, begging him not to reject her because of her jewels. Despite her concern, she began to resent his attitude. He was being utterly ridiculous. Did he really expect his wife to come to him barefoot, in nothing but a shift?

As if realizing this himself, he relaxed and gave her a rueful grin. ''You will be thinking me odd, I dare say. Bear with my idiosyncracies, my dearest. I shall agree to your bringing your mother's jewels as a dowry, as she did.''

She was very much tempted to reply caustically, ''How singularly kind of you!'' But, in the circumstances, considered it best to hold her tongue.

He stood up. ''Well, there is one thing that must be attended to before we are married, and that is to seek out this cousin of yours and deal with him.''

She sprang to her feet, terror clutching at her. ''Oh no, Richard. You cannot. You *must* not!''

''Calm yourself, my love,'' he said in his maddeningly matter-of-fact way. ''How old a man is he?''

''Twenty-eight.''

''Is that all? I had somehow envisaged a very much older man. It will not take much to settle him.''

Rosaline began to shiver uncontrollably at the very thought of Oliver and Richard together. ''He is not like you,

Richard. He plots and—and he plans, like a spider in the middle of a web." She gripped his arm, her fingers digging into it. "He intends to kill me; he told me so. He said that if I didn't marry him, he would kill me."

"What palpable nonsense! No wonder you became an actress! It seems to me that you are well suited to melodrama. I have the distinct impression that you must have grown up on a diet of Mrs. Radcliffe's gothic novels."

His scathing attitude enraged her. "Very well, Mr. Courtenay. Laugh at me if you wish, but I tell you again that while Oliver lives, my life is in constant danger."

"What would you have me do? Seek him out and kill him in a duel?" He was openly laughing now. "Oh, pray forgive me, my dearest little love, but I cannot help it." He took her hands, which now, like the rest of her, were shaking with anger. "I assure you that no man in his right mind would risk being hanged for a minor estate consisting of a farm and . . . what? A few acres of land, perhaps?" He spoke slowly, like a man attempting to talk sense into a stupid child, which further infuriated her.

"Oh! You are—*unbearable*! Condescending and unbearable!" she cried, slapping his hands away. She drew herself up to her fullest height to confront him with flashing eyes. "If you choose not to believe me, then our engagement is at an end." Her voice had risen in her fury.

His smile faded away. "No, I shall not permit you to reject me so easily," he said very quietly. He did not attempt to touch her again. "Merely tell me what it is that you wish me to do, and, pray, do not overset yourself so."

She was forced to turn aside to mop the treacherous tears that welled up in her eyes. She must be exceedingly overtired to be weeping like a silly chit. She sniffed, blew her nose, and stuffed her handkerchief into her sleeve. "I wish us to be married as soon as possible. Then, and only then, shall I feel safe from Oliver. Once we are married, we shall consult a lawyer to see what can be done about him."

"Then that is what we shall do. But, I beg you, my love, no more of this morbid talk of your cousin wishing to kill you. No doubt it was said in his rage at your rejection of him." His jaw tightened. "I must own, however, that I am extremely eager to get my hands on this cousin of yours. Not only does he try to force himself upon you, but, in addition, he subjects you to all manner of irrational fears. He will have to answer to me for all the suffering he has caused you, I can tell you."

Rosaline was too weary to argue any further with him. His commonsensical mind was unable to envisage anyone so complex, so intrinsically evil, as Oliver. And she had to admit that her necessarily abbreviated tale of lust and greed did sound a trifle gothic when related in this cozy setting. It was also likely that he would find her story far more credible if he were to see Beresford Castle—and to know of what the "minor estate" consisted!

"Come, my dear Miss Fleming. Rosaline Fleming." He pondered the name for a moment and then smiled. "Not for long, though. Rosaline Courtenay," he pronounced with a grin. "It has a ring to it, does it not?"

"Yes, Richard, I agree. A wonderful ring to it. Light me up to bed now, or I shall be falling asleep on the hearth rug."

But, in actuality, it took her a long time to fall asleep, despite the warm spot in the bed where the warming pan had been. Her bout of anger had exhausted her, and the talk of Oliver had resurrected all the old, sick memories. She began to doubt that she would ever be safe from him, even after her marriage. Indeed, she also could be placing Richard's life in jeopardy by marrying him without telling him the truth about herself—not only Richard's life, but that of any child they might have.

While Oliver lived, none of them would be safe.

Most of all she wondered, as she lay listening to the early morning stir in the street below, if Oliver knew where she was at this moment.

Chapter Sixteen

The ever-increasing rumble and rattle of carriage and cart wheels over the cobblestones and the yells of milkmaids and sellers of flowers and pies and heaven knows what else ensured that the small amount of sleep Rosaline did manage to get was not of the undisturbed variety, and so she was up and about long before the maid came to open her shutters.

How in the world could anyone sleep in this racket? she wondered as she completed her morning toilette, applying a little more than usual of the pink complexion cream, with which Lord Kenmore had provided her at Luxton, to conceal the dark circles under her eyes. She must try to look her very best for Richard's grandfather.

Mrs. Jennings herself waited upon her. Indeed, so bursting with curiosity had she been that she had followed the chambermaid into the room when Rosaline's early morning hot chocolate had been brought up and remained with her to assist her to dress.

Rosaline took an instant liking to the loquacious housekeeper when she announced without preamble: "Everyone belowstairs is all agog to see Mr. Richard's fiancée. You see, he's a special favorite, is Mr. Richard, and we'd all given up hope of ever seeing him wed. Always remembers everyone's name, does Mr. Richard. Mind you, Miss Fitzgerald, that's not surprising, considering most of our household's been with the family since before he was born. And, of course, we all loved his mother, Miss Amelia, not only because she was Sir John's only child, but because she has such a sweet nature, and Mr. Richard's uncommonly like his mother.''

Mrs. Jennings was almost as small and wrinkled as her husband, but far more rotund. As she helped Rosaline into the simply high-necked jaconet muslin dress with the emerald satin sash, she was continually pumping her for information, seeking to wheedle as much as possible from Mr. Richard's betrothed to relay belowstairs. But Rosaline, having become an expert at subterfuge by now, turned back the questions so adroitly that she discovered far more about Richard and his family than Mrs. Jennings learned about her.

It very soon became evident that, in Mrs. Jennings's eyes, anyone Mr. Richard had chosen to be his wife must be perfect in every way, no matter what her status or background.

To find herself so warmly accepted would have been a heartwarming experience had Rosaline not realized that Sir John would not be so easily won over. Having eaten the light breakfast of poached eggs, tea, and buttered muffins which Mrs. Jennings had ordered brought up to her, it was with a great deal of trepidation that she descended the stairs to meet with Richard and his grandfather, who, she was informed by Mrs. Jennings, awaited her ''at her convenience'' in the drawing room.

''Miss Fitz—er, Miss Fleming,'' Jennings announced. She grimaced at his hesitation but could not blame him, for he had been informed by her only a minute or so before that Fitzgerald was her stage name and Fleming her true name.

When she went in, she saw that the two men were separated by a considerable distance; Richard stood by the large window, and his grandfather had situated himself beside the mantelpiece. Both men turned as she entered. Her heart sank when she saw Richard's tense jaw and the white, set look about his mouth. An atmosphere of friction pervaded the room.

General Sir John Huntley was a tall man of suitably military carriage, with steel-gray hair and a fine old face with the same strong Roman nose that Richard had. Unfortunately, at present, the fine old face was marred by lines of the anger which, as he waited to greet her, he was visibly trying to restrain for reasons of courtesy.

Richard strode forward to kiss first her hand and then her cheek. "Bear up, my love," he whispered with a twitch of his lips. "The worst will soon be over.' He took her hand and led her to Sir John. "Grandfather, I wish to introduce Miss Fleming, my affianced wife."

Sir John gave her a military bow, which was so stiff that had it been someone else she might well have suspected him of wearing corsets. "Miss Fleming" was his frosty greeting as he extended his hand.

"Good morning, Sir John," she countered in her low, musical voice, shaking hands with him. "You must be considering this an extraordinary imposition on my part, to be landing in on you in such an odd fashion." To her relief, the words came out with an assurance she was far from feeling.

He looked surprised at this frontal attack—and at her air of assurance. His eyes narrowed in his attempt to survey her more circumspectly. "Pray be seated, Miss Fleming." He indicated a straight-backed chair whose seat was lower than that of the others. *Designed to put me in my place, well below him, no doubt* was her thought.

She gave him one of her dazzling smiles as she sat down, and he placed himself before her, still surveying her with a puzzled expression on his angular face.

Richard came to stand behind her chair, a move calculated to demonstrate his support. But she was already beginning to feel that she had no need of it.

"Will you take some refreshment, Miss Fleming?" Sir John asked. "Some lemonade, perhaps, or chocolate?"

"No, I thank you, sir. I have only recently partaken of breakfast."

"Very well. You may go, Jennings. We are not to be disturbed until I ring for you."

When the door had closed behind the butler, Rosaline sat waiting, her hands folded calmly in her lap. Her poise and well-bred manner appeared to have taken Sir John so much by surprise that he was at a loss to know how to begin.

Having gazed at her for more time than could be considered polite, he clapped his hands together behind his back and, clearing his throat, fired his first volley.

"I cannot for the life of me make any sense of this cock-and-bull story my grandson has told me. He says that you're an actress, but not one in fact. That your name is Fleming, and also Fitzgerald. That he met you at Kenmore's place, but actually on Exmoor. What the deuce is it all about?"

She could feel the normally unruffled Richard Courtenay bristling behind her and cast him a quick, reassuring glance before she launched, very reluctantly, into an abbreviated version of her invented history. As she went along, she became increasingly aware of the gaping holes in the account.

"Who did you say your father was?" Sir John barked.

"George Fleming. You would not know him, of course, sir. He was a—"

"Fleming. Fleming. I know that name. Deuce take it, I could swear I heard it mentioned only recently."

Fear tightened her throat. "It is quite a common name hereabouts, I should imagine," she said in a deceptively light voice.

She looked up and caught an expression in the troubled old eyes which terrified her.

Richard squeezed her shoulder. "For heaven's sake, sir; you are behaving as if Rosaline were one of your unfortunate subalterns. Have down with all this, I beg of you. I have told you all there is to know."

But Sir John's mind was now on another track. "Rosaline. Pretty name, that. Uncommon. Shakespeare, eh? Ever played in London, Miss Fleming? Used to attend the theater a great deal when Lady Huntley was alive. That was years ago, of course. Saw many great actresses in my day. But there was one you'd never forget, having once see her. Most distinctive face and coloring. Now, let me see, what was her name?"

His eyes were merciless now, hard and cold as gray slate.

She gave him a tiny, almost imperceptible, shake of the head, at the same time striving to involve her entire heart and soul in her expression, her eyes pleading with him, her lips forming one single word: *Please*.

He slapped his forehead with seeming exasperation. "Deuce

take it, Miss Fleming, that's the vexation of growing old, y'know. Memory goes. Ah well, that's no matter. I bid you welcome to my house, m'dear. I wish you and this rapscallion grandson of mine well. Trust you realize you're taking on the most deuced stubborn man in this world."

His sudden change of mood startled Richard. "So, is it all settled, then, sir?"

"Yes, yes. That is, of course, once you have spoken to your parents. They have the final say. But you both have my blessing, for what it's worth. You'd best call on Aunt Agatha and acquaint her with the news, but be sure to warn her that it is not to be told to a single soul; you know your aunt's tongue. And I'll not have her bringing that obnoxious pug of hers into my house. Be sure to tell her that, too."

"I shall be the very essence of diplomacy, sir." Richard came around to face Rosaline. "Grandfather and I have decided that it would be best to ask my Aunt Agatha to remove here to act as your chaperone, at least until the wedding arrangements are completed. But, firstly, we must pay a visit to my parents. As soon as possible, Grandfather says." His eyes danced with excitement, the golden flecks very much in evidence.

Somehow, she managed to summon up a smile. "Yes, of course. How kind" was all she could murmur.

He bent down to kiss both her hands. Above his bronze head, her eyes met and locked with Sir John's.

"You shall call on Aunt Agatha immediately," he told Richard.

"Surely it can wait until this afternoon, sir. I had hoped to escort Miss Fleming around Bath this morning."

"No. Your aunt must be persuaded to move here as soon as possible. As it is, the servants will be making a heyday of all this. Away with you. Surely you can leave Miss Fleming for one hour."

"I'm not so certain I can." Richard grinned and cast a glowing look at Rosaline.

"Good God, man. You'll have the rest of your lives together. Go now, and do not be forgetting to write that letter to your parents when you return. That will give me time to get to know my future granddaughter-in-law a little better.''

Rosaline was fast beginning to comprehend why Richard was so determined to be entirely independent of his grandfather.

''Reluctantly, I go.'' With a wink at Rosaline and a swift bow, Richard strode from the room, leaving behind him a feeling that it had expanded just a little upon his exit.

Nothing was said between Rosaline and Sir John for several minutes. Her host busied himself with throwing another log on the fire and poking it into a blaze, while she stood staring out the window at the to and fro of passers-by.

As soon as she heard the front door close and saw Richard depart, she turned. ''Thank you, sir, for not giving me away.''

He nodded and pointed to the sofa before the fire, waiting until she was seated before lowering himself into a wide-armed wing chair.

''I was right in my thinking, then. You are the daughter of Henry Fleming and, consequently, the new Countess of Beresford.'

''Yes. It is fruitless to deny it. I am.''

''I knew it, of course. You are remarkably like your mother in looks. The name of Fleming confirmed my suspicions. May I inquire what all this havey-cavey business is about, Lady . . . ? Deuce take it, I don't even know what your real name is. I'll wager your father did not name you Rosaline!''

''No. Horatia is my given name. It is a name I detest. Rosaline was my mother's name for me, and she always used it in private.''

''Ah, now I understand. So I should address you as Lady—''

''As Rosaline or Miss Fleming, sir,'' she said firmly. ''At least until I am married. If, that is, I am to be married.'' She blinked several times.

''I may be growing a trifle senile, Miss Fleming, but I cannot make head nor tail of all this. Can you try to explain it to me? But the truth this time, mind. Perhaps it is my military background, but I can sniff out falsehoods a mile away."

"I had been given to understand that Richard's background was a naval one."

She thought for a moment that he was about to expire from apoplexy, so flushed did his face become. "Good Lord, no! The naval connection is all on his father's side, not his mother's. The Huntleys come from a long military line. Yet every one of my only daughter's sons went to sea. Cannot make it out at all."

"Every one except Richard."

"Yes, poor fellow. Fearful handicap those eyes of his. But still I am convinced that he's cut out for far greater matters, if only he would permit us to help him gain some position where his brains and ability would be noticed. But now we're off at a tangent. Tell me, ah, Miss Fleming, what is this escapade all about?"

She proceeded to do so, this time leaving nothing out. It was an enormous relief to be able to confide in a man who, she sensed, was as shrewd as all get-out, despite his advanced years. He did not interrupt her once, apart from one or two indignant grunts when she spoke of Oliver or Lord Kenmore.

"By Jove, you're a woman of pluck, that's all I can say" was his comment when she came to an end. "Now, before I say anything about what you have told me, I wish first to know why you are hiding your true identity from my grandson?"

"Because he told me that he would never marry a woman whose wealth or status was above his, that he must make his own way in life."

"Lord, not that old talk again! The fellow's a stubborn mule. Pride comes before a fall, they say, and if he loses you on account of his pride, then he'll have lost the greatest opportunity he ever had. And I don't mean your wealth or status either, m'girl. It's evident you love him, though I cannot see why when he behaves like a great gaby, with all this farradiddle about wanting to make his own way; and I know he's deep in love with you, which ain't surprising. Do you seriously consider, though, that he would actually break off the engagement if you were to tell him you were the Countess of Beresford?"

"Yes, Sir John, I do."

"Surely not. Dammit, the boy's a gentleman, born and bred. Wouldn't throw over a lady."

"I cannot risk telling him. I own I should prefer to wait until after we are married, but if you think I should not, then I shall tell him after we have broken the news of our engagement to his parents. Meanwhile, there is Oliver to consider."

She broke off for a moment, eyeing the old gentleman with a half-smile. "Would you be so kind as to explain to me, Sir John, why it is you have not even questioned the veracity of my story, when Richard adamantly refuses to believe that I am in any danger from my cousin's threats to kill me?"

"Ha! That's easily explained. First of all, you haven't told him the truth, have you? Deuced difference between being heir to a small farming estate and heir to a large fortune, numerous estates, and a title, to boot. Secondly, Richard is of a phlegmatic nature, slow to be aroused, but once he has been, terrible in his fury. Just the sort of officer I relied on in the heat of battle! In addition, there's this: His life so far has been far too narrow. Schooling at Winchester and Cambridge, occasional visits to Bath and London, a handful of positions as a tutor or private secretary—that is all. He has never even been to the Continent because of this demmed war with the French. He has not mixed in Society enough and judges everyone by his own exemplary standards. He has yet to learn that there are unrelentingly evil men in this world. I believe, however, that by belittling your fears of your cousin, he seeks to offer you reassurance."

"He does not know Oliver!"

"No, my dear, he does not. Which brings us back to your cousin. What was your intention when you fled from Beresford Castle?"

"First of all, of course, to hide from Oliver. Then I

intended to contact an old friend of my mother, Sir Victor Golland, who is a barrister at the Inner Temple."

"Dead."

"I beg your pardon?"

"Golland's dead. Been dead these past three years."

"Oh, I see." So much for that idea.

"Besides, what could a lawyer do? From what you have told me, I gather that you have no actual proof that Prescott attacked you, have you? There was no one there to witness it. On the other hand, he has ample proof that you stabbed him. It was your dagger... and you ran away."

She shuddered.

"Forgive me, my dear, but we must face facts. What about your servant?"

"Lemmy? Of course! She could vouch for the fact that she had been drugged by Oliver, could she not?"

"Doubt if they'd take her word against Prescott's in a court of law. Probably say all the servants had been cast-away after the funeral. Quite common, y'know, for servants to get drunk on their dead master's wine after he's been buried."

Rosaline sighed. "I suppose you're right."

"The worst thing is that your cousin is spreading it about that you are mad. If only your father hadn't kept you virtually locked up all these years, away from Society; bound to make people suspect there's something the matter with you."

"Yes, damn him!"

His faded eyes lit with sympathy as he leaned forward to pat her hand. "Bad lot, Beresford" was all he said, but she felt warmed by his obvious concern

"What am I to do, Sir John?"

He pondered for a while, drawing a battered silver snuff-box from his waistcoat pocket and taking a large pinch in each nostril. Having sneezed twice and blown his nose very loudly, he said: "Remain in Bath for now. Once Richard's parents receive his letter, he should take you down to Ilfracombe to meet them. That will give us a few days to plan our strategy."

"And you agree that I should not tell Richard who I really am?"

"Reluctantly, I do. If he'll not accept assistance from his own grandfather, it's unlikely he'll be willing to pocket his pride and knowingly become betrothed to an heiress." He held up a finger and beamed at her. "I have it! Tell his mother everything when you meet her. She and Richard are as thick as thieves. Ten to one she'll know what's best to do." He hauled himself up from the chair. "Is there anyone who could be in Bath who might recognize you?"

Rosaline rose to stand before him. "I do not think so, but, in truth, I have no way of telling. Any one of Oliver's, or my father's, acquaintances might recognize me—or one of Oliver's spies. He vowed he'd have me tracked down if I ran away."

"Humph! Sounds a deuced ugly customer. Well, m'dear, you cannot become a recluse again, so it's a risk you'll have to take. You have a right to some enjoyment after all these years of being shut away. Indeed, it occurs to me that once your true identity is revealed, it will do your case against Oliver a great deal of good if witnesses can be produced to vouch for you as a normal, sane person who danced at the Assembly Rooms and exchanged gossip in the Pump Room."

The idea of being free to be almost her real self, with Richard at her side, so delighted her that she was tempted to fling her arms around Sir John's neck, but was not at all sure how the upright old man would view such forward behavior.

"That's an extremely pretty gown you're wearing this morning, m'dear," he informed her.

"One of Lord Kenmore's purchases, I'm afraid." She gave him a rueful smile.

"Tell you what, if you're feeling awkward about wearing all the things he bought, why don't you let me make you an advance, so that you may make some new purchases?"

"Thank you, sir, but as Lord Kenmore has exquisite taste, I intend to keep the few things I took from Luxton and reimburse him eventually for them. Richard would not like me to be taking money from you."

To her great surprise, Sir John suddenly slapped his forehead. "Lord, we are forgetting one thing. Mourning!"

"I beg your pardon, sir?"

"Mourning. Mourning. You should be in mourning clothes, for your father."

Rosaline raised her chin, prepared to do battle. "I have already thought of that, Sir John, and decided that to wear mourning would only draw attention to the fact that my father has died recently. I think it would be best, if you are agreeable, if we were to say that Miss Fleming's father died a year ago."

Having received the general's agreement, the last obstacle to her enjoyment was removed, and she prepared to throw herself into the pursuit of the pleasures of Bath with all the enthusiasm of a seventeen-year-old debutante.

"You are like a bird released from its cage," Richard observed three days later as they sipped lemonade and listened to the string orchestra in the Pump Room.

She laughed. "That is exactly how I feel."

"You are easily pleased. Bath is considered *passé* by the *ton* nowadays. Did your parents never take you to Bath or London?"

"No, they did not. You are forgetting that my father was an obscure gentleman farmer." She turned her head aside, so that he could see only her profile. How she hated lying to him! "Exeter is the largest town I had visited until now. You may imagine, therefore, how very exciting all this is to me."

Her gesture encompassed the lofty pillars with their gilded cornices, the three-tiered crystal chandeliers, and, most of all, the crush of people, eager to observe and to be observed.

"My poor darling. What a wretched life you must have led, to be sure, cooped up on a little farm. I am amazed that you are so self-assured and have so many accomplishments, in the circumstances."

Rosaline had to hide a smile. Her father must be turning

in his grave to hear his castle and extensive estates described as "a little farm." "My mother was from a landed family, you must remember," she reminded him. It was essential that she continue to emphasize this point. It might make her eventual denouement a trifle easier for him to accept.

"Of course. The jewels! How could I forget?"

His smile told her that her strategy was beginning to work already. Once he became more inured to the idea of her being the daughter of a woman of substance and breeding, surely it would not prove quite so difficult for him to accept that his betrothed was a countess.

They walked up Milsom Street arm in arm, pausing to gaze into the attractive windows of the various purveyors of books and soaps and prints and maps . . . and then stood outside the bow windows of Mollands, the pastry shop, while Rosaline was introduced to a friend of Sir John—Mr. Sinclair and his wife.

As Rosaline replied to the formidable Mrs. Sinclair's searching questions with the greatest of civility and met her gimlet-eyed perusal of her face and figure with one of her more dazzling smiles, she began to feel glad that they would soon be leaving Bath to visit Richard's parents. All this subterfuge was becoming quite a strain.

"Tomorrow I intend to take you to Mollands for tea and cakes," Richard said as they continued their stroll up the sharp incline towards the intersection with George Street. "Their French pastries are delectable, and the shop is fast replacing the Pump Room as the chief meeting place and gossip center in the town."

"Oh, Richard, I really do not care what we do, just so long as I am with you." She gave him a radiant smile and squeezed his arm. "I cannot begin to tell you how happy I am!"

He looked down at her with such warmth that, for a delicious moment, she thought he would kiss her, then and there, but he merely chuckled and pressed her arm against his side.

This had become their favorite route back to the Circus.

Each time they took it, Rosaline found some new diversion to catch her interest.

They had just stepped off the pavement and onto the street at the corner of George Street and Gay Street, when, above the usual din of street hawkers and carriage wheels, she heard the thunder of hooves.

"Runaway horse!" someone shouted.

She heard screams, Richard's warning shout, felt a rush of wind . . . and the next minute found herself hurled into the gutter with a crash that jarred the breath from her body.

"My God!" she heard Richard exclaim, and the weight of his body was removed from her. Then she was cradled in his arms against his chest, and his voice was urgently calling her name. "Rosaline! Rosaline, my darling! Can you hear me?

Yes, she could hear him, but her head was spinning so fast that she found it impossible to form the words of a reply.

"Fetch a physician. Quickly, now." This time the voice was that of a young woman who was kneeling beside her.

"No, no," Rosaline whispered.

"Thank God!" Richard cried. "She can speak! I'm here, my dearest. Everything will be all right. Are you hurt?"

She raised a trembling hand to his cheek, which was scraped where he had hit his face on the pavement. "No, my love. Thanks to you, I am not."

"Lie still, my dear," the young woman urged. "We should carry her into the shop, I think," she said to Richard. She waved a vinaigrette beneath Rosaline's nose, her attractive face hovering anxiously above her.

"No, please, " Rosaline protested. "I shall be quite well in a moment, once my head stops spinning." She turned her face to Richard's breast. "Take me home, please, Richard," she whispered.

"Call for a hackney," shouted someone in the knot of people that had gathered about them.

A great deal of shouting ensued, all of which filtered through to Rosaline's mind as if it came from a great distance.

"You have been most kind," she heard Richard's voice say to the woman, who was now stroking Rosaline's forehead with a handkerchief soaked in lavender water. "Will you accompany us to our place of residence so that my fiancée and I may voice our gratitude in quieter surroundings?"

"I should not dream of it, but for the fact that I am anxious to make sure for myself that Miss Fleming is none the worse for her accident."

For a short while, Rosaline must have been whirled into unconsciousness, for she became aware of the motion of a carriage over cobblestones, Richard's hand clasping hers, and the softness of a female lap beneath her head.

Richard bent to press his lips to her forehead, his countenance severe in its concern.

"Do not look so worried, my dearest; I shall be recovered very soon," she reassured him.

When the hackney came to a halt, she felt Richard's arms about her, tenderly lifting her down and carrying her into the house. A great hurrying and scurrying, accompanied by the sound of muted voices, followed upon this dramatic entry. Before long, she found herself tucked into her warm featherbed, with a circle of loving, caring faces about her.

But she turned from them all, to bury her face in her pillow, for no amount of loving care could eradicate the icy terror that clutched at her far beneath the strange, floating sensation of unreality.

The question she had been asking for so long had at last received its answer. Yes, Oliver Prescott did indeed know where she was.

——— Chapter ———
Seventeen

"It *was* Oliver! I am absolutely convinced of it. Had it not been for you, Richard, that horse would have run me down." Rosaline tried to maintain as dispassionate a tone as possible, to hide the terror—and anger—that threatened to engulf her.

"My dear, sweet love, runaway horses are an everyday occurrence. How is it possible for you to be absolutely convinced when none of us caught even a glimpse of the rider's face?"

Richard's tone was so calm and reasonable that Rosaline felt like striking him. She twisted her hands together beneath the soft lap robe.

"Even if we had, Richard, it would probably not have helped. It may not have been Oliver on the horse. Indeed, if it had been, I am sure I would be dead or, at the very least, severely injured. My cousin is a crack rider. Whoever the rider was, however, I am certain that Oliver was the instigator."

The argument, begun the day before, was continuing this morning. Rosaline lay on the chaise longue by the window of the sunny breakfast parlor. Her left hip and arm had been severely bruised in the fall, but she was suffering more from shaken nerves than anything else. This wrangling with Richard was doing nothing to ease her mental anguish. He was an impossible person to argue with, remaining calm all the time her fury mounted. By now, her patience had grown exceedingly thin, and she was about to explode.

Apparently sensing her mood, Richard came to kneel beside her; and at the sight of the anxious expression on his handsome face, her anger melted away. She ran her fingers along the scrape on his cheek. ''I hope it won't leave a scar to mar your beauty,'' she said with a loving smile.

''Beauty? You must be delirious, my darling.''

''You do have a beautiful face. Like a Roman centurion's.''

''And you are an incurable romantic, Miss Fleming.''

''It comes from reading too many novels and not having been exposed to Society, I suppose. Do you mind very much?''

He responded by leaning over to kiss her. His mouth moved gently over her lips. She felt a stir of desire and slid her hand to the back of his neck, feeling his thick, wavy hair beneath her fingers. The pressure of his mouth upon hers became more insistent.

''Miss Sidley,'' Jennings announced as he ushered in Anne Sidley, the young woman who had been so helpful after the accident.

''Devil take it,'' muttered Richard. He scrambled to his feet, a tide of red flooding his face.

The visitor appeared no less embarrassed. ''Forgive me. It is an inopportune time. I shall return another day.''

''Not at all,'' Rosaline said, laughing. ''Pray come in, Miss Sidley. Richard was merely trying to allay my stupid fears, that is all. Will you not take some refreshment: coffee, perhaps, or hot chocolate?''

''No, no. I do not intend to stay. I called merely to ask after your health, Miss Fleming.''

''Much improved, I thank you. My left side is rather sore and stiff, but I mean to start walking tomorrow, or it will become even stiffer. Please stay and have some chocolate. I mean to take some. Will you not join us, Richard?''

''Thank you, no. I have business to attend to.''

''Business?'' The austere, set look about his face alarmed her. ''No, Richard, please.''

He frowned and shook his head at her, indicating that he did not wish to speak before Miss Sidley.

Rosaline sat up and swung her legs to the floor. ''It is something to do with Oliver, isn't it? I beg you to wait a while, Richard. He is an exceedingly dangerous man. Why will you not believe me now that you have seen an example of his work?''

"We shall speak of this later."

"We shall speak of it now. Never mind Miss Sidley," she said impatiently. "I consider her my true friend after all her kindness to me yesterday." She flashed a warm smile at Anne, whose kindly face brightened at her words. "What do you intend to do?" she demanded of Richard.

"I mean to make certain inquiries," he replied.

"About Oliver?"

"About the accident—and to ascertain whether or not your cousin is in Bath at present."

"I know he is."

"You cannot know that he is until you have proof of it" Richard said in his most vexing, reasonable tone.

"Oh, do go away," cried Rosaline, suddenly breaking into laughter. "I refuse to argue with you any more." She turned to her new friend. "He always gets the better of me, Miss Sidley, because he refuses to lose his temper. It is exceedingly vexing!"

She threw a loving little glance at Richard to soften her words but saw by his expression that she had failed to bring him around.

"I shall leave you two ladies to enjoy your chocolate and gossip," he said without a smile.

Having made his farewells, he strode from the room, leaving Rosaline with a cold feeling about her heart.

Why, I do believe he is jealous! she suddenly thought. That was it! He was jealous of this new friendship she had made. How very odd! She had not considered that Richard could be jealous of a woman. How silly men were! Did he not realize how wonderful it was for her to have a female friend of her own age for the first time in her life?

As soon as she had given orders for refreshments to be brought to them, Rosaline stretched out her hand to Anne Sidley. "Sit here, beside me."

Miss Sidley did so, drawing off her white cotton gloves and placing them neatly in her lap.

"My memories of yesterday are rather hazy, I fear," said Rosaline. "But one thing I cannot forget is your extraordinary kindness, Miss Sidley. Your presence was a great source of comfort."

"I am glad of it. But I did only what anyone would have done out of Christian charity," protested Miss Sidley.

Rosaline surveyed her new friend for a moment. She could not be called pretty, but her oval face, curling fair hair, and neat figure were certainly not unattractive. She was dressed soberly but in good taste in a high-necked dress of dark blue figured cotton.

"It is not my intention to encroach upon an act of charity," Rosaline said, feeling rather shy, "but I should very much like us to become friends. You see, I have had no female companions of my own age at all. And although my fiancé is, naturally, my dearest friend, it would be extremely pleasant to have someone to talk to about fashions and with whom to go shopping."

"How very odd not to have had friends of one's own age and sex!" Anne smiled. "I should be delighted and most flattered to be your friend, Miss Fleming."

"Rosaline."

"Rosaline," Anne repeated.

Over almond macaroons and steaming hot chocolate topped with thick cream, the two new friends exchanged sketchy histories of their backgrounds, Rosaline adhering to the story she had told Richard. She had been quite tempted to reveal all to her new friend but was prevented by her concern that, as a result, Anne might let something slip to Richard.

They chatted about fashions and music and the latest dances and books, until Anne looked at the watch at her waist and exclaimed: "My goodness, it is almost a quarter past twelve! I promised my mother that I would go to the lending library for her and be back before noon."

"Oh, dear. Will she be very vexed?"

"No, no, not at all. But being an invalid, time hangs heavily for her."

"Does she not venture out at all, not even to take the waters?"

"No. My aunt's servant collects a bottle of the waters each morning for Mama, and she reads a great deal."

"It must be rather a solitary life for you. Are you able to go to any concerts in the Assembly Rooms?"

"I used to do so, but ever since Mama became partially paralyzed I have been much more confined. And my aunt does not care to be left alone with Mama for very long." Anne became engrossed in smoothing out the worn fingers of her gloves, one by one.

"Pray forgive me for asking this, for it is not my intention to pry into your affairs, but have you . . . is there any chance of marriage?"

"Very little, I fear. Although I have received a good education and am of good family, I have no fortune. Besides, I must take care of Mama."

Anne turned her head to look out the window, but not before Rosaline had caught sight of an expression of raw bitterness in her blue eyes. The sweet smile returned almost immediately, however. "But I must not complain. Although my aunt is somewhat difficult to live with, it is thanks to her generosity that we are able to spend a few weeks each year in Bath, and my mother is always patient and uncomplaining. I love her dearly, Miss Fleming, and would do anything for her."

Rosaline was aware of a firmness about Anne's jaw that she had not noticed before, and she was filled with admiration of her stoical patience. She secretly determined to do everything in her power to come to the assistance of Miss Sidley once she was married to Richard and reinstalled at Beresford.

"I must take my leave." Anne drew her gloves over her ringless fingers and stood up. "May I call upon you again?"

"You certainly may." Rosaline swung her legs down again and, holding tightly to the carved end of the chaise longue, stood up. "Heavens," she groaned. "I really must move around a little more. I shall walk with you to the door."

"Are you certain that you should? It is obvious that you are still suffering some pain."

"I shall be well enough once I move around more. I have every intention of going for a short walk tomorrow. I wish to see the memorial to the actor James Quin in the abbey. Indeed, I have seen only the exterior of the abbey so far. We are to leave Bath at the end of this week to visit Richard's parents; so, you see, I must be able to walk freely before then. It would give me great pleasure if you would accompany me to the abbey tomorrow; would that be possible?"

"Certainly. I shall call upon you at eleven, if that would be suitable."

"Eleven will be perfect." Rosaline embraced Anne. "I have enjoyed your visit so very much."

"And so have I. I trust that Mr. Courtenay will have been successful in his quest."

Rosaline shivered, feeling as if a black cloud had passed over the sun. "I am not certain that I wish him to be successful. If he finds Oliver . . ." She left the sentence unfinished, not wishing even to consider a confrontation between Richard and Oliver.

"Surely he would not challenge your cousin to a duel?"

Rosaline gave a faint smile. "No, that would not be Richard's way. Particularly as dueling is against the law. That is really the crux of the problem. I am not sure what we can do about Oliver. All I do know is that however long it takes me, he *shall* be brought to justice."

"Is there not a lawyer dealing with your father's holdings who could help you?"

"No. I cannot place any trust in our lawyer. I believe he would take Oliver's side in a dispute. Richard's grandfather intends to write to a neighboring landowner to enlist his aid." It was not necessary to inform Anne that this neighbor was the powerful Lord Ellington. "Never fear, we shall soon put an end to my cousin's plots."

"I am glad of it. From the sound of it, you have suffered enough." Anne turned abruptly to walk into the hall. "Eleven o'clock tomorrow, then. Goodbye, Miss Fleming."

Rosaline raised her hand in farewell and walked slowly back to the chaise longue, holding onto the backs of chairs for support as she crossed the room. The heavy cloud still hung over her, quite dissipating the pleasure of Anne Sidley's visit.

As she waited anxiously for Richard's return, Rosaline's mind became agitated with all sorts of mental pictures of Oliver's sneering face gloating over Richard's lifeless body. Good God, Richard was right. She really was growing morbid. Thoughts of Oliver always had affected her in this way. She wished she had Sir John's companionship, for his forthright manner would have been a powerful antidote to her sick fears. But Richard's grandfather had gone out to visit a friend who was confined to the house with an attack of gout and would not be back until later that afternoon.

After taking a light luncheon, she remained in the morning parlor, having refused Mrs. Jennings's suggestion that she would be far better off in her bed, and dozed on the chaise longue. But her intermittent sleep was so fraught with nightmarish shadows and nameless fears that, determined to stay awake, she took up her book, Fanny Burney's *Evelina*, an old favorite of hers, having found this copy on Sir John's bookshelves.

She was deeply immersed in Evelina's adventures with the Branghtons when Jennings quietly entered the room.

"Pardon me for disturbing you, Miss Fleming, but there is a gentleman to see you. I told him you were not at home to visitors, but he insisted that I bring his card to you. He is most persistent, ma'am."

She took up the embossed card from the silver card tray, to exclaim "Great heavens!" when she read the name.

What in the world was Lord Kenmore doing here?

_____ Chapter _____
Eighteen

Rosaline threw back the lap robe and sat up, her heart racing. Even a semireclining posture most probably would be viewed by Lord Kenmore as some sort of licentious invitation.

Should she send him packing? No, that would be foolish. Surely she was safe from his advances here in Sir John Huntley's house.

"Show Lord Kenmore in, Jennings, and then bring us some coffee. Coffee only, mind, nothing stronger."

"Yes, Miss Fleming. Are you certain it is wise to see him, considering there's no gentleman at home at present?"

"Yes, Jennings. I assure you that I shall be perfectly safe. You are forgetting that Lord Kenmore was Mr. Richard's employer of late. Show him in, if you please."

Mumbling to himself, the butler went out, to return almost immediately with Francis Kenmore. He followed Jennings into the morning parlor and stood there smiling his habitual one-sided smile.

"Good afternoon, Lord Kenmore."

"Your servant, Miss Fitzgerald."

"You may go now, Jennings. Bring the coffee in here in ten minutes, if you please."

Jennings's expression left no doubt as to his opinion of his young master's fiancée entertaining an elegant buck alone. Reluctantly, he backed out of the room, sending her one of his warning looks before closing the door.

At any other time, Rosaline might have been tempted to laugh, but this was not the time for laughter. "Pray take a seat, sir," she said in a cool voice. "What brings you to Bath?"

He sat down and crossed one slim leg over the other. "You do, Miss Fitzgerald. I beg your pardon; habit dies hard. I should have said 'You do, *my lady*.'"

She flung up her head, her eyes widening. "How did you find out?" she demanded, realizing that it was useless to deny it.

"It was something you said on that last occasion—an occasion which, I should imagine, we both should prefer to erase from our memory."

"What did I say that could possibly have given me away?"

"Oh, it was but a trifling thing, but when added to your imperious manner and your seemingly unassailable virtue—most rare in an actress, my dear lady—it did prompt me to question whether you were, in truth, what you claimed to be. Then I was reminded of something else that had happened on the opening night of Pepperell's play."

"For heaven's sake, sir, tell me what it was that I said."

"You informed me that you once had almost killed a man for having attempted to ravish you. Do you recollect saying that to me?"

"I may have done," she replied. "I was . . . not in control of my senses at the time. It is impossible to say if I did or not."

His lips clamped into a thin line, and he ran his long white fingers up and down the black ribbon of his quizzing glass. "My conduct that night was beneath reproach. I cannot expect you ever to pardon me for it. But we shall come to that later. You did, indeed, say that you had once almost killed a man. It was not until the following day that my mind went back to the supper party with my companions after the opening night of that wretched play of Pepperell's. You came to join us later, you may recollect. One of my friends, Sir Basil Fortescue, began to talk of a man named Prescott who had been stabbed by his cousin the Countess of Beresford."

Rosaline's breathing came shallow and fast, and her tongue flicked out to moisten her dry lips.

"It did not register at the time," Lord Kenmore continued, "but when my mind returned to that night, I remembered that your face turned white and that you insisted upon leaving almost immediately thereafter."

He leaned forward, his dark eyes seeming to pin her to her chair. Even had she wished to, she could not have moved. "With that memory everything suddenly fell into place. It needed only a few discreet inquiries to elicit the information that the young Countess, although a recluse, was known to be extremely beautiful, with the auburn hair and green eyes of her mother, who, by the bye, just happened to have been a famous Irish actress before her marriage to the Earl of Beresford."

Rosaline raised her chin. "And just what do you intend to do with this information?" she demanded.

"I shall tell you that when you have answered me one question."

"What is it?"

"What is your present relationship with Courtenay?"

"We are engaged to be married."

He gave her a long look. "That is what I had heard. Besides, I could not envisage the worthy general entertaining his grandson's *chère amie* in his house, nor the always correct Mr. Courtenay asking him to do so."

"You are insulting, sir."

"To you or to Courtenay? No, no, I did not mean that. Confound it, my wayward tongue always gets me into trouble. It was not my intention to insult you or Richard."

To her consternation, he sprang to his feet and began to pace agitatedly about the room, returning to stand before her. "It was never my intention to offer you insult, Rosaline," he said in a low voice. "But your behavior was beyond my comprehension. To be frank, I did not know how to deal with you. I had never met a woman like you before."

"You mean that women had always fallen into your hands like ripe plums before."

"Well, yes, I suppose that is an accurate, if rather bald, way of putting it." His lips slid into his mocking smile, but this time she knew it was self-mockery. "I had never before met a virtuous actress."

"My mother was an actress, and she was virtuous," she told him coldly. "There are, I am sure, many more who would be virtuous if it were not that their profession leaves them open to the vile attentions and insults of men like yourself, Lord Kenmore."

"*Touché*, my lady. But to be fair, you did offer me a great deal of encouragement. Perhaps it was merely your ignorance of the ways of the world, but I must own that for a time I did seriously consider that you had a *tendre* for me."

Her cheeks grew warm, and she looked down at her clasped fingers. "I had, my lord; that is to say, I thought I had."

"May I inquire what it was that changed your mind?" he asked gently.

"Two things. Your conduct and Richard Courtenay."

"My conduct, I can understand, would disgust you. You must bear in mind, however, that I took you for a female of an inferior class."

"And, therefore, fair game" was her caustic response. "We have covered that ground already. It is no excuse whatsoever for your insulting behavior."

"Very well. I humbly accept your recommendation that, in future, I should treat actresses like ladies instead of treating ladies like actresses."

Rosaline did not return his smile. It was strange that he no longer held any power to charm her.

"What I still fail to comprehend," he continued, "is your relationship with Courtenay."

"It is of a longer standing than you realize."

"Ah, so you had met him before you came to Luxton."

"Yes." She was not prepared to give him any further explanation.

"And you truly love him?"

"Would I be marrying him if I did not?"

Francis Kenmore slowly shook his dark head. "I believe it, but I cannot pretend to understand it. He hasn't a penny to his name, you know, despite his breeding and superior intellect. Told me he won't take help from anyone, even his grandfather."

"I know that."

"Good God, I hope he realizes what a lucky dog he is! He gains the hand of not only the most beautiful woman in the whole of England, but also one of the wealthiest. Well, that political career he has pined for will be his in a trice, and damned good he'll be at it, too."

"He doesn't know."

"Doesn't know what?"

"Doesn't know who I am."

"You're bamming me!"

"No, I am not. I haven't told him yet."

"In God's name, why not?"

She pleated the folds of her skirt between tense fingers. "Because he might not marry me if he knew."

"Might not ... Of all the ... !" Lord Kenmore gave a crack of laughter. "Now I know the pair of you are as mad as March hares! Might not marry you! I cannot think of a better reason for him to marry you, you goose!"

"But then you are not Richard, are you?" she cried. "And kindly do not call me a goose."

"Well, you are one if you think that. Why on earth wouldn't he marry you?"

"Because he told me he could never marry a woman of superior wealth or status."

"What humbug! Sounds like a hero in one of those dashed gothic novels."

"It's true," she told him, flushing with indignation. "Even Richard's grandfather believes it."

"Are you telling me that Sir John is aware of your true identity?" he asked incredulously.

"He most decidedly is. And he agrees with me that we must keep it from Richard, at least until I have made a visit to meet his parents. It would be rather difficult for him to call off our engagement after that, I should imagine. Even then, I fear that he will not be at all happy about it."

"The man must be crazed. Not happy to be marrying a countess!"

"Oh, you would never understand—"

The door opened and Jennings entered, followed by a

footman bearing the coffee tray. "Your coffee, Miss Fleming."

"Thank you, Jennings." She gave Lord Kenmore a little shake of her head to warn him not to speak before the servants. "Thank you. I can manage. You may go."

Once the footman and Jennings had departed, she moved from the chaise longue to the chair beside the tray. Francis Kenmore moved to the chair opposite and sat down, observing her as she poured the coffee.

"Where is Courtenay now?"

"He has gone out for a short while."

"Yes, I realized that. But where? And don't tell me that it is none of my business. I hear there was an accident yesterday. Runaway horse. I could see when you walked that you are still in pain."

His eyes met hers, and they exchanged a long look before she bent her head to pour cream into his coffee.

"Prescott, eh?"

Her hand shook, spilling some of the coffee in his saucer as she handed it to him. When she had finished blotting it with a napkin, she looked up to catch the flash of rage in his eyes.

"So it is true." His expression was grim.

She nodded, biting her lip to prevent the tears that had gathered behind her eyes from spilling over.

"God damn him! Fortescue told me a great deal about your cousin; said he was an extremely dangerous man. Something about some involvement in smuggling off the Cornish coast."

"Oliver is involved in many things. Smuggling is only one of them."

"Courtenay cannot deal with a man like that."

"And why not?" she demanded, bridling at this insult to Richard's manhood.

"Don't get up on your high horse. I don't mean to say he hasn't the courage, but he'll try to do it within the law, and that's not the way to catch a man like Prescott. Got anything on him?"

"I beg your pardon?"

"Have you any proof against him? Did you trace the horse? See the rider's face?"

"No. Richard's out now trying to seek out information. The only problem is that I couldn't give him Oliver's real name for fear he might then trace him back to me, so I said his name was Purvis."

He appeared to find this highly amusing. "That's rich!" he cried, slapping his thigh. "Now, now, don't be flying up into the boughs with me again," he added hastily, for she had confronted him with flashing eyes. "Even if you had given Richard his real name, I'll wager a thousand guineas he wouldn't get a thing on him. The fellow's too fly by half, from the sound of it. I take it Cousin Oliver's out to marry you to gain the Beresford estates for himself?"

"Yes," she whispered.

"I wouldn't give a halfpenny for your chances of staying alive for long after he wed you. He'd want you dead before you bore an heir, I should imagine."

"Can we change the subject?" she begged, feeling very sick. "As you have indicated, there is nothing we can do until we have some proof against him."

He set his cup down on the table. "Oh, yes, there is, my beauty."

"Oh? What, pray tell me?"

"I shall deal with him."

"You? You must be out of your mind. What concern is it of yours?"

He came to sit on the edge of the sofa, very close to her chair. "It concerns me very deeply, Rosaline."

The uncommonly serious tone of his voice disturbed her. "Please, Lord Kenmore, say no more."

"Do not look so troubled. I shall say this only once; the matter will never again be alluded to by me. I give you my solemn oath on it."

He took her hand in his, and for some strange reason she permitted him to do so.

"I have been an utter fool. I had the chance of sublime happiness and threw it away. There was a chance, was there not?"

She could not deny it. Had Richard not been at Luxton, had Francis Kenmore's conduct towards her been that of a gentleman, she might well have fallen in love with Lord Kenmore.

"You do not deny it. Oh, yes, I know there was always Courtenay, damn his eyes, but without him—and if I had behaved with propriety—things might have been different between us, might they not?"

"They might, but I loved Richard even before I knew who he was."

"More riddles. No, do not explain. It is none of my business how or when you met and fell in love with him. What is my business is the welfare of yourself and, ergo, your future bridegroom. There'll be talk enough when the penniless younger son of a sea captain marries one of the wealthiest and most beautiful women in England, but any chance Courtenay might have of a political career would be at an end if he became embroiled in some unsavory scandal involving his wife's cousin and heir."

He was right, of course. Was there no getting rid of Oliver? He was the devil incarnate, seemingly invincible.

His grip on her hand tightened. "My darling Rosaline, you must have realized by now that I love you. I did not know it as a certainty until it was too late. I very much fear that I am doomed to carry that love in my heart forever." He gave a light laugh. "Lord, that sounds like a line from one of Pepperell's appalling plays!" A faint line of red brushed the skin over his angular cheekbones. "Grant me this one favor, therefore: permit me to take this burden from you. There are ways of dealing with Prescott that are open to me but closed to Courtenay. It must be done soon, for your cousin must be growing desperate by now. We shall not tell Courtenay, of course. The man has his pride. I shall—"

The door burst open, to reveal Richard, still wearing his top boots and gloves.

Rosaline hastily withdrew her hand from Lord Kenmore's.

"What do you want here, Kenmore?" Richard demanded.

Francis Kenmore slowly got to his feet, his sardonic smile and raised eyebrows a challenge. "Merely to call upon you and Miss Fitzgerald to convey my congratulations upon the occasion of your engagement."

"Miss Fleming, you mean. And how did you come to hear of it?"

Rosaline had never seen Richard quite so angry before. "Lord Kenmore called—"

A nerve jumped in Richard's cheek. "I have already heard why he called." He moved forward to tower above Lord Kenmore like some malevolent giant. "And I wish to inform you that you are not welcome in this house, Kenmore. Do not come here again."

Lord Kenmore raised his hand in a mocking salute. "Bravo! Well said, my buck. Never darken my doorstep again, eh? Don't worry, I'm going," he said as Richard made another move towards him.

He turned back to Rosaline, who had risen. "Your servant, ma'am," he said, making her a flamboyant bow. As he rose from it, his eyes met hers. He gave her a twisted smile and then turned to Richard.

"Goodbye, Courtenay." His proffered hand was ignored. Kenmore shrugged. "My congratulations again. You are an extremely fortunate man."

He strolled from the room. They heard his voice thanking Jennings for his hat, gloves, and cane, and then the slam of the front door and his quick footsteps on the pavement outside.

"What the devil was Kenmore doing here?" demanded Richard. "And explain to me, if you please, why he was holding your hand."

"Oh, leave me alone," Rosaline wailed, and, to his utter amazement, she pushed past him, tears streaming down her face, and hurriedly limped up the stairs to her room.

Chapter Nineteen

Reconciliation was sweet. It came the next morning, after Rosaline had spent a wretched night, having stayed in her room, stubbornly refusing even to accept Richard's messages.

They sat close together on the little sofa in the morning parlor, their hands clasped tightly as if unwilling ever to let go of each other again.

"I am a dolt," declared Richard. "A thick-headed, jealous dolt."

"No, my darling, you are not. Your reaction was most understandable, considering what had occurred at Luxton. But, as I have already assured you, Lord Kenmore called only to apologize for his conduct and to offer his congratulations to you, nothing more."

Nothing more than a declaration of undying love and an offer to rid her of Oliver, she reflected wryly.

"Will you forgive me for having for even one second mistrusted you?"

"Of course I shall, my darling, foolish one."

"It is only that I love you so much and at times find it difficult to believe that you could bring yourself to love a prosaic, penniless pedant like me."

His eyes twinkled at her, and she smiled back at him, pressing her hand against his cheek, which was healing nicely. He clasped his hand over hers and then turned it over to kiss the softness of her palm, employing his tongue as well as his lips. She had never realized quite how sensuous a hand-kiss could be.

He gazed at her, fire in his gold-flecked eyes. "God, how I love you." As he spoke he pulled her against him and buried his face in her neck, his breath warm beneath the tendrils of her hair.

A cough and a step in the hall forced them apart. Smiling mischievously, she patted her hair into place and by the time Sir John entered, they were consulting a book of Italian prints, their heads close together.

"Message for you, m'dear," Sir John said. "I was coming in any case, so I told Jennings I would give it to you. Messenger's waiting for a reply."

He handed her a folded note, which she opened. "Pray excuse me while I read this. It is from Miss Sidley."

Ignoring Richard's quick frown, she read the note aloud: " 'I regret that I shall be unable to call upon you this morning for our visit to the abbey, as it is necessary for me to run an urgent errand for my mother. Would two o'clock this afternoon be convenient for you? Kindly send your reply by the bearer of this note.' "

She folded the note again and looked at Richard. "Had you any plans for this afternoon, Richard? For us, I mean."

"No, for I must write a letter to my parents, confirming our expected arrival on Saturday. I also have an appointment with Mr. Briggs of Pennington and Briggs, a firm of solicitors."

"Oh, and what is that about, might I ask?" Sir John's tufty gray eyebrows rose in disapproval.

"It is to discuss the possibility of my articling with the firm."

"If you're going into the law, you'll read for the bar," his grandfather spluttered. "I'll not have my grandson becoming a confounded law clerk."

"I cannot afford to read for the bar, Grandfather, and it is imperative that I find permanent employment as soon as possible if I am to be married."

"Humbug! I'll not be able to lift my head in this town with you pushing a pen at a demmed desk in a solicitors' office."

"Then I shall apply in some other town," Richard replied in a calm voice. "We cannot be living off your charity forever, you know."

Seeing that Sir John's face was beginning to turn positively purple, Rosaline hurriedly intervened. "Then I am free to go to the abbey with Anne?"

"If that is what you wish," Richard agreed. Then his face brightened. "Tell you what, I shall meet you at Mollands at four o'clock. Two hours should be enough time for you to see the abbey, should it not?"

"More than enough. I do not wish to be walking for over-long on my first day."

"Are you certain that you should be walking at all today?"

"Of course. In any event, I can always remove to the Pump Room if I grow fatigued and wish to take a rest."

She wrote a quick note of reply to Anne at Sir John's desk in his study and gave it to Jennings to give to Anne's messenger. When she returned to the parlor, it was to find the two men in earnest conversation, which they immediately broke off upon her entrance.

She started forward. "You have news of Oliver. Do not deny it. I can see it in your faces. Tell me."

"It is not precisely news, my love. I merely learned yesterday that a man matching your cousin's description hired a black horse from Green's stables the day before yesterday."

"I knew it."

"I regret to inform you that that is not sufficient evidence to have a man arrested on a charge of attempted murder. Apparently the man gave his name as Atkins, a common enough name. But there is no sign of an Oliver Purvis having resided in Bath recently."

There wouldn't have been! She could see that the necessity of giving Richard a false name for her cousin was making matters even more complicated, if that were possible. She knew that Sir John also had been making discreet inquiries, using Oliver's true name, of course. The fact that he had not communicated anything to her probably meant that he too had not been successful in his search—as she learned after luncheon, when Richard had left for his appointment.

"Everywhere I went I drew a blank," Sir John told her. "Oh, his name was known all right, particularly in the more unsavory gaming hells, but no one admitted to having seen him in Bath recently."

"I thought as much. He is far too cunning to provide us with any evidence against him."

They were prevented from any further discussion by the arrival of Anne Sidley. Rosaline had dressed in a short spencer over her striped percale dress, but Anne advised her to change into a warmer pelisse.

"Although the sun is shining, there is a biting wind which is particularly cutting in open spaces."

The abbey courtyard being in the lower part of the town, Rosaline was not quite sure why the wind would affect them, but, taking her friend at her word, she donned her pelisse of cobalt blue trimmed with gold braid in the hussar style.

Rosaline had been awed by the exterior of Bath Abbey, with its pale-gold stone and magnificent gothic arched doorway, but the beauty of the interior impressed her even more. She had seen one other large church, Exeter Cathedral, but that had been several years ago. It occurred to her, as she stared at the east window's glorious stained-glass panels, how very much she had missed by being shut away in Beresford Castle, and she knew a sudden longing to have Richard by her side to share her pleasure.

She determined there and then that when she gained complete control of her home, she would have nothing but beautiful things about her. The castle's interior would be gutted, and all the dark memories would go out with the massive oak furniture and the faded wall hangings.

Having seen the memorial to James Quin, the famous actor, and read Garrick's epitaph upon it—

> *That tongue which set the table in a roar*
> *And charmed the public ear, is heard no more—*

Rosaline was content to come out into the open courtyard and the warm sunshine.

Anne consulted her watch. "There remains almost three

quarters of an hour before we are to meet Mr. Courtenay at Mollands. Knowing how difficult walking is for you, I have planned a surprise."

"Oh, I do enjoy surprises. Do tell me what it is."

"I thought you might like to take a short drive to Beechen Cliff to see the panorama of Bath from there. My aunt has kindly lent me her carriage this afternoon, and it awaits us just across the bridge."

"What a splendid idea! How very kind you are! Richard has taken me to Sydney Gardens, and he drove me out to Landsdown Hill earlier this week, but I have not yet been to Beechen Cliff. So that is why you told me to change into a warmer pelisse! I must own I thought it a trifle odd, for it is, in truth, extremely warm in town."

"Yes," Anne replied, "that is why."

She did not say any more but began to walk briskly in the direction of Stall Street.

"Pardon me, Anne," Rosaline said after a few minutes, "but I cannot keep up with you at this pace."

Anne halted. "We shall take a hackney, then."

"Nonsense. You have only to walk just a little more slowly, that is all. It is only because I have not been walking since the accident."

Anne's eyes seemed to focus on her for the first time in quite a while. "Of course. Forgive me. It was thoughtless of me."

It occurred to Rosaline that her friend was not feeling quite the thing today. Her face was very pale and, in retrospect, she had appeared somewhat preoccupied all afternoon.

"Are you feeling unwell, Anne?" she asked, touching her arm.

"Not at all," came the sharp reply. "Why do you ask?"

"Merely because you have not seemed quite yourself today. You appear anxious about something."

Anne gave her a forced little smile. "I am perfectly well, I assure you. My only source of anxiety is that we may be late for our meeting with Mr. Courtenay."

"Oh, Richard will not mind. He is inordinately fond of Bath buns, you know. I have seen him devour six at one sitting!"

Again, the forced smile. "I must insist that we take a hackney. There is one now, at the corner of the street."

Before Rosaline could stop her, Anne had hailed the coach, and in a moment they were inside its shabby interior, seated on the cracked leather cushions, and being driven through the busy streets and over the bridge to Holloway.

Once they had left the crowded streets of the town behind, Anne appeared to find it necessary to lean out the window and direct the driver, which seemed a trifle odd to Rosaline.

Eventually, they rattled onto a dusty stretch of unpaved road and into a dilapidated stable. Rosaline was surprised that Anne's carriage had not waited in one of the main stableyards on the southern outskirts of Bath.

Once the hackney came to a full halt, she carefully descended, wincing at the soreness in her bruised hip, which had been accentuated by the bumpy rude. The yard was deserted but for a few hens flapping about in the dust. Then she saw the solitary carriage drawn up beside a roofless barn.

Anne grasped her arm as they walked across the yard. "Get in quickly or we shall be late."

Rosaline found herself thrust unceremoniously into a corner of the carriage. "I was expecting an open carriage so that we would be able to view the scenery." Her tone was cool, for she was exceedingly vexed at her friend's strange behavior.

"It is all my aunt has. Not all of us are excessively wealthy, you know."

An icy chill swept over Rosaline. "What do you mean by that?" she demanded, gripping Anne's arm.

The other woman shook off her hand, refusing to meet Rosaline's eyes. "Oh, I do wish he would make haste," she said distractedly. She pulled on the window lever and thrust her head out the open window. "Thank God. He is coming at last." She spoke to herself, not to Rosaline.

Rosaline looked at her white, rigid face and made to rise. "I think, after all, that we are too late to drive up to the summit," she said, trying to control the tremor in her voice.

The carriage moved off, making a sharp turn, the movement unbalancing her so that she was forced to sit down again.

"Too late, indeed," echoed Anne in a hollow voice. Her breathing was hurried.

The carriage was moving fast now, rattling over the unpaved road, jolting them so severely that they had to cling to the leather sidestraps to avoid being flung out of their seats.

"The driver must be mad to be going at such a pace," Rosaline cried above the thunder of hooves and creak and clink of leather and metal. The dust the wheels were raising was so dense that she could see nothing from the small window.

"I demand that you order him to stop!" she shouted. "Did you hear me, Miss Sidley? Tell him to stop."

She launched herself across the carriage to attempt to rap on the small square window beneath the driver's box to attract the coachman's attention, but Anne gripped her arm, forcing it down. "Sit down," she ordered her.

Rosaline's eyes narrowed. She no longer merely suspected, she now knew that Anne Sidley was, for some obscure reason, her enemy. She also sensed that she was in great danger.

"Get out of my way," she told Anne. "I am larger than you, and I shall not hesitate to employ physical force if I must." Her stomach churned at the thought of wrestling with another woman, but she was prepared to go to any lengths to escape.

As she confronted Anne Sidley in the swaying carriage, the other woman suddenly turned and, to Rosaline's great surprise, hammered on the coachman's window.

Rosaline felt lightheaded with relief as the carriage began to slow down. As soon as it had come to a complete stop, she would order the coachman to drive directly back to Bath. If he refused, she was prepared to make her way back on foot. Anything, rather than spend one more minute with this false friend. From Anne's remark about her wealth, she suspected her of being involved in some conspiracy to abduct her and hold her for ransom.

"It won't fadge, you know," she informed Anne with a look of utter disdain. "I shall offer the coachman a sum vastly superior to what you are paying him and order him to drive me back to Bath. And you, my dear Miss Sidley, shall walk."

Anne Sidley sat back with her arms folded, totally ignoring her.

Rosaline heard the coachman climb down from the box. She leaned forward to open the door, to find the light blocked by a dark figure. The door was flung open, and the figure's head and shoulders came into view.

"I bid you good afternoon, Cousin Horatia."

It was Oliver.

Chapter Twenty

As Lord Kenmore was pulling on his leather driving gauntlets, there came a great knocking at the front door of his town house in the Crescent. Not content with plying the knocker, the caller was also, apparently, pounding on the door with his fist.

"See who it is," Lord Kenmore told his valet, who had just assisted him into his many-caped white drab driving coat. "But remember, whoever it is, I am not at home."

The sound of raised voices emanated from the hallway, one in particular resounding through the house. "Damn you, I know very well that he is here. I demand to see him!"

"Confound it," Lord Kenmore muttered. His eyes darted to the small side door that led from the library into his study.

"As soon as the carriage arrives, tell Berry to drive to the corner of Brock Street and pick me up there," he instructed his valet. "Meanwhile do your best to fend Mr. Courtenay off for as long as possible. He must not know where I have gone."

But as his hand touched the brass handle of the side door, the main doors of the library were thrown open.

"As I suspected, you are here," Richard Courtenay said.

Francis Kenmore sighed and turned back. "You appear to be in the habit of making spectacular entrances, my friend. It occurs to me that you should seriously be considering a career in the theater, not politics." He waved an airy hand at his valet. "Cancel that message for Berry, Carter. I shall call you when I have need of you."

Courtenay closed the doors behind the departing valet. He was breathing heavily, as if he had been running, and his hair was wind-blown. "What have you done with her, Kenmore? And don't ask me who, or I shall take you by the throat and choke it out of you."

The thought of those large hands about his throat caused Lord Kenmore to swallow hard. "I gather you mean Rosaline?"

The desperate man made a threatening move towards him, his eyes glaring wildly behind his spectacles.

Kenmore cursed beneath his breath. Hell and damnation! He could not waste any more time. Every second was precious. There was nothing for it but to tell him. It was the one thing he had hoped he would not have to do. Curse Berry for being so damnably slow!

"She's not anywhere to be found," Courtenay said. "Not at home, not at Miss Sidley's house. I was to meet her at Mollands at four. She never came."

"Before we waste any more time, where is Sir John?"

"My grandfather? What the devil has that to do with it?"

"Answer me, man. Where is he?"

"Gone to Bradford to visit a friend. Won't be back until nine or so. Why?"

"Is there any possibility that she might have gone with him?"

"None at all. He left the house long before she did." His eyes widened with sudden realization. "Good God, Kenmore. Do you mean to tell me that you don't know where she is either?"

190 / Elizabeth Barron

"Exactly so. Am I correct in thinking that you suspected me of abducting her?"

"Naturally."

"You know, Courtenay, it occurs to me that my life was infinitely less complicated before your future wife came into it. This is no time to be bandying words with you, however. Tell me quickly, have you any idea where she might be?"

Courtenay ran his hands through his hair. "Lord, I don't know. All I *do* know is that I'm afraid Miss Sidley may be involved somehow."

"Miss Sidley being . . . ?"

"A friend of Rosaline's. She gave us assistance at the time of Rosaline's accident."

"And you don't trust her?"

"No. I haven't from the start. Immediately after the accident, she called Rosaline by her name, yet no one else had mentioned it. I decided later that she must have learned it from some mutual friend and that I was being ridiculous in mistrusting her."

"And Rosaline was with Miss Sidley this afternoon?"

"Yes, they were to tour the interior of the abbey."

"Very well. Now let me tell you very quickly what I know. I gave Rosaline my word yesterday that I would make inquiries regarding her cousin for her."

"Good God, why should you—"

"For God's sake, man, permit me to speak, or we shall get nowhere. I've scoured the gaming dens—of which there aren't many since Bath became so deuced dowdy and respectable—and the various stable yards. Everywhere I drew a blank, until not one hour ago I learned that a man answering to Prescott's description hired a closed carriage and a slap-up pair for the first stages of a long journey."

"Who the devil is Prescott?"

"Your fiancée's cousin, Oliver Prescott."

"You're an imbecile, Kenmore," said Courtenay in a withering tone. "Her cousin's name is Purvis, not Prescott."

"Believe me, it is Prescott."

The appearance of another person at the door interrupted

what appeared to be an imminent explosion on the part of Richard Courtenay.

"Ah, Berry," Lord Kenmore said to his groom. "All set? Good. Keep them on the move for a few minutes longer, and I'll be with you."

"Where are you and Berry going?" demanded Courtenay.

"I had hoped to keep it from you, but I am about to try to follow Prescott. The longer you hold me here, the further will be the distance between us."

"I warn you if it is an Oliver Prescott you are tracking you have the wrong man." He met the other man's eyes and was forcibly struck by what he saw there. "You really believe this man to be her cousin?"

"I have irrefutable proof."

Courtenay pulled on his gloves in a decidedly business-like manner. "Then I am coming with you."

"I regret not. Your weight would slow us down."

"Do you seriously imagine that I would permit you to chase after my future wife and her abductor without me?"

Lord Kenmore sighed. "No, regrettably I do not. Very well, then. Accompany me if you must, but I give you due warning that it will only slow us down."

"Not so. I can take my turn at the ribbons when you are fatigued."

"Now there I draw the line. I'll not have my cattle's mouths mangled by your great fists."

"Damn you, Kenmore. Take that back. I'd knock you down if it weren't for—I'll have you know I can handle a team as well as anyone!"

"Forgive me, old fellow. I'll accept your offer if I am in need of it, I assure you. I also assure you that I shall drive my team as hard as possible. But if you do come with me, you will have to act as my groom, blow up at the tolls, open gates, et cetera, for I cannot take a third man in the curricle." He clapped Courtenay on the arm. "Now let us be off. I have a great deal to tell you, but it will have to wait until we're clear of Bath.'"

It took them more than half an hour to return to the stable yard where Prescott had hired the chaise and to question the coachman who had driven it out the Holloway road, and another twenty minutes for him to lead them to the deserted farm off the Wells road.

"This be the place, sur," the coachman said, sliding off his nag. "'E made me stop afore the gate and bade me walk back to Bath. Paid me right well, 'e did, so I asked no questions of 'im."

There was no one there but a simpleton minding a few bedraggled hens and one pig in the dusty yard. They had already learned from the coachman, however, that he thought the gentleman, who had been dark-featured, intended to drive a considerable distance. "Aye, sur, 'e asked me all manner of questions about which inns were best for posting."

They still did not know if Rosaline had been with Prescott after he had taken over the driving from the coachman. No amount of questioning could elicit any information from the simple lad in the filthy smock, but as they were about to drive off, he muttered something.

"Eh, what was that?" said the coachman. "Speak up, you gawkey!"

"Pretty ladies," the lad said.

Admirably restraining his impatience, Courtenay smiled at him. "Pretty ladies? How . . . many . . . pretty . . . ladies?" he asked very slowly.

The lad held up two dirty fingers and laughed, displaying toothless gums. "Two. Two pretty ladies."

"That's it," Kenmore shouted triumphantly. "Get up, Courtenay. He's got Rosaline and the other woman with him." He tossed a golden coin to the coachman, who deftly caught it and bowed low before remounting his nag.

As Kenmore turned the curricle, Courtenay took out a small notebook. "What the devil are you doing?" demanded Kenmore.

"Keeping a note of all expenses incurred. I regret I do not have enough on me at present, but—"

"For God's sake, man!" At the sight of Courtenay's expression, Kenmore added, "Oh, very well. Keep your damned expense book if you must."

"You shall be reimbursed for every penny you spend, I

give you my word. She's to be *my* wife, Kenmore.''

"Yes, Yes. Get down. You'll have to open that damned gate.''

Courtenay sprang down and ran to open the ramshackle gate, and then closed it again after the curricle had gone through. Kenmore had already started up the horses again so that Courtenay was forced to run along beside the curricle and jump onto the step and haul himself in.

"In another hour it will be dark, so I intend to spring 'em for the first stage," Kenmore said. "We'll leave the talking until the second stage, if you don't mind.''

That would also give him time to work out exactly how he was going to break the news about Rosaline's true identity to Courtenay. Of course it might be to his advantage to tell him bluntly and hope that he might cry off the engagement then and there, but he had the distinct notion that all this havey-cavey business about hiding Rosaline's true identity had been unnecessary. Courtenay's grim face and tense jaw hid an inner turmoil that came out in flashes of impatience that were most unlike him. No, this man would not relinquish his Rosaline so easily, damn his eyes!

When they halted to make the first change, they received their first confirmation that they were on the right track. A party answering to the description they had given had changed horses at Midsomer Norton.

"I think we'll press on and make our first change at Wells," Kenmore said, having cast an eye over the post-horses in the yard. "Mine are good for at least another ten miles, and we should get better cattle at the White Hart.''

It was an ideal night for traveling. The road was dry and relatively quiet, and the full moon and starlit sky made the going much easier now that it was dark. Courtenay removed his spectacles and, to Kenmore's amazement, was able to see way ahead, so that he was forewarned of any unlit, slow-moving carriages or lumbering stagecoaches ahead of them.

"That's a remarkable talent you have there, Courtenay. You'd be invaluable in a race.''

"But then there's the disadvantage of my weight," Courtenay reminded him.

"Yes, there is that. Still, I'm not certain that having telescopic eyes doesn't outweigh the weight."

Their combined laughter was the first moment of relaxation they had shared.

"You said that you had a great deal to tell me," said Courtenay, still scanning the road ahead.

Kenmore shot him a glance and then kept his gaze on the space between his two horses. There was no easy way to tell him, he decided. Straight out was the only way. No beating about the bush.

"By now you must know that I was telling you the truth when I said that Prescott is Rosaline's cousin," he began.

"Then why the devil did she tell me his name was Purvis?"

"Because if she had told you his real name, you might have discovered who Oliver Prescott is."

"Who he is? Is the blasted villain something special, then?"

"Well, yes, in a way he is. He's the sole heir of the Countess of Beresford."

"'Ware broken-down coach!" yelled Courtenay.

Kenmore maneuvered the curricle onto the crown of the road and ripped past a coach which had lost its offside wheel.

"I regret you've quite lost me," Courtenay said once they had safely passed the coach. "The Countess of Beresford. Wasn't that the madwoman who tried to murder her—"

"Cousin? Correct."

"I recall reading about it in some paper at Luxton. If I remember correctly, she had been locked away by her father for many years, and this cousin was her heir and she stabbed him. That must have happened—"

"About six weeks ago. Just before you came to Luxton."

"Yes, that is so. But . . . My God, Kenmore!" He gripped Kenmore's arm

"Hey! Let go. You'll have us in the ditch."

"You cannot mean . . . I cannot believe . . . Where is Beresford Castle?"

"Close to Exmoor."

"Exmoor!" A long silence ensued. "No wonder she thought I was her cousin's spy!"

"Exmoor? Is that where you met? Good God! You must tell me all about it."

"No," Courtenay said.

"No, perhaps not." Kenmore gave Courtenay a sidelong glance.

Courtenay sank back in the narrow seat. "Then Rosaline is the Countess of Beresford."

"She is."

"And the story of her insanity was invented by Prescott to cover his villainy."

"No doubt. He had to hide the true reason for his cousin's attack upon him and her subsequent flight."

"Why in the name of heaven didn't she tell me?"

"Because she was certain that you would not marry her if you knew she was a countess."

"She told you that?

"She did, indeed. Apparently you repeatedly told her that you would never marry a woman of superior wealth or status," said Kenmore.

"Yes, I did. That was how I felt."

"You put it in the past tense."

Courtenay sat up straight. "Good Lord, man, of course I do! I own I still don't like the idea, but at the time I was speaking of some nebulous woman, not of Rosaline."

"I thought as much. Told her so. But she said that even your grandfather had agreed that you should not be told who she was."

"Don't tell me he was in on this, too! Does everyone in the world know except me? What a great gaby I must appear. When was I to be told, might I ask? On the wedding night? Perhaps she discussed that with you as well, considering she confided everything else to you." His tone was understandably bitter.

"I believe she was going to tell you after the visit to your parents. Said she didn't think you could cry off then."

Courtenay struck one large fist into the palm of his hand. "Damnation, what a fool I've been! A blind, stupid fool!" He struck his forehead with his clenched fist.

"Don't be so hard on yourself, old man. I didn't twig

until she let something slip that last night at Luxton. I had all the details from Basil Fortescue. He has an acquaintance who knows Prescott.''

"That bloody villain. I suppose his aim is to marry her so that he can gain control of her estates?''

"And the accident with the horse was a mere warning, you mean? I regret to say that, from what I have learned of him, I rather think that Prescott's aiming a little higher than merely being Rosaline's consort.''

The ensuring silence was punctuated only by the pounding of the horses' hooves on the hard road.

"She told me he had threatened to kill her,'' said Courtenay. "She repeatedly told me, and I wouldn't believe her. God help me, I accused her of behaving as if she were in a melodrama. Curse it!'' He struck the side of the carriage with his fist.

"Save your curses and your spleen for Prescott.''

"I'll kill him!''

"Yes, I rather thought you might,'' muttered Kenmore. "Blast it!''

"When we reach him,'' Courtenay said in a fierce voice, "keep out of it, Kenmore. Hands off! He's mine, understand?''

"I understand.''

"And if he has harmed Rosaline in any way, I shall make his death a slow and exceedingly painful one.''

"I shall be happy to hold him down while you do so. What will you do with Miss Sidley?''

"I'll have her shipped to the other end of the world.''

"Bloodthirsty devil. Can't say I blame you, though.''

"Where are they making for, do you think?''

"We'll have a better idea when we reach Wells. Bear up, old man. We shall reach them in time, never fear.''

At Wells, they learned that they were gaining on them, but they were still almost two hours behind.

'He's driving at a neck-and-neck pace, I can tell you,'' Kenmore said.

At Glastonbury, they found that they had gained another twenty-five minutes on them according to the posting records. They decided not to make a halt for dinner, but procured some legs of roast chicken, a loaf of bread, and a bottle of claret, and consumed them as they drove.

The next stop was Bridgwater. By now Kenmore had been driving for several hours and his arms were growing numb. Reluctantly, he handed the reins over to Courtenay.

"Not bad, all things considered" was his grudging opinion after a while. "After all, you cannot have had a great deal of experience. Never mind, you'll have abundant opportunity to improve your driving skills once you marry Rosaline."

"Dammit, Francis, don't rub it in."

"Don't tell me you won't enjoy having your own carriages. A great advantage over walking, Richard."

This witticism was greeted with a reluctant grin.

From then on, they took turns driving, so that each could catch a little sleep.

It was early in the morning by the time they reached Minehead. There they struck a piece of good fortune. One of the stable lads had overheard the dark-haired gentleman say to one of the ladies that they would arrive at the castle in time for breakfast.

"That confirms it," Courtenay cried. "He *has* taken her to Beresford Castle!"

Chapter Twenty-One

Rosaline opened her eyes long enough to enable her to recognize her bedchamber at Beresford Castle. Then she squeezed them shut again and groaned. The incessant pounding in her head was like the relentless surge of waves against a rock, and she felt extremely sick. She could still smell the sickly sweet fumes of whatever it was that Oliver had clamped over her mouth and nose.

She had been unconscious for most of the ensuing journey but eventually had begun to regain consciousness, waking at intervals, aware only of the nauseating sway of the carriage and the shadowy figure of Anne Sidley in the corner before she slipped back into merciful darkness once more.

Now she was back at the castle again. She had come full circle. As she was being carried from the carriage, she had seen its towers and battlements against the gray light of the early morning sky and immediately abandoned the last lingering shred of hope that Richard might rescue her.

Again she opened her eyes, and this time she was determined to remain awake. If there was to be any chance at all of outwitting Oliver, she must strive to clear her mind, for, most certainly, she could not fight Oliver physically this time. As she had discovered when she first attempted to sit up, she was extremely weak.

She heaved herself up against the pillows, her gaze taking in the familiar furnishings, the objects she had known since childhood: the massive oak clothes-press; the carved chest of Lebanon cedar that had been in the family since the seventeenth century; the portrait of her mother as Portia, her coloring even more vivid against the severe black legal gown and white bands. But now everything was tainted with Oliver, with the memory of what had happened here between them. As the memories of that night flooded over her, she was seized with a grim determination to confront Oliver *now*, at whatever cost. She could not endure the thought of waiting—waiting for him to come creeping up to her room to do whatever it was he intended to do to her.

Sick and giddy, she swung her legs over the side of the bed, clinging to one of its carved bedposts for support. One hand clutching at the bedcover to save herself from falling, she dragged herself along the side of the bed. When she reached her dressing table, she bent to peer into the mirror and saw an ashen-faced figure in a crumpled dress, with tousled hair loosened from its braids.

Ruefully, she reflected that if she were to be seen like this, it would not be difficult to persuade people that she was indeed a madwoman.

Determined not to give Oliver the satisfaction of seeing her thus, she splashed her face with water from the porcelain basin. Then she took up her hairbrush and, with great effort, managed to tidy her hair. To complete the transformation, she brushed a touch of rouge paint on her cheeks and lips. It made a world of difference. She felt almost human again.

She poured a glass of lemonade from the jug by her bedside, silently thanking whatever unseen hand had placed it there. Its tartness was invigorating. Drawing herself up tall and straight, despite her swimming head, she began the long walk across the room, along the landing, and down the wide staircase.

Although the great hall was empty, the sound of voices issued from the parlor beside it. She crept down, to be brought up short by the sight of two of her footmen standing at the foot of the stairs. From the lack of servants elsewhere, she had surmised that Oliver had sent all of them away. She decided, therefore, that these two must be in his pay.

"It is not necessary for you to announce me to your master," she said, sweeping down the last three stairs.

As one of the footmen ran to warn Oliver, the other made as if to bar her way.

"How dare you! Get out of my way," she commanded him, her eyes flashing. He stared insolently at her and then his gaze fell and he stepped back, permitting her to pass by him.

As always, it was cold in the hall, a damp cold that chilled her to the bone. She walked to the large stone fireplace. "Throw some logs on this fire," she ordered the footman, her voice ringing confidently through the hall. "And then bring me some breakfast. Where is Mrs. Lemming?"

The footman, who had taken up one of the huge logs from the box and was adding it to the fire, looked up at her. "She was sent home weeks ago, your ladyship."

"Home? This is her home."

The man flushed scarlet. "Yes, your ladyship. I meant to say . . . That is—"

"Your old nurse has been sent to live with her daughter, the farmer's wife, who lives near Combe Martin, you may recall," Oliver said from behind her. He had entered with his habitual catlike tread.

Heart pounding, Rosaline turned to face her cousin, steeling herself not to shrink from him as he drew nearer.

"Good morning, fair cousin" was his greeting. "I am delighted to see that you are sufficiently recovered to be able to join us." He was dressed in his customary black, with a simple white linen neckcloth, the lack of color serving to emphasize his pallor and the sloe-black, watchful eyes.

Anne Sidley hovered behind him, as if she wished to be hidden by his figure. Her expression was one of extreme wariness.

"Ah, my dear friend, Miss Sidley," Rosaline said, choosing to ignore Oliver. "May I bid you a belated welcome to my home?"

Anne Sidley's cheeks reddened. She made a move to retreat into the parlor.

"No, no, Miss Sidley. Do not think to be depriving me of your excellent company. I have given orders for breakfast. Come, sit before the fire and we shall eat together." Rosaline sat down in the high-backed carved oak chair, knowing full well that her shaking legs would not support her for one moment longer.

Frowning, Oliver pushed Anne Sidley forward. "I regret having to inform you that there is no time for eating, my dear cousin. Your giant friend, Mr. Courtenay— By the bye, I shudder at your taste in men, Horatia. I understand, from my informants, that he has been employed as a tutor and a secretary. Hardly the consort for the Countess of Beresford, surely? Your father certainly would not have approved. In any event, as I was saying, your suitor by now will have been making efforts to trace your whereabouts for several hours. Although I deem it highly unlikely, it is possible that he might have been able to track you down or, at the least, hazard a guess that you might be here. It is necessary therefore to expedite matters. I had hoped that you would have remained unconscious for a little longer," he added in a tone of regret.

"So much easier to kill me when I cannot fight back, is that it, Oliver? How very sporting of you!"

Miss Sidley spoke for the first time. "He has no intention of killing you. He merely wishes to marry you because it was your father's dearest wish."

Rosaline laughed. "Oh, my dear, naive Miss Sidley. Is that what he told you? What a tale of romance! But you surprise me. I had thought Mr. Prescott might have induced you to betray a friend by promising you marriage."

Now it was Oliver's turn to smile derisively. "Marriage! Hardly." Miss Sidley bit her lip and flushed at the scornful tone of his voice. "Gold, my dear cousin. The key to all men's—and women's—baser instincts: the glitter of gold."

"I see." Rosaline bent her gaze on Anne Sidley's defiant countenance.

"You do not know, you cannot know, what it is like to live a penny-pinching existence," declared Miss Sidley, flags of red flying in her white cheeks. "Living on other people's charity. Seeing the mother you love wither away in not much better than a servant's apartment for the want of a little money."

"Why, yes, now I recollect that you once told me you would do anything for your mother. Doubtless I should have taken that as some sort of warning. But then, the entire episode of the horse running me down was a masterpiece of ingenuity. I congratulate you, Cousin Oliver. You surpassed even yourself there. I gather it was your intention not to cause me any severe injury, but to inveigle Miss Sidley into my household, so that I could be enticed back to the castle."

"Exactly so." Oliver gave her an unpleasant smile and consulted his watch. "We have talked enough."

"I beg you to permit me just a few more words with my friend, Cousin. Even a common executioner gives that to the condemned man—or woman." She turned again to the other woman. "I merely wish to tell you, my dear Anne, that it was a trifle shortsighted of you not to realize that you would have gained far more from your friendship with me than from this conspiracy with Mr. Prescott."

Miss Sidley's cheeks reddened again. "From you? Why should I gain anything from you?"

"Of course. How very silly of me to think that a woman who could sell her friend would be capable of comprehending the tangible as well as the sentimental rewards of friendship. Never mind, my dear Miss Sidley. As the hangman places the hood over your head, you can make a speech, saying you did it all for the sake of your mother."

Anne Sidley darted forward, her eyes bright with anger. "You truly are mad, as he told me you were. Your cousin is not going to kill you."

Rosaline sat upright, her hands gripped together in her lap, striving to present a picture of calm assurance. "Ask him." She nodded towards Oliver.

But there was no need to ask him. "You were given the opportunity to marry me once," Oliver declared. "I shall not repeat it."

"I did not think you would. For one thing, you know very well that I would find some way to kill you myself before I would bring myself to marry you. Only, this time I would make sure I was successful!" She gave him a mocking smile. "So, Cousin Oliver, what is to be your plan?" she asked in a conversational tone.

"My poor mad cousin is about to attempt to set fire to the castle and will then throw herself off the battlements."

"Astounding! Mr. Pepperell would be proud of you! What a truly sensational scenario for the conclusion of a play!"

"You have omitted one thing," said a quiet voice from behind Oliver. "The hero's rescue of the heroine."

Rosaline leaped from her seat to see Richard step out from the shadows behind Oliver, a long-barreled pistol in his hand. She made no move, but her eyes met his across the space dividing them and she read the unspoken message: *All is now well, my darling.*

Wide-eyed, Oliver spun around and, upon seeing Richard,

gave an ugly laugh. "Mr. Courtenay, I presume. My congratulations. I fear I have underestimated you. I own I did not consider it possible for you to reach me in time."

"Take care, Richard," Rosaline called out. "The two footmen, if not others here, are in his pay."

"I believe they have been dealt with," Richard replied.

Now she came forward. "He may have a weapon on his person. Shall I search him?"

Richard nodded. "But mind you do not get between Prescott and me," he warned.

From behind, she ran her hands down Oliver's coat, flinching at this unwelcome contact with him. She discovered a small pistol stuffed into the waistband of his breeches, and she removed it and held it trained on him.

A short laugh, hinging upon a sob, burst from her. "My God, Oliver. You have been beaten at last." Tears filled her eyes as she looked at Richard.

Oliver glanced from her to Richard and back again, and then crossed his arms. "Now that you have me, what do you intend to do with me?" he asked with a shaky attempt at a smile.

"I am going to take you outside and kill you," Richard replied.

The smile broadened. "In cold blood? Well, well."

"Not exactly. You will be given the matching pistol to this one."

"A duel?" Oliver raised his thin, dark eyebrows. "With you?" He gave a short grunt of amusement. "I was right. You are a fool. I must own, however, that the idea intrigues me. I have never before killed a man who wore spectacles. Tell me, what distance do you propose? Two paces?"

"You underestimate Mr. Courtenay," said another voice from the screen end of the hall. Lord Kenmore sauntered across, the companion to Richard's pistol in his hand. "He's a crack shot."

"Lord Kenmore!" Rosaline cried, bewildered. "What on earth are you doing here?"

"I accompanied my friend, Courtenay, merely to witness

this highly entertaining scene. Ah, Miss Sidley, I believe. We have not met. Kenmore, ma'am. Your servant.''

He bowed to Anne Sidley, who stood with her hands and back pressed against the wall, as if she longed to disappear through it.

"The servants?" asked Richard.

Lord Kenmore nodded but said nothing. His pistol was still pointed at Oliver. "Lady Rosaline, be so kind as to give me the small pistol, would you?"

She was almost reluctant to give it up. Knowing Oliver as she did, she still was afraid that he would manage somehow to spirit himself out of this predicament. She handed the small pistol to Francis Kenmore, who put it in the pocket of his greatcoat.

"Now Richard's pistol, my dear," he said in a soft voice.

Startled, she flung up her head. "Richard's?"

"Yes," Lord Kenmore replied. "Remember our conversation?" he said, an expression of intensity in his eyes. "Give her your pistol, Courtenay."

"I'll be damned if I will. What's your game, Kenmore?" Oliver's gaze flickered from one to the other, evidently attempting to assess the situation.

Lord Kenmore smiled. "Rosaline will explain it all to you when I have gone, Courtenay."

"Gone?" Richard started forward. "If you're in league with this devil, I swear I'll kill you both where you stand." His expression was terrifying in its ferociousness.

"It pains me that you should suspect me of such a thing, my friend, but in the circumstances I forgive you. Give Rosaline your pistol, if you please."

"I'll see you hanged first. I warned you before, Kenmore. Keep out of this. It is my business, not yours." He prodded Oliver with the pistol. "Walk to the main entrance" was his order.

"One more step, Courtenay," Lord Kenmore said, "and I shall not hesitate to shoot you."

"You would not do so!" cried Rosaline.

"I most certainly would. A nice neat graze along the

right shoulder or wrist, I think—just sufficient to mar his aim."

"Damn you, Kenmore. I warned you, this is none of your business. Rosaline is my fiancée. I shall deal with it."

"You said something about your brother's merchant ship sailing from Plymouth this week, if I recall, Courtenay. Will you permit me to use your name as recommendation to procure a passage? Always wished to go to the West Indies. They say there's a fortune to be made there."

"And you are in such dire need of a fortune!" Richard said in a withering tone.

"I must own that I find it extremely edifying to have two men fighting over me," Oliver interjected. "Perhaps someone would kindly inform me as to exactly what is going on?"

"Why certainly, sir," said Lord Kenmore. "I shall be only too happy to do so. It was my intention all along to challenge you, once I learned of your abduction of Lady Rosaline. Unfortunately Courtenay arrived on the scene before I was able to get away from Bath. Naturally, he would prefer to kill you himself, a sentiment with which I have the greatest empathy. You must understand, however, that he is engaged to be married to your cousin, Lady Rosaline. If he were to slay his wife's cousin and heir he would create a great public scandal—apart from the more obvious fact that dueling is prohibited by law. It is best, therefore, that I be the one to kill you, Mr. Prescott. One thing is certain: Whichever one of us does it, before one hour has passed, you shall be dead."

Rosaline went to Richard and looked up into his grim, drawn face. "Francis is right, my love. If you kill Oliver, it will create a dreadful scandal. Not only you but also I would be seriously implicated."

"You are taking Kenmore's side in this?"

"Yes," she said simply. "Give him the pistol, Richard."

"And is it *your* intention to shoot me down in cold blood?" Oliver asked of Lord Kenmore.

Lord Kenmore looked profoundly shocked. "Nothing so unsporting, my dear fellow. I dispatched a note to Sir Basil

Fortescue when I reached Minehead, asking him to bring two of his friends and a physician to the stretch of Exmoor nearest Beresford Castle. It will all be quite aboveboard, I assure you. You shall have a second and your choice of pistols."

"You are very sure of yourself," said Oliver. "It does not appear to have occurred to you that I might win this duel."

"No" was Lord Kenmore's succinct reply. "Come, what are we about, discussing such matters before ladies?"

He turned again to Richard. "For Rosaline's sake, Richard," he said quietly.

"Damn you, Kenmore, you know you have me hipped when you bring Rosaline into it." Richard handed the pistol to Rosaline, who passed it to Lord Kenmore.

He thrust it into his pocket and then took out the small pistol. "Take this and give it to Richard once I am gone," he said to Rosaline, not taking his eyes off Oliver. "Farewell, my lady. One day, with your husband's permission, you shall do *She Stoops to Conquer* at Luxton. But for now I bid you *adieu*."

"Not *adieu*, Francis," she whispered, pressing his hand. "*Au revoir*. God bless you."

Lord Kenmore turned away abruptly and gave Oliver a vicious jab in the back with the pistol. "*En avant*, Prescott." He motioned to him to go before him down the hall and out the main entrance. "I am taking the carriage, but I leave Miss Sidley in your charge, Richard," he shouted, and the next minute the two men were gone.

They heard the crunch of footsteps on the gravel driveway, and shortly thereafter the sound of carriage wheels and horses' hooves in the distance, and then silence.

It was Anne Sidley who broke the silence eventually. "What will you do with me?" she asked in a scared voice.

"For now," Rosaline said, having cast a quick glance at Richard's grim profile, "I intend to lock you in my bedchamber, for I cannot bear the sight of your face one minute longer. We shall think of what to do with you later."

She took Anne Sidley's arm and marched her upstairs,

leaving Richard alone to compose himself. The past dozen or so hours had been a shattering experience, one that she would not easily forget, but she knew that it would prove even harder for Richard to come to terms with what had passed between him and Francis. His integrity, his very honor was at stake, and it would take a while for him to recognize that he had made the right decision.

When she returned to the hall, he was standing in the same spot, alert, his very stance suggesting that he was listening keenly for something.

"What if Kenmore does not win?" he asked fretfully.

She had the impression that he did not know that she had left the hall. "He will. Besides, having met Lord Kenmore's friends, I suspect that Oliver would not escape with his life even if he were to kill Francis Kenmore. Rough justice, I know, but it occurs to me that it is the kind of justice that Oliver himself would choose. Far better to be tried and executed by your equals than to suffer the ignominy of a public trial, followed by transportation in the company of felons and the lowest dregs of humanity to an alien world."

He seemed to drag his mind back to acknowledge her presence and took her hands in his, summoning up a smile. "What a pleasant change to have you being so full of common sense and me imbued with morbid fancies. You are in the right of it, of course. If Kenmore is as good a shot as he is a whipster, I have no doubt whatsoever that he will win the duel. If he does not, then I myself shall finish Prescott off, and we shall have a prolonged honeymoon in the West Indies."

He pulled her against him and gazed deeply into her eyes. "My God, here am I concerned about Prescott when I almost lost you. Had I arrived but one half hour later—"

"Well, you didn't, so you may set your mind at rest." She scanned his beloved face. "Was it Francis Kenmore who told you my true identity?" she asked hesitantly.

"Yes, and I have a score to settle with you there, my girl. All this nonsense about you and my grandfather hiding it from me until after you had met my parents! What a pair of precious idiots!"

"Idiots, indeed! It was you who said you would never marry a woman of wealth."

"So I did. I begin to think I was right in saying so," he added, looking about the hall. "My God, I have heard of ancient piles, but this place is beyond belief. My poor darling, however did you survive living here?"

A shiver ran across her shoulders. "I trust it will not deter you from marrying me."

His arms tightened about her. "Nothing could do that, my precious love. Not your wealth, nor your title, nor even this gloomy vault. I suppose we do have to live here?"

"No, we do not. I have three other estates: one in Scotland, one in Cornwall, and another in Kent, together with a town house in London."

"Good Lord." He looked extremely alarmed.

"But although I loathe the castle, I love Beresford itself: the sea, the rugged coastline, the moors." She gave him a mischievous grin. "Most especially the moors."

He grinned back. "Perhaps Prescott had the right idea after all. Set the castle on fire."

"I have a better idea. Why not completely redesign the interior? It has been done most effectively at Warwick, I know."

"You must do what you think fit, my love. It is your home."

"And very soon to be yours, whether you like it or not," she reminded him. "So it shall be a mutual decision."

"As you will. Then I shall say here and now that I consider yours to be an excellent notion. But before we become embroiled in a lively discussion concerning interior decorating, I regret to have to point out that we did not have time to stop for breakfast this morning, and for some reason I have suddenly realized that I am ravenously hungry. Do you think there might be any food in the kitchen?"

"I am certain of it. Indeed, I had ordered breakfast a short while before you arrive. By the bye, that was a splendidly effective entrance you made, if I may say so."

"Yes, it was, was it not? Kenmore says that I have a talent

for making good entrances and should consider entering the theatrical rather than the political arena."

"Good heavens, I sincerely trust you did not take him seriously!"

"Not I. I consider that we two have had more than enough drama to last us a lifetime. But come, my dearest countess, let us make a grand entrance into the kitchen before I expire from hunger."

Their mingled laughter as they set off, arms about each other's waists, in search of food prevented them from hearing the distant report of two pistol shots, one immediately following the other, from the direction of Exmoor.

——— Epilogue ———

26 January 1814

It was extremely cold in the vast amphitheater of the Theatre Royal, Drury Lane. The snow left by the storm that had hit London a few days before had melted to slush, and the seeping drizzle that ensued seemed to have permeated the theater itself, the chill dampness subduing the usual exuberance of those patrons sitting on the benches in the less than half-full pit and gallery.

Only one of the dress boxes was occupied, its occupants being a woman who was wrapped against the cold in a long cloak of black sable and two men who retained their velvet-lined cloaks for warmth.

Tonight's play was Shakespeare's *Merchant of Venice*. The cold and the lack of a decent-sized audience appeared to have affected the actors, for their performances were desultory, to say the least. Indeed, those who were there had begun to mutter among themselves and were preparing to call it a night and make for home, when the Shylock made his first entrance.

Immediately, a whisper of surprise ran through the meager audience, for the small, thin actor who was playing the Jew was wearing a black beard and wig rather than the customary red.

But this was not to be the only change in the usually predictable portrayal of the moneylender. Before the end of his first scene, a ripple of excitement ran from pit to gallery. This was not merely an actor playing Shylock. This *was* Shylock. The comedy had become a tragedy centered around the small, lonely, defiant figure of the Jew.

Who was this unknown who employed his entire body, his ringing voice, the veritable gamut of emotions, to portray Shylock? Not only did he eschew both the stock comic trappings of the usual portrayers of the role and the classic gestures and graceful poses of Charles Kemble, their favorite, but this unknown actor also drew the audience into the drama, exciting their pity and anger. In stature, this man was but a pygmy beside Kemble; yet with a total lack of artifice, a naturalness that was almost supernatural, he moved them to tears.

By the start of the third act, word had spread, and people were coming in from the streets to see this remarkable new actor who had arrived, unheralded, on the theatrical scene. His speech *If you prick us, do we not bleed? If you tickle us, do we not laugh?* was greeted with thunderous applause. And, in the fourth act, the anguish and rage at his crushing defeat, when he had been quite sure of victory, was so terrifyingly real that the audience was momentarily stunned, sitting in utter silence until its members rose to their feet as one in unanimous acclamation of this great new actor with the piercing dark eyes.

As Edmund Kean, for once groggy with success rather than drink, made his way to the corner of the common dressing room beneath the stage, he was accosted on all sides by his fellow actors, the stagehands, and members of the management.

"You have made a hit, a positive hit!" the stage manager cried.

Three people, two men and a woman, came to see him when he had removed his makeup and costume.

"Kenmore," Kean cried, his swarthy countenance animated at the sight of his old friend. He regarded Lord Kenmore's companions with a puzzled expression. Their faces were vaguely familiar.

The woman put back the hood of her sable cloak, and he saw the glory of her auburn hair, piled in coils with tendrils about her beautiful face.

"Good God! You are—"

"Permit me to present Mr. Edmund Kean, Lady Rosaline. Mr. Kean, may I present Lady Rosaline Courtenay, the Countess of Beresford," Lord Kenmore said.

"Courtenay... Countess..." Mr. Kean shook his head, utterly bewildered.

Lady Rosaline gave a peal of delightful laughter, her green eyes shining as brilliantly as the emeralds about her creamy throat. "Never mind, Mr. Kean. We shall explain it to you some other time. For now, I must tell you how very much your performance moved me. You will remember my husband, Mr. Richard Courtenay?" She indicated the tall man in gold-rimmed spectacles who stood beside her

"Of course. Now I remember. Kenmore's secretary." He took the man's proffered hand, feeling even more than usually aware of his own inadequate height and also quite certain that he had committed some sort of *faux pas* by mentioning Mr. Courtenay's previous employment. He had a sudden longing for a good stiff shot of brandy.

"Mr. Courtenay is newly elected a member of Parliament," Lord Kenmore told the actor.

Mr. Kean murmured suitable congratulations.

"A magnificent performance, Mr. Kean," said Mr. Courtenay.

Edmund Kean felt himself out of his depth, as he usually did in the company of members of the ruling class. In addition, his memories of those days at Luxton House were not happy ones. Indeed, his stay at Luxton had been one of the low points of his life.

"A truly remarkable performance, Kean," Lord Kenmore said. "My faith in you has been rewarded at last. My only regret is that it has taken so long. It was unfortunate that I myself was unable to come to your assistance before now."

It was impossible to tell if Mr. Kean's success had brought him any happiness. If it had, it certainly did not show in his expression. "I have fought long and hard for this recognition," he said through tight lips. "But now nothing can take it away from me. Nothing." He turned to drag down his multi-caped greatcoat from a cloakstand and pulled it on, its size dwarfing him.

"Now, if you will forgive me, I am going home to my wife," he told them, a light of quiet triumph at last evident in his aspect, "and I shall tell her that she shall have her very own carriage and our son Charles shall go to Eton."

He looked at them, through them, as if he did not see them. "If you will excuse me . . . I thank you for coming to see my London debut. I trust we shall meet again . . ." And he turned on his heel and, like a whirlwind, was gone.

"What a strange little man he is," declared Rosaline. "But strange or not, I shall never, never forget his performance here tonight. Thank you a thousand times for your kind invitation, Francis."

"Ah, but wait until you see his Richard the Third," Francis replied. "Will you both do me the honor of joining me for supper? It is, after all, a long time since we were last together."

"And much has happened since that time," said Richard.

"Yes, indeed." They all fell silent for a moment, but Francis lightened the sudden gloom by adding, with his tilted smile: "So I observed, my lady, when you loosened your cloak. May I be so impertinent as to ask when the great event is expected to take place?"

Rosaline blushed and laughingly pressed her hands to her swelling abdomen. "You may, indeed. In April—another three months."

"I suppose it would be too much to ask if I could be appointed one of the godparents?" Francis said, sounding surprisingly wistful.

Rosaline exchanged glances with Richard.

"Becoming a godparent means to undertake a solemn obligation to be an example of good living to your god-child," Richard said.

"Lord, it all sounds exceedingly daunting. But, believe it or not, I have already taken a vow to become a sober peer of the realm. I have decided that I must marry, for I should be thinking of an heir. I have even thought of taking my place in the House of Lords, God help me, so that I shall, perhaps, be seeing something of you at Westminster, Courtenay."

"A grand reformation, indeed," Rosaline observed.

"I shall believe it when I see it," mocked Richard.

Francis Kenmore's eyes gleamed. "Would you be willing to make a small wager on it?"

"I'm not usually a gaming man, but I'll not turn down the chance of a certain win. What is your wager?"

"That I marry within six months."

"Oh, that is far too easy for you," interjected Rosaline. "It is a simple matter for a man of wealth and title to ask the first eligible woman he meets to marry him."

"Very well, then, my fair Rosaline. You shall set the terms."

"It should be that you must *fall in love* and marry the object of that love within six months."

"Done!"

"Not so fast. There is one more proviso: the object of your love must also love you. It must be mutual. Neither party must pretend to love. You will not find that quite so easy, I believe."

He met her eyes and gave her a rueful smile. "You are right, for my heart belongs permanently to another, alas."

"Humbug! as dear Sir John would say. There are many more fish in the sea."

Francis gave his hand to Richard. "Your wife is, as

always, infallible. You're a lucky dog, Courtenay, but you know that already, no doubt."

"I do, indeed. How much, Kenmore?"

"How much? One hundred guineas."

"Phew! That's a trifle steep." Richard turned to Rosaline. "Still, I consider we can afford to lay out that much, can we not? After all, it is a pretty sure thing."

"We can," she said firmly. "Particularly in such a good cause. But I trust you will not mind paying up, Richard, for I have the distinct feeling that we shall lose this wager."

"Shall you mind losing, my dear Rosaline?" asked Francis Kenmore with the mocking smile she remembered so well from the past.

"Not one whit, my dear Francis. This is one wager I shall be delighted to lose." She smiled at both men. "Come, my lord, you said something about supper. I wish to hear all about your sojourn in the West Indies, *and* we are weak with hunger."

"We are?" Richard responded with a lift of his eyebrows above his spectacles.

"Not you, stupid. I mean the Courtenay-Beresford heir and I are hungry." She grinned at her husband and then turned back to Francis. "Another thing, Francis. If you manage to fall in love and marry someone whom I deem suitable before the day of our firstborn's christening, then you shall be chief godfather. Agreed, Richard?"

"Agreed. But if you're thinking to find Rosaline's equal, Kenmore, I warn you, you've not a hope of winning that wager."

"You, sir, are a highly biased gamester," the Countess of Beresford informed her husband.

Uncaring of Lord Kenmore's presence, she stood on tiptoe to kiss Richard and then, tucking her hands within her escorts' arms, she marched both men off to supper.